An Irresistible Temptation

DEFIANT HEARTS BOOK 2

Sydney Jane Baily

cat whisker press
Massachusetts

Published by **cat whisker press**

Cover: Philip Ré
Book Design: **cat whisker studio**
Editor: Chloe Bearuski

ISBN-13: 978-1957421001

DEDICATION

To my children,
Pandora and Jasper
who fill my heart with love

You give me so much joy.

OTHER WORKS

The RAKES ON THE RUN Series

Last Dance in London
Pursued in Paris
Banished to Brighton
Gretna Green by Sunset

The RARE CONFECTIONERY Series

The Duchess of Chocolate
The Toffee Heiress
My Lady Marzipan

The DEFIANT HEARTS Series

An Improper Situation
An Irresistible Temptation
An Inescapable Attraction
An Inconceivable Deception
An Intriguing Proposition
An Impassioned Redemption

The BEASTLY LORDS Series

Lord Despair
Lord Anguish
Lord Vile
Lord Darkness
Lord Misery
Lord Wrath
Eleanor

PRESENTING LADY GUS

A Georgian-Era Novella

ACKNOWLEDGMENTS

I offer heartfelt gratitude to my enthusiastic beta readers: Renee Sevelitte, Tammy Thompson, Pamela Hodgin, and Holly Meyerhoff. Thanks to the informative man at the San Francisco Cable Car Museum (whose name I failed to obtain), and to Wendy Kramer, librarian in the San Francisco History Center at the San Francisco Public Library for sending much-needed primary sources. Thanks to my cheering section. You know who you are. And, of course, thanks to my mom, Beryl Baily, who read the nearly final draft, chapter by chapter, right along with me. We had a fun time that night.

A NOTE FROM THE AUTHOR

Dear Reader,

I must confess that I took a few liberties, time-wise, with creating the San Francisco Symphony. It did not form officially in the mid-1880s as it does in my story. In reality, it was not until after the terrible 1906 earthquake that a group of businessmen decided that a world-class symphony should be part of the re-built city.

Though there were some local symphonies with whom Sophie Malloy might have played, including the San Francisco Symphony Orchestra in 1896, the San Francisco Symphony Society in 1897, and the Philharmonic Orchestra in 1898, none of these were long-lasting.

The symphony I refer to in this story came to be in 1911 when Henry Hadley, on December 8, 1911, conducted its first performance. Hadley is also in this story, along with many real-life musicians that accompanied him to San Francisco. I also changed their playbill, having them concentrate, in their opening series, on one classical composer each night. In truth, Hadley hit the audience with four big names on opening night: Wagner, Tchaikovsky, Haydn, and Liszt.

Sherman Clay & Company was a real music store that opened in 1870. It was founded by Leander Sherman, who left Boston for San Francisco, just like Sophie. The store might, indeed, have provided the symphony with its concert grand piano. In fact, all the pianos mentioned and described were real, and some still exist, including Sophie's exquisite Broadwood and Sons grand that her father bought her.

Cheers and happy reading!
Sydney Jane Baily

CHAPTER ONE

1886, Spring City, Colorado

The train rocked sharply to the left, and Sophie smacked her head against the window for the umpteenth time that day.

Really! She rubbed her temple, running her hand over her dark hair. This was certainly not the smooth ride between New York and Boston, or even between Paris and Rome, for that matter. This was the West.

This was freedom, she thought to herself with the merest hint of a sad smile.

As the train crossed over into Colorado, heading for tiny Spring City, none of the other passengers would suspect she was anyone out of the ordinary. Looking at her, in her custom-made blue dress, her hands folded neatly in her lap, no one would know or care that she was a world-class pianist. Her studies at The Boston Conservatory of Music under its famed director Julius Eichberg and then at The National Academy of St. Cecilia in Rome were of little use to her at that moment.

Sophie stretched delicately before turning her face once again to the window. Briefly, she caught sight of her own reflection. Although the man she'd believed she would marry had torn her heart asunder the previous year, destroying her composure with all the roughness of a piano's dissonant second interval, she decided her appearance remained unchanged.

Perhaps a bit weary-looking around her eyes, which stared solemnly back at her.

On the inside, however, Sophie struggled to regain the self-possession she'd felt before Philip went to Oxford University to study philosophy. Without her.

What was the point, she had wondered aloud to him, *to debate life and God and Heaven and whatnot?* When she played her pianoforte, she knew the meaning of life. And she even suspected she'd heard the sounds of Heaven in many a concerto. Why debate and deliberate? Why not just live life and be grateful?

Philip had not invited her to Oxford, and she'd left Rome alone, returning home to Boston.

Focusing on the vastness outside the train, she felt a twinge of disappointment at having seen so few buffalo. No great herds were left. However, her sister-in-law, Charlotte, who had lived in Colorado until she'd met Sophie's brother, Reed, nearly a year and a half earlier, had told her about the inspiring immensity of the wide-open spaces. Having never before seen the magnificent plains, Sophie was truly impressed.

However, she had to admit that each time the train pulled into a station, no matter how small the pocket of civilization, she would breathe a sigh of relief. And when the long sequence of passenger cars, sleeper car, dining car, and baggage cars left a town behind and wound its way farther across the deserted prairie, anxiety gripped her anew. Despite being pulled by a strong locomotive and guarded at the rear by the caboose, the train seemed to Sophie as nothing more than a tiny boat in a nearly limitless ocean.

When she finally arrived in Spring City, Colorado, Sophie stood on the station platform, which was merely a few boards nailed together, looking expectantly for Dr. Cuthins and his wife. Doc and Sarah were old friends of Charlotte, who was now the toast of Boston's literary circles, as well as being Reed's adored bride. The Cuthins had attended the Malloy-Sanborn wedding in Boston the year before. Having them there, representing Spring City, had been a generous gift to her sister-in-law.

Sophie's gift for Reed and Charlotte had been an original composition, which she played at the reception hall while they danced. After the wedding, she'd waited patiently through the long winter that turned into spring and then the insufferably hot months for their first baby to be born. At last, she made her escape from Boston's smothering atmosphere in early August.

And here she stood, thousands of miles from home.

Sophie waited and waited, until the train had departed and the platform was empty. Licking her lips, she tasted dust and couldn't help making a sour face. Offering—no, insisting—on handling the task of packing up Charlotte's things had seemed a brilliant idea a few months ago. Despite her brother's hesitation over her safety and despite Charlotte's own brother's offer to complete the task himself, Sophie had claimed the job. She'd dismissed Reed's concerns and then pointed out Thaddeus's lack of reliability. After all, he was still a bit of an unknown entity, who never stayed in one place very long.

It was the perfect excuse for Sophie to get away, see the West, and forget Philip. Or at least, she would try to.

Sitting upon her trunk, she placed her carpet bag on her lap and wondered what she should do. This was not Boston. No cabriolets happened by to take stranded passengers to their destinations.

She sighed. It was not the first time she'd found herself either alone or stranded, or both, in a strange city. But this was the first time she'd seen a mule pass by, looking as if it were more composed than she, in fact, felt. Now that she was off the train, the big open space all around the small town seemed even bigger, and the town, itself, seemed to shrink, becoming the littlest oasis in a massive landscape.

Humming to herself, she jiggled her leg, checked the pins holding her hat, and desperately wished for a cafe offering some strong Turkish brew and a pastry.

Just then a strange noise took her attention to the sky. An ugly black bird with a small head and large black body was cruising lazily back and forth, making a warbled bark. She shuddered and rose to her feet. This was the "wild West," as Thomas Reid had described it, and not for the first time, she wished she hadn't read her younger sister's copy of *The Scalp Hunters* before traveling.

What to do? Obviously, there was no telephone nearby, and a telegraph office wouldn't help her now. There wasn't even a real station house. If there had been, she knew with her luck the ticket window would be closed and shuttered.

With resolve, Sophie half pushed, half dragged her trunk off the crude boards until it landed on the ground next to the platform. Taking the two steps down to street level, which in this case was mere dirt, she grabbed the handle. Luckily, having traveled extensively, she was not one to over pack. Still, it was a struggle as she resorted to pulling the trunk along the dusty road with her carpet bag perched on top.

Spring City was not big by any standard, and the station was at one end of the town, but which end was Charlotte's home? That, Sophie didn't know.

"Main Street" stated the sign, as she approached the first block of buildings, and she paused. It had to be a joke as she saw no other streets at all. But on the horizon were mountains, grand and awe-inspiring. She shivered despite the heat of the day and the difficult task at hand. She really was on the edge of nowhere.

All the buildings looked similar, with flat fronts and squared off tops, although behind the frontage, she could see the roofs were slanted as any in New England. Some had a second story, with two windows over two, but that was the highest she saw. No wonder her sister-in-law had walked Boston's streets staring up at the buildings for months after she'd first arrived.

Sophie had no idea a town could still look so . . . so primitive in this day and age. She saw no brick at all, only wood, even the sidewalks were wood, raised up a step from street level.

Along the sidewalk was the occasional barrel, a trough, or a hitching post. Wagons were parked and horses pawed at the road that bisected the town before stretching, it seemed, all the way to the mountains in the distance. And, of course, there were people—not a lot, but some, either sitting on benches in front of stores or standing in doorways. And every one of them turned to look at Sophie.

She knew what she needed to find, either Fuller's Hotel and Restaurant or Doc Cuthins' surgery. She had to locate the people whom Charlotte considered friends and whom Sophie could ask for help. Dragging her trunk a few more yards, she wished she could set it down and walk briskly along unhampered, but she feared everything she'd brought would disappear in the blink of an eye.

With almost all the strength gone in her arms, she was attempting to heave the trunk up onto the sidewalk, perching one end on the wooden planks, when someone collided with her from the rear.

"Oomph," she expelled all the air from her lungs as her stomach caught on the tilted edge of her trunk, then she slid slowly down the length of it back onto the dirt road, head and hands first. For a dreadful moment, she sprawled there, knowing her dress had flipped up at her waist and over her back, leaving her drawers, lavender-colored and lacy, on view.

"Shit," she heard before she could right herself. The man's sentiment echoed what was in her head, although she was too much of a lady to voice it.

And then, "Oh, sweet Jesus, ma'am," as strong arms lifted her off the ground.

Sophie was not one to take offense, although she was getting sorely tired. Anything she was about to say, however, died on her lips at the spectacle of the man who now had hold of her.

To compose herself, she looked down to see what had happened to her things. Her beloved carpet bag was upended in the street. Frowning, she looked back to the man's mud-splattered boots, up his worn, well-fitting blue jeans, and to what had once been a pale-blue shirt now covered in grime.

Her gaze traveled higher to his equally grubby but ridiculously handsome face that had stopped her cold for a moment, with his burnished brown eyes, dark eyelashes, and inviting mouth, curving slightly as though he tended to smile often.

He tipped his black brim to her, with a quick tap of his hand.

"Ma'am," he said, before giving her a brief smile that showed a dimple in his right cheek, his teeth looking all the whiter for appearing in the midst of his dirty face.

Dirty and devastatingly attractive—a combination she hadn't experienced before!

He was tall, clearly, for she had to look up at him, despite her own uncommon height for a woman. And she realized he was still holding her arm with one hand, a strong capable hand. She felt his warmth right through the fabric of her dress and her traveling mantle.

Letting herself feel his fingers gripping her for a moment more, she then shook him off by taking one step back.

"Are you all right?" he asked.

Sophie looked at her hands, stretching them in front of her and wriggling her fingers. Everything seemed fine except for her white gloves being torn and filthy.

"I'm fine," she said at last, seeing as he was watching her careful examination. "I'm sorry. I wasn't looking where I was going."

"Me neither," he offered. "I was talking to Dan and walking out of Drew's." He gestured to the feed store. A man standing in the doorway, wearing a heavy apron, chuckled.

"Yup, he was," Dan confirmed. "Riley, don't you know better than to leave a store ass first? Unless you're trying to drum up future business for yourself."

Riley laughed and looked back at Sophie, who tamped down an inappropriate thought about his very sweet, even sexy laugh, and his eyes that sparkled wickedly when he was amused.

"Most women would have given me a tongue-lashing for knocking them into the street and ruining their gloves."

"As long as you don't make a habit of it," she said, glad she hadn't been in Boston, where she would have been run over by a brougham within seconds.

"I'll try not to." He treated her to a broad grin—a very sensual grin, too, Sophie mused. *She must be extremely tired and lonely to keep having these incorrigible thoughts.*

"Can I make it up to you?" he asked.

Without waiting for an answer, he lifted up her traveling trunk as though it weighed nothing and deposited it on the sidewalk in front of the feed store.

Hurriedly retrieving her carpet bag from the street, making sure everything was still inside, she stepped up beside him.

"Thank you. Can you tell me how to get to Fuller's? Or better yet, to Dr. Cuthins?"

"Well, which do you need?" He crossed his arms. "A place to stay or a doctor?"

"Riley could give you either one," Dan said, before turning and going back inside, as the man beside her dismissed him with a wave of his hand.

"Neither, really," Sophie said, "but Dr. Cuthins was supposed to meet me at the train, with his wife."

"Maybe he had an emergency," Riley said. "Though I'm sure Sarah would've come herself."

"It could be they didn't receive my last telegram with the correct date of my arrival," Sophie suggested. "If you direct me to Fuller's, I'll—"

"I'll do even better," he said. "Follow me." And with that, he heaved the trunk up onto his shoulder and started along the sidewalk, Sophie trailing behind.

"Are you kin?" he asked. "To Doc or Sarah, I mean."

"No," Sophie said, not wanting to elaborate on her personal life. It was bad enough a stranger was carrying her luggage and had most likely seen her fancy pantalets.

"I didn't get your name," he said over his shoulder.

"No, you didn't," Sophie said, unused to the familiarity. He hesitated, and she nearly ran into the back of him. Then he resumed his easy saunter.

"You're not from here?"

"Obviously," Sophie agreed.

"Hey, Riley," came a voice from the next shop they passed, a barber standing in the doorway, arms crossed.

"Hey, Ely," Riley said without stopping.

Sophie nodded to the man who gave her a long friendly look as she passed by before he called out, "You-know-who's gonna be hopping mad."

Riley just flapped his free hand back at Ely, either to acknowledge or dismiss the sentiment. *The man was referring to a jealous wife, perhaps,* Sophie mused.

"I've been away for a while," Riley continued their conversation, "but I still would have remembered you."

Sophie supposed some women might have simpered or blushed, but she merely shrugged.

"It's a small town," she pointed out. "I'm sure if I'd grown up here, we would have run into each other."

Then she did run into him, as all of his six feet and two or three inches came to an abrupt halt.

"Why have we stopped?" she asked, touching her nose where it had collided with the back of his shirt and trying to peer up at her own bonnet to see if the brim had been utterly crushed against his broad back. He lowered the trunk to the sidewalk.

"Doc's place," Riley said, gesturing toward the white door in the one-story building.

She looked up to see a shingle that had 'Cuthins, Physician' in plain black lettering on a painted white sign. Riley opened the door for her and stepped aside.

"Why, thank you, Mr. . . . ah?"

"Dalcourt, but you can call me Riley."

"Thank you, Riley." It felt strange, indeed, to call this man by his first name, but she didn't want to seem stuck up. As he still held the door, she went in. Scanning the tidy waiting room, she noted a door in the back wall, probably leading to the examination room and surgery.

Sitting at a desk was a middle-aged woman, dressed in pale gingham, with glasses perched on her nose, perusing papers.

"Sarah, you have company." She looked up at Riley's voice.

"Oh, my word! Sophie!" Sarah came out from behind the desk. "But how can you be here today?" She took Sophie's bag without asking and set it down on a chair. "Gracious, I forgot how much you are the spitting image of your brother."

Sophie winced slightly. With her striking height, dark hair, and vivid blue-black eyes, she knew she looked a lot like Reed, only she hoped a tad more feminine.

"Mrs. Cuthins, I fear you didn't get my last telegram."

"Please, call me Sarah," she said, coming forward to hug Sophie, who stiffened. Right then, the inner door opened and Doc Cuthins emerged.

Sarah laughed and released Sophie. "I forgot. You East Coasters aren't quite as relaxed and friendly as we are."

"Stop teasing the girl," Doc Cuthins said to his wife. "Not everyone wants to immediately be your kissing cousin. Now, where are your things, Sophie?"

"Mr. . . . that is, Riley, has my trunk," Sophie said and turned to see he'd already stepped back outside and was loading her trunk into a wagon.

"Oh, I—"

"That's our trap," Sarah reassured her. "I'm gonna get this girl home and fed, lickety split," she told her husband. "I'll see you later." And she placed a big kiss on Doc's lips, leaving him with a smile, before she ushered Sophie back out the door.

On the sidewalk again, Sophie turned to Riley.

"I appreciate your help."

"Anytime, Sophie," he said, shooting her a grin, evidently pleased at having gained this piece of personal information.

With another tip of his hat, he walked back the way they'd come. She watched him a moment before getting up into the wagon next to Sarah, unable to completely tamp down a vague happy feeling at having met him. Perhaps she would even admit to a flutter of excitement.

"Charlotte's house is ready for you. I've dusted and made up the bed, but I haven't stocked the pantry," Sarah fussed as they drove along Main Street.

Sophie had heard of Sarah's fervent desire to feed every stray soul who came through Spring City or who had the poor sense not to cook, like Charlotte.

"I'm sure I can come up with something," Sophie said. "If you drop me off at Charlotte's—"

"Nonsense, we'll stop at my house for a cup of coffee while I pack you up some home cooking, then when Doc gets home, we'll take you over together. And we'll bring Alfred along, too."

"Alfred?" Sophie repeated. For some reason, her mind went to Riley Dalcourt, as if somehow Sarah was going to produce a man for Sophie to borrow as well.

"Charlotte's old horse. He's been great company to my Bonnie here, but you can use him to get back and forth."

"That's very kind, Sarah, but I won't be here very long."

"Long enough to need a horse and wagon, I'm sure," Sarah said, ending the discussion and turning instead to questions about Charlotte and Reed and their new baby.

It hadn't been more than a few minutes when Sarah said, "We're here," and turned the trap into the small yard of a neat little house, all whitewashed boards and blue-painted trim, with flowers everywhere. Before she could say another word, a horse went galloping by.

"Purple!" came an exuberant voice that trailed after the rider. Both the women turned to see man and horse already yards away, a black hat raised high in the air in salutation.

"Riley!" declared Sarah, with a chuckle. "What in the heck is he saying?"

But Sophie had gone quite still for she had the nasty feeling he was referring to her undergarments.

Riley continued riding far into the foothills. He urged his horse faster until they were both breathing hard, and finally he pulled back on the reins. Turning his mount, he regarded Spring City and could make out the Sanborn house where Sophie was staying. He didn't even know the woman's last name.

Spitting into the long grass to get the grit out of his mouth, he spurred his horse homeward. It didn't matter anyway. So what if, back when he was a younger, more idealistic man, he'd pictured a woman exactly like her. A woman with dark hair and intelligent eyes, full pink lips, and a tall, curvy body.

Reality had a way of chasing off frivolous dreams, or outright killing them. After all, he had a fiancée, a good woman to whom he'd promised himself, body and soul.

CHAPTER TWO

Sophie packed the last of Charlotte's old clothes into the trunk and closed the lid. On hands and knees, she pushed it across the wide pine floor, arranging it in an orderly fashion next to the other two trunks. Soon, they would hold the rest of the items Charlotte had asked her to send.

Her sister-in-law wanted nothing in the way of furniture from the house. Charlotte had already retrieved her father's desk and books, as well as her grandmother's oval mirror, before the wedding. Sophie could see why Charlotte didn't want the rest. The furnishings were shabby at best or simply functional with nothing of beauty to recommend them.

Even the ancient upright, although Sophie had been delighted to see it in the sitting room, was one of the most pathetic excuses for a piano she'd ever had the misfortune to play. But play it she did, on the very first day, as soon as Doc had dragged in her trunk and Sarah had given her a basket of food, and they'd left. Sophie whipped off the sheet covering the old instrument and settled down to play.

Terribly out of tune, the piano still bent to Sophie's artistry, and the resulting music made her mind calm and her heart peaceful. Ten minutes passed, half an hour, an hour. She was starting a new life, she reminded herself. She simply wasn't sure what that new life entailed yet, whether heading back to Boston or to Europe, or where.

However, for the time being, she was satisfied with having put even more distance between herself and Philip's familiar, beloved face, his warm smile, and his even warmer hands. And his treacherously fickle heart. And his unthinkingly cruel words.

She pounded the keys, all dissonant bass chords, until the sounds drowned out the thoughts in her head. So much for a peaceful heart.

At least, she'd stopped crying.

When the sun was midway across the clear blue sky on her third day in Spring City, Sophie left the Sanborn homestead and walked to town. It wasn't far, especially on a beautiful, late summer day. She felt as if she knew at least some of the people from Charlotte's animated stories of her home.

Walking into Webster's store, she met the owner, Jeremiah, and his granddaughter, Anna, who talked a mile a minute when she found out who Sophie was. Naturally, the young woman was full of questions about Charlotte, the town's renowned literary daughter. Sophie smiled. Only her brother Reed could go halfway across the continent to a dried-up little town on the most solemn of legal tasks and find the brightest gem of a female to take for his wife.

Sophie bought new gloves and headed for Fuller's, which Charlotte swore served the best turkey pie. Sophie sat in the window and ate, not concerned by the curious stares of the townsfolk. Some had greeted her, already knowing she was Charlotte Sanborn Malloy's sister-in-law, thanks to Sarah Cuthins.

"Thank you," Sophie said as the waitress came back with more coffee. "Charlotte was right about the pie."

Jessie Hollander smiled broadly. "Shoot. That ain't nothin'. Wait till you try my lemon cake."

"That's what I'm here for, too," said a voice behind her, and Sophie turned to see Riley, not any cleaner than the last time she'd seen him. But she was damned if, even dirty, he wasn't the most attractive man she'd ever laid eyes on. *Why hadn't Charlotte mentioned him?*

"Sophie," he said, tipping his black hat. His eyes were fixed on hers, with a small frown between his eyebrows. He looked like a man bothered.

"Riley," Sophie returned, by way of greeting.

Jessie stood, hands on hips. "Riley, what do you think you're doing, coming in here covered in trail dust, unsettlin' my customers?"

Sophie watched him shrug. "You know what *she's* like when she wants something," he said by way of explanation. Sophie's ears perked up. Was this another reference to the mysterious woman who might be "hopping mad"?

Jessie nodded. "Oh, I know, all right. But I thought she didn't like lemons."

"Never mind that," he said, his glance darting back to Sophie. "I'm here for cake."

"Very well," Jessie said. "I'll be back in a jiffy. Two pieces?"

Riley raised his eyebrows. "Might as well. I would've eaten hers before I got back, I suppose."

Jessie turned back to Sophie.

"And you, miss? A slice?"

Sophie shook her head. "No, thank you. Another time, perhaps."

Standing up, she started to sort through her purse for the right change, feeling Riley's eyes on her, but then, that had been the case with all the townsfolk all day.

"You're missing out," he said, making her jump. "The lemon cake is just the right blend of tart and sweet."

Philip would have philosophized about how the cake held all the elements of life if it truly blended those two opposing elements so perfectly. She sighed. *Why did her former beau have to pop into her brain without bidding?*

She tried to smile at Riley, but felt the ache in her heart grow again. Was it simply because she was near a man, reminding her of what she'd lost? Or was it being near a man who had absolutely no feeling for her? She belonged to no one now. As she tugged on her gloves, she wondered what Riley's woman was like, the one who apparently could be a handful when she wanted something, a little like Sophie's younger sister, she guessed.

"Good day," she said, as she passed him.

"G'day, ma'am," he called after her.

Walking slowly up Main Street, she passed the feed store, the general store, Webster's, Ada's Saloon. People were all going about their business. Tomorrow, she would set about working a little more quickly and perhaps finish the packing. The sooner she sent the trunks back to Boston, the sooner she would be free to decide what to do next.

"Hey, Sophie."

She slowed her pace as Riley fell into step beside her. She was unsure whether it was allowed for her to walk with this man she barely knew. But things were different in Spring City, Charlotte had assured her, not as rigid as in Boston's society, which was ruled by propriety and a bewildering array of social mores. One false step and you could be ruined there. Here, Sophie supposed she could walk without recrimination along the town's main thoroughfare, next to this tall, easygoing man.

"Where're you headed?" Riley asked, swinging a small, white cake-box by its string with such vigor, it could only mean disaster for its contents.

"Home," Sophie said, distracted by his motions. "Um, you might want to be careful with that." She indicated the box now being twirled nearly upside down. "If you want to have any semblance of cake left to give to your . . . wife?"

Riley's faced grew serious. "Fiancée," he corrected.

"Congratulations," Sophie offered, not sure what else to say despite the lack of joy in his expression.

After the briefest of pauses, Riley laughed.

"What is it?" Sophie couldn't help asking.

"No one else in this town has congratulated me on my engagement. Rather the opposite."

Sophie was intrigued and, despite her better manners, was going to ask about the situation when Riley stopped.

As she had done earlier in the week, she asked, "Why have we stopped?"

He gestured to a two-story, yellow house behind him with painted shutters, a carefully tended yard, and a wraparound porch with a rocker begging to be sat on.

"Yours?" Sophie guessed.

"My fiancée's family home."

"Then you'd best be taking her the cake, post haste," Sophie advised, tilting her head to the side and finding herself more than a little curious as to this man's story and his fiancée's, for that matter.

"I hope I'll see you again," he said to her, touching the brim of his hat.

She smiled at him and took a step back. Riley moved forward toward the porch.

"It was a pleasure," he added, seeming to mean it, with a half-smile on his face and small crinkles at the corners of his eyes. She had to own up to feeling a frisson of pleasure herself, just looking at the man.

"Thank you," she told him and took another step, still facing Riley who was framed from behind by the pretty house. But she had to ask him.

"Riley, what do you do to get so dirty each day?"

As soon as the words were out, she clapped a hand to her mouth. *Oh my God, what had possessed her?*

But he didn't take offense. Instead, his smile turned into a genuine grin that made Sophie's insides do a little dance.

"I ride," he said.

"Ride?" she repeated.

He nodded and looked past her toward the open landscape beyond the town.

"I ride, just for the hell of it. Pardon my language. I've got a great mount right now, and he loves to run, and so do I."

She must have frowned because he laughed and said, "You look puzzled."

"I . . . I guess I thought." She closed her mouth. *What had she thought?* That he would tell her he was a stable hand or a horse trader or even a rancher. How odd. Clearly, he wasn't a farmer. *Hm*, he had time to gallop on his horse for sheer pleasure. Perhaps no gainful employment, yet how did he keep a fiancée? Whom no one congratulated him on having?

"Never mind," she said, giving a little shrug and taking another step. She wanted to ask him a whole host more questions, but he wasn't her business.

"You should deliver that cake."

"I should," he agreed, but his eyes were locked on hers, and he wasn't moving.

"Yes," she heard herself say. Then, finally, she turned toward Charlotte's house. After a few paces, she felt the urge to look back, certain for some reason Riley was standing still, watching her walk away.

Yet she didn't turn. As she passed Drake's barn, she considered how quickly Charlotte and Reed's romance had heated up in there, at a town-wide dance, according to Charlotte's telling. Sophie hummed to herself.

If Riley—such a devilishly handsome man—were looking at her with some measure of interest, she would consider it the first small binding of the tatters of her heart. Sophie decided to hold onto that thought rather than turn her head and look.

Riley watched her until she was out of his sight. He had been unable to resist going into Fuller's after he saw her through the window. *Shit!* Why had he wasted his time talking about lemon cake he would end up eating himself, since Eliza hated citrus? He should have asked Sophie the million questions going through his mind, like what hocus-pocus she was using to make his mouth go dry each time he saw her.

And how in the heck was he going to stay away from her when all he wanted was to get closer?

CHAPTER THREE

The knock on her front door could only mean one thing, Sarah Cuthins had brought more food. Reluctantly, Sophie lifted her fingers from the piano keys. At this rate, she would be as big as Charlotte in her last month before she'd given birth to baby Emory.

"Come in," she called out, rising from the stool. But even before she exited the parlor, she had a feeling it wasn't Sarah—a feeling and the wafting scent of some floral perfume.

Sure enough, standing in her front hall was a petite woman with hair in the fairest shade of blond Sophie had ever seen, all in ringlets. After getting over the shock of what seemed to be an angel's visitation, Sophie settled her gaze on the crystalline blue eyes, so light compared to her own and which were carefully taking in their surroundings.

She had the absurd notion this delicate creature was lost, perhaps having fallen off a cloud and ending up on her doorstep.

"Can I help you?" Sophie asked.

"It's I who should be offering you help. I hear you've been in Spring City for three days and I had yet to meet you or welcome you."

"Oh, well, how kind." Sophie had heard of a welcome wagon that came around when someone moved to a new territory or city. "But I'm not staying long. I don't need any help."

The woman laughed, a sweet tinkling sound, and her curls shook as she did so. Sophie failed to see what was amusing.

"I'm Miss Prentice. Eliza Prentice." She said it as if Sophie should know the name. "Perhaps you've heard of me. Or my father?"

"I'm afraid you have the advantage, Miss Prentice. I don't really know anyone in town except the Cuthins. Would you like to have a cup of coffee?" Sarah had made sure Sophie had a tin full of coffee, enough for a month, and plenty of milk and honey to go with it.

"That's very kind of you, Sophie. Is it all right if I call you Sophie?"

It's a bit late to ask, she thought, but all she said was, "Certainly."

Leading the way to the kitchen, she gestured for Eliza to sit at the well-worn, plank table. After filling the kettle and lighting the stove, Sophie turned to see her visitor had grabbed a kitchen rag and was wiping the bench with it.

Sophie smiled. She'd done the same thing a couple days earlier but had got used to the fact this town was dusty. Without paved streets, dirt seemed to get tracked in with every step and float uninvited through the doors and windows.

Eliza saw her watching and returned a sweet smile. "My dress is new," she explained.

Sophie nodded. It was a lovely dress indeed, all pinks and creams, and seemed the height of foolishness in this environment. But that was not her concern.

When the coffee was poured and Sophie had taken a seat, a few moments of uncomfortable silence passed, but Eliza merely looked around and sipped her coffee.

"It was nice of you to call on me," Sophie offered, although she would rather be playing the piano and brooding, as she found herself doing more and more.

"It has been many years since I was in Charlotte's house," Eliza offered.

Oh. Suddenly it was clear to Sophie. Eliza had to be one of Charlotte's old friends and had come for news of her. She relaxed. Her unexpected visit didn't seem so odd after all.

"She is doing very well," Sophie said. "It was an uneventful pregnancy, and Emory came out healthy and hearty."

"So, she had a baby?" Eliza looked smug. "That's what happens when—"

"Yes, Reed is over the moon happy." She smiled at the memory of her brother's extreme delight.

Eliza's mouth pursed slightly for a moment. "Still together, then?"

"But of course," Sophie said, her smile faltering. "I thought you would know that. They were married last year."

"Before the baby?"

Sophie's mouth dropped open, and she snapped it shut. She was starting to get the first inkling Eliza might not have been a friend after all.

"Mr. Malloy and Charlotte," Eliza continued. "What a surprise that was. Right under all our noses."

"I guess it must have been a surprise," Sophie agreed. "And perhaps not entirely welcome, to have Spring City's famous author whisked away to Boston."

Eliza leveled her gaze. "Oh, I'm not sure she is all that famous. I, for one, have never read any of Charlotte's writing. But her carrying on like that in this very house." She shook her head slowly, her blond curls swinging right and left. "With those two children nearby. Charlotte very nearly became *infamous*, if you ask me."

"They fell in love," Sophie said.

"They fell into bed," Eliza snapped.

Sophie set down her cup. "You are speaking of my brother and my sister-in-law. They are good, upstanding people. They deserved—"

Eliza put up her hand and smiled a most beatific smile. "They deserved each other. I'm very happy for them." Her happiness didn't reach her pale-blue eyes. "And what of Charlotte's brother? How is he faring?"

Sophie shrugged lightly. "I have no idea about Thaddeus Sanborn." It was clear the woman was looking for more gossip about Charlotte's family.

"Miss Prentice," Sophie began.

"Call me Eliza, please."

Sophie started again. "I don't wish to be blunt, but did you come calling for a particular reason?"

The golden-haired angel seemed to take no offense. "When the first Malloy came to town, he made such an impression on everyone, I was eager to meet you. I'm quite curious as to why you'd follow in your brother's footsteps and come to Spring. Also, I wanted to ask after Charlotte and her brother, too, of course."

Sophie rose. This tête-à-tête was over. The woman was a snoop and a busybody, and Sophie wanted her out of the house as soon as possible.

"Thank you for coming over," Sophie said, stepping into the hall, so Eliza had to stand up and follow. "But I have to get back to the packing. I'm trying to get Charlotte's things on the train in the next day or so."

It wasn't a lie, although Sophie had spent more time playing the piano and sitting on the porch swing than packing.

"So, you'll be leaving soon?" Eliza persisted.

"Yes, I believe I already said that." Eliza's obvious interest in her imminent departure made Sophie want to stay longer, just to spite her. Why the woman provoked her ire, Sophie couldn't really say. What a shame Miss Prentice could look so lovely and yet seem so unfriendly at the same time.

"I won't take up any more of your time then." With a backward wave of her hand, Eliza was gone, strolling out to her awaiting buggy with its blue hood to keep the sun off her unblemished skin.

"*Hm,*" Sophie muttered. Had Charlotte mentioned something about Miss Prentice? Perhaps it would come to her. She turned and looked at the two open trunks, each partially filled, and sighed. Maybe tomorrow she would finish them. Right then, she wanted to lose herself in her music. And brood.

With the late afternoon sun on her back, Sophie strolled into town, nodding at Dan, the feedstore owner, and then at Ely. She was headed to Doc Cuthins' practice to find Sarah. They were going to eat at Fuller's, Sophie's treat for all Sarah had done to help so far.

But when she pushed open the door, Sophie saw no sign of Sarah. Deciding to wait, she sat down on one of the comfy seats set out for the doctor's patients. She'd quickly discovered he was very well-respected in town and had been ever since arriving as a young doctor over twenty-five years earlier.

Next to her chair was an old newspaper, and she was surprised and delighted to see the article on the front page had the byline "Charles Sanborn." *What a smart sister-in-law she had!* And, it was clear Sarah loved Charlotte, like a daughter.

Picking up the paper, she started to read. A few minutes later, the door to the examination room opened.

"Sophie," came a masculine voice that was definitely not Doc Cuthins.

Riley Dalcourt! Now, why did his voice cause a subtle reaction in her body and brain, as her pulse quickened and her mind cast around for something to say. Perhaps it was the same reason she'd taken care with her hair and clothing before walking into town, on the off chance she might encounter him again.

Sophie slowly put down the newspaper, giving herself time to get a hold of any wayward emotions, then looked up, knowing she would see his strikingly handsome face.

She gasped. "Sweet mother," she said aloud, rising to her feet. "What happened to you?"

He laughed. His face—and she assumed the rest of him, too—was scrubbed clean, and without his hat, she could see his hair was as russet brown as Alfred's mane and looked soft to the touch. And touch it, she wanted to do.

Gracious. Clean pants, bleached shirt, even clean boots.

"Are you finished looking me over?" he asked, arms crossed.

She blushed for the first time in years. She only hoped her mouth hadn't been hanging open.

"I didn't know you had it in you to tidy up so well." She tried to sound nothing more than casually jovial.

He rewarded her with his dimpled grin that actually made her stomach flutter.

"Believe it or not, beautiful lady," he said, "this is how I look every morning and every evening. It's the in-between hours that give me a bit of trouble. At least, when I'm in Spring."

She was thinking about how he'd called her beautiful and about seeing him in the mornings and last thing each night. Sophie nearly shook her head to clear away the wicked thoughts.

"And when you're not in Spring City?" she asked.

He shrugged. "Then I look like everyone else, I guess. I don't have a reason to get covered in dirt in San Francisco."

She was just thinking how Riley Dalcourt could never look like everyone else, not with that face, those eyes, that smile, when his words caught up with her.

"San Francisco?"

"Yup. I thought Sarah might've told you."

"Told her what?" Sarah asked, coming in the door with a package in one hand and her purse in the other.

"That I don't live here full time, but am—"

"Riley, why would we be talking about you, son?" She looked at Sophie. "Men! They believe they're all we think about and all we talk about."

Sophie smiled. Actually, she would have liked to have heard more about Riley, but she wasn't about to say so.

Sarah put her things down on her table. "Are you all done in the back?"

"Yes, ma'am. Bottles labeled, samples checked, instruments cleaned."

"Good, then you can take Sophie here along to Fuller's. I'll be over as soon as I can."

"Oh," Sophie said, feeling immediately awkward at imposing on Riley. "If you're not ready, I'll wait here with you."

"Nonsense. I have a quick letter to write to catch the afternoon post. A bit of a supply issue," she said, looking at Riley as she wrinkled up her nose. "You know that cramp bark from Eli Lilly. They keep telling me it's on the way. Very frustrating." She turned back to Sophie. "But it's past lunchtime, and I can't have you wasting away to nothing on my account. Get along, and I'll follow right quick."

"If you're sure," Sophie said and found herself being pushed out the door by Sarah, followed by Riley, who had grabbed his hat off the hat stand and closed the door behind them. But she didn't take a single step along the wooden sidewalk.

"Really, I'm perfectly fine, happy even, going to Fuller's by myself," she insisted. "I don't need a keeper or a babysitter."

He fingered the brim of his hat, then rubbed his hand along the back of his neck. Obviously, he didn't want to go against Sarah Cuthins.

"How about we go as friends, then? I'm getting hungry myself."

Sophie paused. *What was the harm?*

"Oh, well, in that case." She started walking toward Fuller's, and he fell into step beside her. They were silent for a moment, but not awkwardly so.

"You were right, by the way," he said casually.

"I usually am. Right, I mean. That's what my brother says. But about what precisely?"

He shot her a grin, apparently appreciating her sassy retort.

"About the cake. It was only a box of crumbs by the time we opened it."

We . . .

"I ate it anyway, still tasted fine. But some people like things just so, I guess."

"Some people, such as your fiancée?" Sophie bit her tongue. She shouldn't have pried. But Riley chuckled.

"She's particular, all right."

"Most women are," Sophie agreed, trying to redeem herself for snooping.

"Sit anywhere you like," Jessie offered, taking a second look when she saw Sophie and Riley together. She clucked her tongue and walked away.

"Why am I getting the feeling this is not a good idea?" Sophie asked, tilting her head and looking at this umber-haired man who seemed to have the easiest smile of anyone she'd ever known. There it was again.

"No reason on earth," Riley said, evidently not wanting to discuss his fiancée anymore. "Two friends having lunch, that's all. And the only thing better than the turkey pie—"

"And the lemon cake," Sophie cut in.

"And the lemon cake," Riley repeated, "is the meatloaf. Better than my mother used to make, and that's saying something."

"Where are your parents?" Sophie figured since she'd already asked him why he was filthy, she could at least ask him something a little more appropriate.

"I don't rightly now." He chuckled at her expression, but paused as Jessie took their orders. "My father's a cartographer, and my mother loves him very much. So when he's out surveying, she's by his side. But our house is out of town about a mile. Dad likes it quiet."

Now it was Sophie's turn to laugh. "Spring City seems quiet enough without needing to move out of town."

"It wasn't always this way. We used to have a gold rush going on, but that all died out years ago. Anyway, even then, it was probably nothing compared to Boston."

He knew where she was from, which meant he must have asked Sarah.

"Or San Francisco," she added, remembering their conversation that had been cut short.

"True. First time I got off the train there, whew, I was gawking like a greenhorn. The number of ships, the military contingents, the prostitutes—sorry, but I'm just telling you—so many people, Mexicans and Chinese, and Chinese ladies dressed up as Mexicans, and the Barbary Coast. Sophie, you'd have to see it for yourself." He paused. "Well, you can't, you're a woman! They have gambling dens with two hundred men in them at a time. That's like all the population of Spring City in one place."

He stopped and took a bite of the hot food. Sophie couldn't help but notice his eyes had taken on a certain spark. Obviously, despite being born and raised in Spring City, Riley Dalcourt was taken by the excitement of a real metropolis.

Swallowing, he continued. "Less than a decade ago, with what they called the Big Bonanza, a million dollars a day for two months came flowing into the city. Can you imagine?"

She couldn't. Everyone had heard stories of the gold rush and the Comstock Lode, but the amount of wealth was truly staggering.

"And you notice how quiet it is here?" Riley asked.

She nodded. She'd noticed little else since she got off the train.

"In San Francisco, it seems as though music is on every corner as soon as the sun goes down. Everything from accordions to violins and everything in between, including bagpipes. Sometimes, you just have to stop and listen and toss coins in 'cause you can't believe how beautiful it sounds, all mixed together, the hand-organs and flutes, the banjos and even pianos."

"Pianos! On the street?" She nearly choked on her bite of meatloaf.

"No, no," he said and laughed. "The pianos are in the saloons, but all the windows and the doors are open, and it all floats out, along with some of the saddest looking folk you'd ever care to see."

"Who could be sad with all that music?" Sophie wondered.

"Well, the gambling is bad, the drinking is worse. And the women!" He stopped abruptly, and she detected a flush under his tanned skin. "In the Barbary Coast, everyone seems addicted to something and can't help themselves."

"And what about you?"

He smiled. "The only thing I'm addicted to is riding as far and fast as I can when I'm here, where there's plenty of open space to do it. I don't have a lot of space in San Francisco."

Sophie felt a sharp desire to see this coastal city, to compare it to her own beloved Boston, and to explore its differences. Maybe she would make that her next destination. But before she could say anything more, Sophie realized the restaurant had grown exceedingly quiet, the stillness broken only by sharp footsteps rapping quickly across the floor, until they came up directly behind her chair and stopped.

CHAPTER FOUR

"**R**iley," the voice was soft, but it made the hair on the back of Sophie's neck stand up, and she swiveled her head around to see who it was.

The seemingly angelic Eliza Prentice stood there, her face flushed, her lucent blue eyes flashing. She looked down at Sophie, who found her own mouth had fallen slightly open although she had nothing to say.

"Hey, Eliza," Riley said, seemingly unbothered by whatever scene the rest of the diners were anticipating.

"Don't you 'hey, Eliza' me." Her voice was still so soft and low Sophie was sure only the three of them could hear. Then it rose considerably. "What in the hell do you think you're doing?"

"Miss Prentice," Sophie began as the shoe dropped and she realized Eliza must be the formidable fiancée. "I hope you're not imagining—"

"Why is she speaking to me?" Eliza said, still looking solely at Riley. "And not you?"

"Now, Eliza. Don't get all ruffled. Sit down, if you want. We're merely having a meal."

"You are not to sit down and have a meal with another woman. Do you realize what that looks like? What people are already saying? Do you realize how that makes me feel?"

Sophie saw Riley's face change at his fiancée's words, expressing an emotion that ended up looking like regret.

"Sit with us Eliza," he said, with infinite patience, "and then it won't look like anything. I'm not trying to make you feel bad."

He shot Sophie a quick rueful glance, which made Eliza stamp her foot. Luckily, since chairs hadn't been thrown or a table immediately overturned, the other customers had returned to their food and conversations.

"There's room for only one woman at this table," Eliza insisted.

Sophie did not want to be the cause of an ultimatum that would surely end either in damage to Riley's engagement or humiliation to herself when he was forced to ask her to leave. She found her voice.

"Miss Prentice, I was just leaving." She pushed her chair back, causing Eliza to take a hurried step sideways. Riley stood as well.

"Thank you for keeping me company," she said to him, and she meant it. Turning to Eliza, she added, "Thank you for your graciousness in letting me borrow your fiancé."

Eliza sucked in her breath, about to let loose with an expletive, Sophie imagined.

"There you are," Sarah Cuthins said, after hurrying over and astutely taking in the tense scene. "I'm sorry I took so long. John Worthen brought in his boy, and luckily Doc had just come back. But that young'un wouldn't stop crying even though it was only a boil on his foot."

She took hold of Sophie's elbow. "I know you've probably eaten already, but stay and keep me company." She looked back at Riley. "Thanks, for escorting Sophie to lunch." To Eliza, she said, "Good day, Eliza."

Eliza pursed her lips in reply.

"Ma'am," Riley said, nodding to Sarah. Then his eyes fixed on Sophie's for a moment.

"Sophie," he said with another nod. "I enjoyed the conversation."

He tossed some bills onto the table and turned to his fiancée. "Eliza, I'm done here. If you intend to eat, perhaps you can join these ladies." And he walked out, slowly, deliberately.

"Well, I never," Eliza declared. And without a word to either of them, she strode out after her man, pausing to kick at an empty chair by the door, sending it skidding a few feet before she slammed out of Fuller's.

Sarah still had hold of Sophie's arm, which she quickly released. "Sorry about that. I hope she wasn't too unpleasant."

They sat down at the same table in the midst of the plates. Sophie shrugged. "I've seen worse." She thought about her brother's former paramour, Helen Belgrave. The widow could make women tremble and grown men cry. Eliza wasn't even in her class.

"I really did enjoy the company. Riley told me all about San Francisco." She lapsed into silence while Sarah placed her order and chatted with Jessie.

It suddenly dawned on Sophie that Riley, with his seemingly good nature and easy smile, had been foolhardy enough to ask a woman like Eliza Prentice to marry him. She sipped at the fresh cup of coffee placed before her and thought about that puzzling fact. He must truly love Eliza, much more than Philip had loved her.

Obviously, Eliza was beautiful, but Sophie couldn't picture her even standing close to Riley when he was covered head to toe in trail dust. It made no sense, so it must be true love for both of them—either that or he was easily caught by a swaying bustle and a shock of golden hair.

As for Eliza, Sophie could see why the woman would put up with dirt and separation for the opportunity to be in Riley's muscled arms and kissing his sensual mouth. Shaking her head to clear it, Sophie tried hard to focus her attention on what Sarah was saying.

A day later, a telegram came from Charlotte asking Sophie how she was faring. Sarah brought it out to the house, and Sophie used the excuse to write back and ask Charlotte what she could discover about the music opportunities in San Francisco. She thought she'd recalled they had an opera house. If so, they might need a pianist. Or perhaps a music conservatory needed a teacher. It was useful having a sister-in-law who knew editors around the country and had the wherewithal to investigate nearly anything.

Sending the telegram the next day, she had only to wait for a response. Sophie was in no hurry to vacate Spring City after all. Everything seemed calm there except for the incident at Fuller's. As long as Sophie avoided Riley and steered clear of any further interaction with Eliza Prentice, she would enjoy the peace of the little town before moving on.

However, two days later, while Sophie sat chatting with Sarah in the doctor's office, Eliza marched by the window, looking strident.

"What is that woman's problem?" she asked. "She seems very . . . tightly wound."

Sarah laughed. "That's a kind way to put it." But she sighed. "Let's see if I can shed a little light on her. An unhappy little girl, with no mother from when she was very tiny, and a powerful but distant father. Eliza grew up to be a spoiled young woman." She tapped her fingers on her desk. "That's our Miss Prentice's story. Don't worry about her, dear. She's either a force to reckon with or to avoid. Charlotte always chose the latter."

"Charlotte is a better person than I am, then. I feel as if I want to poke Eliza with a stick, just to see what she'll do."

"Like a rattlesnake?" Sarah suggested.

"How does Riley stand her?" Sophie wished she could retrieve the words, as she saw Sarah pause. She'd gone too far now into the familiarity of their lives. But it seemed so removed from her own real life it was almost like watching a play, and she wanted to know more about the actors.

"I apologize," she said immediately. "It's none of my business."

"That's all right. Between Riley and Eliza, they've made it everyone's business anyway."

"What do you mean?"

"Public displays like the one in Fuller's the other day are nothing new. We've all been treated to an Eliza tantrum of one kind or another. It's better when Riley's away, of course. Though this time when he leaves, I believe he's planning on taking her with him."

That thought made Sophie cringe inside. "So, their wedding is planned?"

"Yup, but Eliza has put it off. Twice, I believe."

"And what does her father think of these delays?"

"Ah, Elijah Prentice is an odd one. Surly, controlling, except where Eliza is concerned. He owns most of these buildings, and makes us pay our rent on time, let me tell you. But he never leaves his house anymore."

"How unusual," Sophie commented.

"He may be an invalid. Only Eliza and their housekeeper, and Riley, of course, see him."

Sophie started to feel sorry for the young woman. Maybe she was tormented by an unhappy home life and thus tormented everyone around her in turn.

"You're best to stay out of it," Sarah cautioned, seeing the thoughtful look on Sophie's face.

"No doubt," Sophie agreed, "although maybe—"

The sound of an explosion and the shaking of the ground stopped her mid-sentence. The two women looked at each other, eyes wide. Doc came flying out of the back room.

"What in the name of God almighty?" and he ran straight out the door. They picked up their skirts and high-tailed it after him.

The groans of the injured came through the black clouds of smoke. The train's engine was on its side as was the first car that followed, and the second was tilted wildly, with the last car and caboose having jumped the tracks while remaining upright.

Everywhere was pandemonium. Most of the town's people had come running. Sophie watched Doc disappear into the acrid smoke that burned her throat with every breath. He came back moments later to bark out orders for stretchers to be made and for Sarah to grab his medical bag. Sarah was already kneeling beside a crying woman lying prone with her child in her arms.

"I'll get the bag," Sophie called out to no one in particular, and she started to run. Breathless by the time she got back to Doc's, she saw Riley's horse tethered outside, panting as hard as she was. The door was open, and she wasn't surprised to find Riley in the exam room, already gathering supplies. He looked up at her footsteps.

"I came back for Doc's bag, but you already have it," she said.

"No, this is mine." He was stuffing bandages into it. "Doc's is over there." He gestured with his head. "Grab it, would you?"

She was frozen for a moment, confused as to why he had an identical black medical bag.

"Sophie, please hurry," he urged her, and she reached for the bag.

"And smelling salts, right?" she asked.

"Yes," he said, "in there," gesturing to a cabinet. She grabbed a handful of little vials.

"Are you ready?" he called over his shoulder, already striding out.

Her arms full, she struggled to stuff everything into Doc's bag and ran after Riley. He was waiting next to his horse, his bag by his feet. Without a by-your-leave, he snatched Doc's bag from her, set it down, and assisted her into the saddle.

"Oh," she started to protest she couldn't possibly take his horse, when he thrust both bags into her arms.

"Hold these," he ordered before swinging up behind her.

"Oh," she said again, as his arms came around her to grab the reins. She was well and truly squished between the pommel, the two bags . . . and Riley.

"Hold on," he said against her ear, and they were off, the fastest ride she'd ever experienced, right past Jessie carrying blankets, right into the thick smoke, right into the injured and the saviors. Riley slid off his horse before they'd even stopped. He grabbed both bags and looked back up at her.

"Tether him to a tree, out of the smoke, will you?"

"Of course," she said.

He gave her a grateful nod and turned away. He hadn't asked her if she could ride, she thought, gripping the reins and gingerly squeezing Riley's horse to stay on. If a carriage was attached, even a fast-as-lightning Tilbury, she'd be in her element, but astride a large, muscular horse was another matter altogether.

Managing not to fall off, she made the horse go in the direction of the trees, at which point, Sophie half slid, half fell off its back before securing the animal to a branch.

Then, she dove back into the chaos. Everywhere people were reaching out their arms for assistance. Stretchers had been fashioned out of broom handles and blankets, or even plain old boards, and the injured were being carried back, some to Doc's waiting room, some right into his exam room and surgery, and some to spare beds at Fuller's Hotel.

For her part, Sophie found it easy to offer comfort wherever she could, either wrapping a blanket around someone in shock or holding a person's hand until either Riley or Doc came over to examine them for broken bones or worse. At last, she found Sarah, blood on her hands, grime on her face, matching Sophie's own appearance.

With their arms around each other's waist, they walked back to the surgery. Sarah explained they would be needed long into the night if there were bones to set.

"Are you up to it?"

Sophie was about to answer when she saw Eliza Prentice sitting on her comfortable front porch, with a book in one hand and what appeared to be a glass of iced tea in the other.

Sarah followed her gaze. "That's just how the Prentices are. She doesn't know any better."

"Ridiculous," Sophie muttered. Then she called out, "Miss Prentice, why don't you bring some of that refreshing tea to people who may be parched from the smoke?"

Eliza stared her down coldly, and Sophie tried to put her out of her head by the time they reached Doc's practice. A crowd of people were milling around, some passengers from the train, trying to check on loved ones, others just curious.

Sarah pushed through them, dragging Sophie with her.

"Good people, please go to Fuller's where Jessie will be sure to take care of you if you're hungry. Let the doctors do their job." And they went into the packed waiting room where many lay on the floor looking only slightly better than they had earlier.

Another table had been set up next to Sarah's desk, with a sheet over both. Together, they made a makeshift examination and surgical table. Riley was already busy setting a man's broken arm while he groaned in pain, his wife holding his other hand.

"What shall I do?" Sophie asked.

"Whatever Riley wants," Sarah said. "Ask him. I'll go help my Doc." Sophie watched her go and swallowed. She felt out of her element, having only ever seen the occasional carriage accident but never having had to nurse anyone sicker than a sibling with a fever.

"Riley?" she said, after going up to him on quiet feet, careful not to disturb his ministrations. "I'm here to help."

He shot her a grateful glance. "I could use some water. You, too, I bet," he said to his patient. "You're gonna be just fine. My pretty nurse here has all sorts of tricks up her sleeve."

He turned away from the patient, his mouth close to Sophie's ear, so she alone could hear his next words. "Quickly now, grab the morphine bottle from my bag. There's a measure with it. Put a teaspoon into half a glass of water and let's get it into this man. His arm is broken in three places, and it's gonna hurt like hell."

She did as she was told. And she kept on doing it for the next seven hours until everyone was bandaged or stitched and resting on a bed somewhere in the town.

After the last patient had been tended, Doc lay on Riley's makeshift table, his coat balled up under his head, with Sarah in her chair, her head resting on her husband's stomach. Riley and Sophie were on the waiting room chairs, their legs stretched out in front of them.

"Jesus! What a day," said Doc without opening his eyes. "Makes me remember why I went into medicine. Not for boils and women with the vapors."

Sarah chuckled against her husband's belly, not even lifting her head, and Sophie opened her eyes to see Doc stroking his wife's hair. She looked at Riley, whose head was back against the wall, his eyes closed.

"Why didn't anyone tell me Riley was a doctor?" Sophie wondered into the silence.

"I'm not," Riley said, eyes still closed.

"Yet," said Doc.

"Less than a year to go," added Sarah.

"That's what you do in San Francisco, attend medical school?" Sophie asked.

"Yup."

"Hell," said Doc, "he knows more than most of them doctors anyway. Been helping me since he was thirteen."

"Twelve," Riley corrected.

Sophie was impressed by his skill. She'd flinched when having to help him clean a leg wound, and thought she would faint dead away when he started stitching the man's flesh neatly together. How she stayed on her feet to blot the blood so Riley could see to finish, she didn't know.

"You did great, by the way," he said, lifting his head and looking straight into her eyes. She felt a flush of warmth rush through her.

"Didn't she though?" Sarah agreed. "Maybe you want to go into nursing."

"No, thanks. I'm just glad it's over. Does anyone know what happened?"

"A buck," Doc said.

"A large one, on the tracks," Riley added. "Maybe it was deaf or plain ornery, but it's dead now."

"No one on the train died, did they?" Sophie asked.

"Nope," said Riley. "They were lucky. The railroad will send out people to clear it all away and get the trains moving again. Nothing stops the railroad."

It was dark out, and Sophie realized all she wanted was to get home and go to bed. And Alfred needed feeding and watering. She rose to her feet.

"If you don't need me anymore, I'll be heading home."

Riley stood up immediately, then stretched his arms and twisted his neck, side to side. "I'll take you."

"No, that's all right," Sophie said, looking to see if Sarah and Doc were coming. She imagined riding on his horse again, pressed back against the length of his lean, muscled body, and she knew that wasn't a good idea, not when she was tired. Luckily, Sarah stood up.

"Sophie and I will head home together," she said, brooking no argument.

"I'll see you both home," Riley said. "It's on my way."

"What about Doc?" Sophie asked.

Riley laughed as if it were an absurd question.

"He'll sleep in the back room, just in case. It's what he's always done, when someone's birthing, dying, or anything in between."

The three of them stepped outside into the cool night air. As if she'd been waiting, Eliza alighted from her wagon. She had a basket with her.

"Here's my talented man," she said. "I've brought you a hot meal, some soup and fresh-baked bread."

Riley sighed. "I think I'm too tired to eat, Eliza. I'm going to head home."

Sophie couldn't help but notice how clean and fresh Eliza looked in comparison to the rest of them, for whom the term "battered and bloodied" came to mind.

"Nonsense, you have to eat. See, I had your horse brought up." He was tied to the back of Eliza's wagon. "Get in, Riley. I'm taking you home and feeding you. And that's that."

"What about the ladies?" he asked, casting a look at them, his eyes fixing on Sophie's.

"Don't you worry about us, Riley," Sarah said. "You were a wonderful healer today. Now, go spend some time with your fiancée. The two of us will get ourselves home."

Sophie spared him a glance and found him still staring at her. Quickly, she looked away, grateful when Sarah grabbed her hand and started across the street to the wagon.

"Thanks again," Riley called after them, and Sophie knew it was for her.

She simply nodded and waved, not wanting to look back and see Eliza with her perfectly clean hand on Riley's arm. But she heard Eliza add, "Riley, I even made you some fresh iced tea."

That made Sophie turn, just as Eliza shot her a glance of pure malice.

Sophie shuddered. *All of a sudden, she couldn't get out of this town fast enough.*

CHAPTER FIVE

The sun splayed across Sophie's face, waking her the next day. Stretching, she sat up and realized it was late. Very late for her. Back home, noises of the city always had her up early. Here, no noises intruded, and she'd found herself sleeping longer each morning. Today, she had an excuse. The previous evening's toil could be blamed for her staying in bed until the sun was high in the sky.

After dressing and eating, she went to the piano, working on a song she hadn't realized she was writing in bits and pieces over the past few days until it came out of her all at once, flowing easily from her head to her fingers.

Lost in the music, she didn't hear him until he spoke.

"Damn. That was beautiful."

She jumped and rose from the piano stool.

"Riley, how did you . . . ?"

She left off, trying to catch her breath at finding him standing in the parlor doorway. Her heart was racing, she couldn't deny it. He wasn't covered in grime. In fact, he looked very good, as if he'd taken extra care with his appearance. She wanted to tell him he looked fine either way and bit her own tongue, unsure what impropriety might pop out.

"I was about to knock when I heard the most unbelievable music. And it was coming from you," he said, wonder in his voice, his eyes fixed on her as if he hadn't seen her before. "The door was unlocked," he added.

Sophie was blushing again for the second time in as many days. *What was it with this man?* However, she saw no reason to pretend modesty. She was talented and she knew it. So all she said was, "Thank you."

Then what? What did he want? "Can I make you a cup of coffee?"

"I'd rather hear you play some more," he said, coming closer and taking a seat in the parlor.

Sophie stared at him a moment. She'd played for large audiences with nary a qualm when performing at school. Now, however, wanting to play flawlessly for Riley, a few raw nerves made her stomach spasm. It was an odd sensation. Imagining the worries as fireflies trapped in a jar, she opened the lid and set them free.

"All right." Sitting again, she flicked her long, nearly black hair over her shoulders and closed her eyes a moment, deciding what to play. Not her own composition, which he'd stumbled upon, but something really spectacular. Of course— Mozart's *Rondo alla Turca*.

She played for five minutes, then ten, not noticing the passing of time but occasionally looking over at him. He sat with his eyes closed, taking it in. She liked that. It was easier to play without him watching her. When she finished, after the last resonance receded, there was only silence. Then Riley's chair creaked as he stood up and came over to her.

Wordlessly taking her hand, he drew her to her feet. Then he took her other hand and brought her round to face him. She thought he would say she'd played well. It was, after all, a difficult piece. Yet as she looked up into his warm brown eyes, she caught her breath at what she saw.

Instantly, she knew what was coming. She'd seen that look on a man's face before, and she couldn't move even if she'd wanted to.

Sure enough, Riley lowered his mouth to hers and kissed her.

Sophie remained frozen. She knew she should step back and slap him. She should scream at his outrageous behavior. She did neither. Instead, she leaned in toward his tender kiss, and as she did so, whatever was happening between them ignited like wildfire.

His mouth slanted across hers and his lips moved against her own, while his hands dropped hers to encircle her waist and pull her closer. Her nostrils were filled with the scent of him, clean vanilla-scented soap and a hint of leather. Her own hands moved up to rest against his broad chest, and she could feel the staccato of his heartbeat, loud and fierce against her sensitive fingers.

When his mouth became more insistent and opened against hers, she felt his teeth tug at her lower lip, and her knees went weak.

"Sophie," he half-whispered, half-groaned against her mouth.

She was about to pull away, knew she had to, but before she did, she barely touched his upper lip with her tongue.

Suddenly, his hands were buried in her hair, holding her impossibly closer, and instead of letting go, she lifted her arms around his neck and stood on tiptoe to give him better access.

She relished the feel of her breasts grazing the front of him and of her taut nipples being crushed between them. His tongue urged her lips apart, and she opened them, letting him slip inside. Instantly, she felt a low flutter in her stomach and, a moment later, dampness between her legs.

"Riley," she said, her voice and her breathing ragged. "Please." *Stop this madness, for I cannot. Let me go*, she urged silently.

As if he'd heard her unspoken pleas, he did stop, pressing his forehead to her own. Eyes closed, breathing heavy.

"Damn."

She was caught by the husky tone of his voice, shaken, stunned, and sensual.

"Damn," she said back.

He laughed softly, still locked in their close embrace, so she could feel all his body moving as he did. But she had the distinct notion he didn't think it any more amusing than she did.

"What *was* that?" he asked at last, leaning away so he could look into her face, keeping his hands on her waist.

That was splendid, she wanted to say.

However, as he gently ran his thumb across her lower lip, she stepped away, out of the circle of his arms and shivered.

"It was completely wrong, that's what it was." She went down the hall to the kitchen on unsteady legs.

"Because of Eliza?" He was following closely behind her.

"Of course," she said without turning around. "You are engaged to be married. You are in love with your fiancée." She hated that her words sounded more like a question than a statement. *Wasn't he?*

"I *am* engaged," he agreed, causing her a pang of regret she had no right to feel.

He sat down heavily at the kitchen table and, still without looking at him, Sophie lit the stove with shaking hands before putting on the kettle. When she had her emotions in check, she turned. He had his head in his hands.

"But I don't love her," he said without looking up, muffled into his hands. "I care about her because I've known her so long. I wouldn't want anything bad to happen to her."

Like having a broken heart. Sophie could easily imagine Eliza's pain.

"But I don't ever feel like I *need* to kiss her." He raised his head and looked at her, his tawny eyes locking with her dark-blue ones. "Sophie, I was desperate to kiss you. And I want to do it again. And more."

She swallowed. "I think this is . . . lust," she told him, not denying that she wanted him, too.

He dropped his head back down and laughed, but it wasn't a joyful sound. Running a hand through his hair, he asked her, "Have you ever been in love?"

She hesitated, pouring the water into the coffee-pot. She thought of Philip and how many tears she'd cried. She would have married him if he'd proposed to her. She'd let Philip kiss her many times, and they'd touched each other in ways that probably should have waited until after their wedding vows.

But Riley's kiss! That was something else entirely. It was overwhelming in its intensity, and she had to curl her fingers into her palms to finally speak without trembling. *Had she ever been in love?*

"Yes."

Riley raised his head from his hands again. "Where is he?"

"Perhaps he felt about me the way you say you feel about Eliza." It hurt her to think Philip could dismiss his feelings for her as easily as Riley had for Eliza. "Unlike you, though, my beau, Mr. Wainright, didn't seem to mind how he hurt me." That made her want to have another good cry. She ought to be alone. "I think you better leave."

"You just made me a cup of coffee," Riley reminded her.

"Yes, yes I did." She was dazed, shocked even by the fierceness of the desire she had felt—still felt—for this man seated before her, the very instant he'd touched her.

"All right, you can stay for coffee." She sat with offerings of milk and sugar, and they both slowly stirred the dark, steaming liquid. Now that her heart had stopped pounding, Sophie decided she was glad he wasn't going to jump up and ride away too quickly.

"Why did you come here?" she asked him.

He pulled a piece of paper out of his pocket. "You have a telegram."

He handed it to her. It was folded in three but not sealed. *There was no privacy in this town.* She wondered if Riley had read it. She set it down. It had to be from Charlotte and might mention San Francisco. *What if he thought she was following him?*

"Aren't you going to read it?"

"Later."

He shrugged. "I don't read upside down very well."

She rolled her eyes and opened it, holding the paper closely.

Dearest Sophie,

Too much info about San Francisco to put in this telegram. Yes, music. Loads of it. You would love it. Reed is furious and thinks I'm pushing you farther west. Sending you long letter today. Love, Charlotte.

She folded it again and laid it carefully beside her cup. They both sipped in silence.

"Is it from this Wainright character?" Riley asked abruptly.

"No." *Why would he think such a thing?*

"He's an idiot, then. He ought to be begging your forgiveness." He stood up. "I have to go. I promised Doc I'd pick up some supplies in Denver."

They were at the front door before he spoke again. "I'll do some thinking while I'm riding. I have to figure out what to tell Eliza."

What to tell—

Sophie put her hand to her mouth. Was he going to rip the girl's heart out as Philip had done hers? And all because of her?

"Riley, what do you mean?"

He looked into her face, and his jaw clenched. Very slowly, he reached out and curled his hand around the back of her neck. Mesmerized by his gaze, Sophie didn't flinch as he held her steady, then drew her in. She held her breath as Riley lowered his head, but this time, his kiss was feather light. Even so, she was unable or unwilling to pull away until he released her. She drew in a long, ragged breath.

At last he answered her question. "I don't know, but I can't imagine going through the rest of my life without *that.*"

And he was gone.

Without that, he'd said. Heading to her place of solace, she sank down onto the piano stool. Without *that feeling,* be it desire or passion, whatever it was he was missing with Eliza Prentice.

He hadn't said "without you," Sophie noticed, but such a sentiment would have been unthinkable. They'd only known each other a week. Despite the short time, though, it was quite obvious she'd awakened something in him Eliza didn't fulfill.

Plainly, Riley wanted her. To be honest with herself, Sophie wanted him, too. But she squared her shoulders. She would tell him no if he tried to kiss her again.

Riley pushed out of Sophie Malloy's house and vaulted onto his horse in one angry bound. *Damn him for a fool!* Why had he even ventured over there, knowing the temptation, knowing how irrationally he behaved in her presence? And now he'd gone and kissed her!

He spurred his mount into a gallop, hoping the dry breeze would blow away the lascivious thoughts in his head, thoughts that were sending heat shooting straight to his groin. He ought to be hanged for even thinking them.

The thundering hoofbeats beneath him merged with the memory of Sophie's piano playing. He took a deep breath, puffed out his cheeks, and released it. The music he'd heard when he walked up to the Sanborn home had gone right inside him and grabbed his heart. It was so sad and so beautiful at the same time. Like Sophie.

And then she'd played only for him, complex music that seemed to build and grow and expand in the room. It was as if she were giving him a gift with each note, each chord. How could he *not* kiss her? He'd been compelled to. He still was.

He'd meant what he said to Sophie. It seemed unimaginable never again to experience what he'd felt when holding her. He certainly hadn't felt anything like it before, not with Eliza and not with any other woman he'd ever touched. He couldn't know for sure, but he was fairly certain Sophie had felt something special, too.

But what in the hell could he tell Eliza that wouldn't destroy their carefully negotiated engagement? Absolutely nothing. He wouldn't disappoint her for the world, and the option to sweep away his obligations simply did not exist. Nor could he ever bring himself to hurt a woman whom he had known his entire life and who trusted him.

In the end, he'd lied to Sophie, hadn't he? For he had no choice but to live without her. If he was smart, he'd never go near her again.

"Done and done," Sophie said, brushing off her hands while Sarah mopped her own forehead with a handkerchief.

"We did it."

"Yes," said Sophie, feeling satisfied.

"We should have asked for help, perhaps." Sarah eyed the two trunks in the back of the wagon. It had taken them nearly ten minutes to push them up the makeshift ramp they'd created.

"But we didn't." Sophie didn't want to ask Riley for any favors. He was not her man, and Doc was busy. "Let's get them to the platform."

"And then we'll come back for the other one."

Sophie looked at the last trunk. If they could make the ramp higher . . .

"Forget about it," Sarah said, guessing Sophie's thoughts. "It won't take but a few minutes to get to the station, unload, and come back."

As it turned out, they didn't have to do it by themselves. Dan from the feed store was loading sacks when they arrived at the platform.

"Good day, ladies." He tipped his hat to them. Before they knew it, he'd not only unloaded the trunks destined for Boston, but scooted with Sophie back to Charlotte's house to get the last one.

As they turned the wagon into Charlotte's homestead, with Sophie seated next to Dan, they heard horse's hooves.

"Hey-ho, Riley," Dan called out.

Sophie turned to see him, but except for staring in their direction and raising his hat, Riley made no answering call.

Sophie wanted to tell him why she was driving with Dan to her home, feeling uncomfortable he might get the wrong idea.

The next second, she realized how silly that was. How could she care about the opinion of a man who had two-timed his fiancée by passionately kissing her?

But she did.

CHAPTER SIX

Sophie went to the post office in the general store for two days in a row, hoping to receive Charlotte's missive. She'd seen neither hide nor hair of Riley Dalcourt, which had made her a tad edgy, although she knew it was for the best. *Temptation had never been her friend.* She remembered how she'd been sick on chocolate as a child and on absinthe in Paris, much to Philip's amusement.

She had to admit with every fiber of her being, she would like to be kissed by Riley again, but every ounce of moral character she owned knew it was wrong. She would avoid temptation and its consequences, she vowed.

Seeing how she hadn't heard a bloodcurdling scream from the direction of Eliza's house, Sophie figured Riley had not, in the end, said a word to his fiancée about their kissing. She assured herself that was for the best. But what if she ended up being neighbors with him and his new bride in San Francisco?

Ridiculous! What a silly notion. In such a large city, if she indeed decided to go, she might never run into them at all. Why, even here in Spring, she hardly had set eyes upon Eliza since the train accident. And then her luck ran out.

"You-hoo," Eliza called to her as Sophie left Webster's store.

Sophie considered breaking into a run. After all, the woman had packages in her hands and could easily be out-maneuvered.

"Sophie," Eliza called again, and Sophie slowed to a stop, just as Eliza planted herself right in her path.

"I want to say I'm sorry for my behavior in the restaurant." Her pale-blue eyes were peering up at Sophie sincerely.

"No, please don't." Being apologized to by someone whom you have actually wronged was about as uncomfortable an experience as sitting on a pin cushion. Sophie feared somehow Eliza would see evidence of Riley's betrayal, written on her own guilty face.

"I mean, it's unnecessary."

"Yes, it is necessary," the petite blond continued. "I have a temper and I use it without thinking."

That seemed rather self-aware for someone whom Sarah Cuthins seemed to think was a spoiled brat. On the other hand, if that was the reaction when all Riley did was eat a meal with another woman, what would Eliza do if she discovered his latest indiscretion?

Sophie didn't want to find out. All she could do was smile in what she hoped was a friendly way. Eliza smiled back.

"To make it up to you, I want you to come to my house for dinner on Saturday."

That was a surprise, an unwelcome one, too.

"Well, I . . . uh . . . *hm*." Sophie could think of no plausible excuse. Except one. "I may have already left Spring City by then. But thank you, all the same."

"Oh, so soon." Did Eliza look happier? "But if you're still here, then you'll come? Yes?"

Sophie stalled. "I'll have to check with Sarah. I may have mentioned I would dine with—"

"Oh, Sarah won't mind one way or the other," Eliza interrupted. "Please say yes. It's the least I can do."

"All right, then," Sophie said at last, not seeing any way to get out of it, short of leaving town.

"Wonderful," Eliza said, as if she meant it. "And do bring Riley's friend Dan. I hear you're sort of sweet on him."

At Sophie's open mouth, Eliza added, "I can invite him separately if you like."

"No, I'm not. That is, please don't—"

Eliza laughed. "It can't be only you and me and Riley. We need a foursome, and I'm sorry to say Daddy can't join us for dinner."

Sophie blanched. Now it was a dinner party of four?

"Then it's settled. You go ask Dan, and we'll see you on Saturday. Ta-ta." And she was gone.

What the devil just happened? Sophie watched Eliza walk back toward her house. Why did Eliza suppose she liked Dan? Unless Riley had mentioned seeing them together. How odd! But Eliza was correct on one count. They certainly couldn't have a dinner with the three of them. It would be the height of discomfort. It would be bad enough with the four of them, but at least Dan would be a distraction. He had not only been helpful with her trunks, he'd displayed good humor, as well.

Sophie supposed engaging in a little social interaction would be welcome. Charlotte had survived there with not much besides Sarah for companionship, but Sophie was used to friends gathering in each other's parlors back home, as well as in the little apartments in Rome when she'd stayed there studying music. Truthfully, she couldn't deny a curiosity, if not eagerness, to see Riley again.

Perhaps she would find there was nothing between them after all—that the kiss had been the result of a peculiarly tempting situation which, upon seeing him once more, she felt no inclination to repeat.

So, she found herself asking Dan to accompany her to dinner on Saturday.

He looked stunned, then gladdened by the invitation.

"You know, it's been a long time since I was inside the Prentice house. It'll be interesting, I reckon."

"I reckon," Sophie murmured under her breath, having never used the word before.

He picked up a sack of grain and hoisted it over his shoulder heading to the back of Drew's feedstore. The ground sloped sharply away at the back, and the rear door led to a deck built on stilts.

"You can see over the whole valley back here," Dan told her, inviting her to look.

Sophie ventured after him, to see the view she'd experienced from the train when she'd arrived. It was lovely, but so empty, with nothing on the horizon but trees and mountains. She missed the city, no doubt about it. Right then, movement on the right caught her eye.

As the ground sloped away and curved right, it met up with Main Street and the Prentice house a few blocks down. Part of the house was visible from where she stood, but mostly she could look down into the backyard, which stretched on forever until the cultivated area ended and the wild landscape began. And in that yard were Eliza and Riley, walking toward a small flowerbed with a bench and behind it, an arbor. Sophie was transfixed.

The couple stopped, and she held her breath. Their heads were bent close as if talking, and then she watched Riley put his hands on Eliza's tiny waist, pulling her against him. He had to bend way down because she was so short in stature.

Gasping, Sophie could almost feel Riley's hands on her own waist. When their lips touched, she turned to flee the deck, bumping into Dan's chest.

"Steady," he said, and then looked past her shoulder. She turned to see Riley and Eliza still kissing.

"Woo-wee," Dan exclaimed. "Those two are usually colder than an icehouse in February. Something has sparked his fire all right!"

Sophie managed to murmur something incomprehensible about needing to get home and succeeded in making her escape.

With extra special care, Sophie dressed in the best dress she'd brought with her—a satin gown in violet, her favorite color, which contrasted strikingly with her dark hair. It had a form-fitting cuirass bodice, giving her a slim silhouette, with a small train and a hint of a pad for the bustle.

She pulled her hair up and back on top and left the rest to cascade over her slender shoulders. It wasn't Parisian or London fashion, she thought, eyeing herself in the one small mirror resting on the dresser, but it would definitely do for Spring City.

She heard the wagon and couldn't help wishing it were Riley picking her up.

"Stop that," she scolded her image sharply before going downstairs. Dan knocked once and she opened the door to his appraising gaze.

Then he laughed. "Oh, Miss Sophie. Eliza won't like that, not one bit. Oh no, she won't."

"Whatever do you mean?"

He shook his head. "This is gonna be interesting, that's all I can say." And he offered her his arm.

The Prentice house was fastidious, from the tidy front porch with plump pillows on the swing and rocker, to the cool tile entryway with its hallstand and vase of freshly cut flowers. Nothing was out of place. Except Sophie, who immediately wanted to be just about anywhere else, than walking into Eliza's parlor.

They were greeted by a housekeeper, perhaps Mr. Prentice's nurse, and the aroma of roast pork. A few steps farther in and she saw Riley, whose jaw clenched tightly as he took in her appearance, his eyes clearly appreciative. He stood up from the sofa with a tentative smile for her and a firm handshake for Dan.

"Eliza," Riley called out, as if a husband summoning his wife, and the blond woman came from another room, wiping her hands on a kitchen towel, which she dropped on the credenza.

She wore a simple, well-made dress in the perfect blue to bring out her light eyes with matching ribbons in her hair. And startling to Sophie, Eliza wore a spotlessly clean and pressed white apron tied around her waist. No doubt, it was for effect and not for cooking. She was the picture of domesticity. The perfect housewife.

Sophie felt too tall, overdressed, and even garish.

Eliza came to stand by Riley, resting her hand on his sleeve.

"So glad you could both come," she said, eyeing Sophie's gown. Her nostrils flared slightly, but she kept a smile in place. "I guess they dress up more in the city for a friendly dinner than we do here," Eliza commented. "You look so lovely, doesn't she, Riley?"

Oh my God. Sophie felt herself blanche. *Does she know?*

She watched Riley swallow, as his eyes flicked over her from neckline to hem. "Yes, she does."

It took Sophie a moment to realize he was answering Eliza and not her own unspoken question.

Sophie was only glad Eliza hadn't stepped forward to kiss both her cheeks as would have happened in Boston, no matter the level of friendliness or enmity.

"Good evening, Dan," Eliza said, holding out her hand, which he took awkwardly, obviously unused to dinner parties. He held on, looking unsure whether to kiss it or shake it.

"Miss Eliza," he mumbled and let her hand drop. Then he added gallantly, "You look fine yourself."

Eliza smiled again, but it was clear to Sophie it wasn't genuine. Glancing at Riley, she found his brown eyes were locked on hers until she lowered her gaze. Nothing about this felt right.

"Let's sit, shall we?" Eliza said, moving away from the silent group. "Riley, why don't you get everyone a drink. I made some punch. And dinner is almost ready."

Sophie didn't miss Riley's quizzical glance at Eliza. Apparently, this wasn't a usual occurrence. It was too "normal." And if she'd gleaned one thing about Eliza Prentice, it was that she was a hellion, willful, spoiled wildcat, not a simpering female who was happy to cook a meal for her man.

She heard a crash in the kitchen and a muffled oath. Eliza's cheeks turned red. "I'll go see about that." And she was gone. Evidently, the meal's real cook was about to get an earful from the hostess.

Riley turned back to them and shrugged.

"How's business?" he asked Dan.

"Good, but only 'cause Millan's Feed went under in Dorset."

"Dorset?" Sophie repeated. And at her voice, Riley's gaze swung to her lips. Her eyes widened. *How in blazes was she going to get through this evening?*

"Next town over," Dan offered. "The train doesn't stop there."

He trailed off, and they sat in silence again until he turned to her.

"Was that the last of the trunks?" Dan asked her.

Sophie beamed at him, placing her hand on his arm. "Yes, thanks. You are my hero." His cheeks turned a decided shade of pink at her words.

She turned to include Riley in her smile but froze at his narrow-eyed look, and she immediately dropped her hand from Dan. Now why, she scolded herself, was she feeling guilty for being nice to Dan?

"Dan helped Sarah and me to get Charlotte's trunks onto the train," Sophie told him, keeping her gaze steady. "I'm nearly finished here." She felt a twinge of melancholy at the thought of leaving, but leave she must.

"We all wouldn't mind, Miss Sophie, if you stuck around a while longer, right Riley?" Dan said, but Sophie didn't get to hear his reply. At that moment, Eliza returned.

"What did I miss? It's no matter. Dinner's ready. Shall we go in?" and she led the way into the dining room.

They stood, and Riley let Sophie pass first, feeling the heat of his body through the fine fabric of her gown as she brushed past him. She curled her fingers into her palms at the wave of desire that hit her.

At the round table with the pretty lace cloth, Sophie couldn't escape sitting in close quarters. The ladies faced each other, as did the men. Sophie spent the meal making small talk, answering Eliza's stream of questions about Boston and Rome. She couldn't help noticing out of the corner of her eye that Riley was watching her. In turn, Eliza watched Riley.

Sophie wanted to bolt for the door, so bizarre was this little gathering. She was only grateful that Dan seemed guileless and unaware of any tension.

"Your father is unwell, I hear," Sophie said, when all other topics had been worn out.

"Yes, he stays in his room most of the time. His body is weak now, but he's still strong of mind and personality. I don't know how I could leave him." Eliza's voice sounded full of genuine concern.

"You mean when you get married and move to San Francisco?" Sophie asked.

Riley seemed very intent on his potatoes, and Eliza sighed.

"I suppose I must." She looked at Riley who shot her a quick glance. "But I seem to be dragging my feet, don't I? Poor man has been asking and waiting, and waiting and asking for years, it seems."

Riley coughed. "A couple at any rate."

"But I don't think we'll end up in San Francisco in the end. Riley's almost done with training, and then he'll take over for Doc."

"That was the plan," Riley said, sounding to Sophie about as excited as a boy being told to practice scales instead of play outside on a warm summer day.

"I always wondered why you two didn't up and get the wedding over with?" Dan said, before stuffing roasted pork in his mouth. "I mean, you're not getting any younger," he added, jabbing his fork toward each of them.

Sophie would have laughed if Eliza hadn't blanched and excused herself from the table. "I'll go check on my father," she said and hurried up the stairs.

What the hell was going on here? Sophie wondered. After Riley's kiss, she would find it difficult to wait a day, let alone a year or two, to consummate that spark of passion. But maybe Eliza and Riley hadn't waited. She'd seen them kiss. Maybe they enjoyed all the pleasures of husband and wife without the sanctimony of marriage. They wouldn't be the first.

But why not marry, even if Eliza couldn't join him in San Francisco when he'd first started school?

"She's a devoted daughter," Sophie said, thinking perhaps the sick father was the reason why Eliza had postponed the wedding twice, as Sarah had indicated.

"Yup," Riley agreed. He put his fork down. "But it won't be long now."

"Is that right?" Dan asked.

"'Fraid so. Mr. Prentice has fluid in his lungs and can hardly breathe."

"It may be a relief to both of them, then," Sophie said, barely above a whisper, thinking of when her own father passed away after a blessedly brief illness. No one had wanted to see him suffer or deteriorate from the strong man she and her brother and sisters had known all their lives.

"My apologies," Eliza said, when she came back, moving as swiftly as she'd left, and giving them all a watery smile. "He's sleeping peacefully. Now, who wants some pie?"

Sophie watched Riley put his hand on Eliza's shoulder to offer her his strength and saw the special look he received in return. It was touching and made her throat close, and she started counting the minutes until she could escape.

"They should marry and get it over with," Dan said as soon as they were in his wagon. That was just what Sophie had been thinking through dessert and brandy. She had found it increasingly difficult to sit in Eliza's firelit parlor, watching Riley's hands as he held a glass and his mouth when he spoke, all the while feeling ashamed of their earlier behavior.

"Perhaps Miss Prentice is waiting for her father to pass," Sophie offered. "She wouldn't want to move out and set up a home while he is so ill."

"I always thought she was waiting for Riley to come back a full-fledged doctor before she'd marry him."

"Maybe both," Sophie said, not enjoying the idle gossip but unsure how to stop Dan. "You and Riley have been friends a long time?"

"Grew up together," he said, seeming happy to talk about Riley. "He always wanted to tend things, whether a hurt dog or a bird with a broken wing or any of his friends. Hell . . . uh, I mean, heck, I think he caused half my boyhood injuries just so he could patch me up."

Sophie laughed, imagining them as young, troublesome boys. But she was glad when she was back at her own front door. The evening had stretched her nerves to breaking.

"Thanks for asking me," Dan said, walking her to the front porch, nervousness apparent in his faltering step and his hesitant look.

"Thank you for accompanying me." Sophie tried to put him at ease. As far as she was concerned, they had not gone to dinner as a couple, but she was unsure if he knew that. When he leaned toward her, perhaps to kiss her cheek, she stuck out her hand. Dan paused, looked at it, and then grasped hold.

"Goodnight, then," he said.

"I'll be seeing you at the store," Sophie offered, opening the front door with her free hand behind her back, "as soon as I need something for Alfred." Although she would probably be gone before that happened, and Sarah would have Alfred back in her paddock.

"Yes, ma'am," he agreed, still gripping her hand and staring at her.

Smiling, she extricated her hand from his with a small tug.

"Goodnight then." With mercy on the man, she gave him a quick peck on his cheek and vanished inside. *Good lord, but that was awkward!* Sophie leaned her back against the door and listened. She heard his footsteps and then the horse's hooves as Dan drove his wagon away.

"Piano, piano, piano," she muttered to herself and within minutes was lost to the music—melancholy music, both for Eliza and her father, and for herself and Riley, too.

CHAPTER SEVEN

She'd been expecting him all morning. When Sophie heard his sharp rap at the door, she jumped up from the sofa in the parlor where she'd been reading and rereading Charlotte's letter. As she'd hoped, it contained information about a music school and a performance opportunity and even a rooming house. She was to expect a letter of introduction to the San Francisco Symphony from an editor for whom Charlotte had written an article and who also was a San Francisco patron of the arts. Sophie's stomach was fluttering with excitement.

Hesitating at the front door, without even thinking, she raised her hand to smooth her hair. Today, it was coiled in a neat, "no-nonsense" bun, as her mother called it. She took a long breath and then opened the door.

Riley was covered in dust and holding a package in his hand. Her heart sped up, and she half-clung to the door, excited, nervous, wishing she felt nothing at all.

"Cake?" she asked, letting a smile tug at her lips, but he gave none in return.

"Actually, cookies." Riley took her in from head to toe in a swift, serious glance. "From Sarah. I ran into her earlier. You looked gorgeous last night. You still do." His words tumbled out all at once.

Sophie straightened and took a step back, deciding to ignore his immediate venture into inappropriate territory with his comments on her appearance.

"You told Sarah you were coming here?" Wouldn't his visit raise eyebrows, even in Spring City?

"I did." He held out the package, which she took, careful to keep her fingers from touching his. She gave the box a delicate shake, and it rattled noisily.

"Hey," he warned, this time offering a wry grin. "It sounded that way before I rode over here." He took off his hat and whacked his knee with it absently, sending up a grimy cloud.

She knew Sarah well enough by now. "What did you tell Sarah when she asked why you were coming here?"

He reached into the side pocket of the lightweight tan-colored duster he was wearing. A cream-colored envelope was rolled up but not folded.

"For you."

Thank goodness he'd had a legitimate reason to ride over. But she couldn't think of a single reason to invite him in and a million reasons not to.

"Thanks, Riley. Good day." And she started to close the door.

His arm shot out, and his hand stopped the door with a resounding thwack, making her jump. The smile was gone from his face, replaced by something that looked like sadness.

"May I please come in?"

She shook her head immediately. He was playing with fire.

"I don't think that's a good idea. I don't think *you* think it's a good idea, either."

"No," Riley said, looking down at his boots and shaking his head. He stayed that way a moment, pausing thoughtfully. "No, you're right." Then he raised his eyes to hers, and his look went right through her, striking a chord that made her yearn for something more.

"But let me in anyway." His voice, gone low and rough, perhaps with emotion or desire, made her swallow hard. All the reasons to keep him at bay evaporated like morning dew at noontime. She stepped back and held the door open wide.

When he slipped inside, the small front hall shrank, making Sophie feel prickly. Walking back to the kitchen, she placed the box of cookies and the envelope on the table. She could feel him at her back and didn't turn to face him.

Until he touched her, his hand gentle on the small of her back, and then she spun around as if burnt.

"What can we possibly need to say?" she asked. *Stay calm, stay even. Keep her emotions in check.* She conjured up the image of him kissing Eliza in the Prentice's backyard, but it dissolved as he took her hands and held them in his.

His face already seemed dear to her, and she wanted to chide herself, feeling a heaviness in her heart, knowing this could not end well. She knew she was going to get hurt, but hopefully not too badly, if she kept her head about her now. Sparing Eliza, who was going to lose her father and did not deserve to also have a broken heart, sparing her any more pain—that was the only thing Sophie could hope to accomplish. She pulled her hands from his.

"You should not have come."

"I had to," he said, "particularly after that fiasco of a dinner."

She nodded her agreement. True. He pulled out a handkerchief and wiped it over his face, removing a layer of trail dirt, before stuffing the small square of fabric back in the front pocket of his denim trousers.

"Are you sweet on Dan?" It rushed out of him all at once.

She laughed, so surprised by his question. But she didn't want to disrespect Dan who'd been so helpful. "He seems like a good man, kind and funny."

"None better," Riley agreed. "He's my friend." He searched her face. "But I felt like popping him one right in the mouth, every time he looked at you. In that dress."

She swallowed, feeling her throat close at the emotion in his eyes. "There is nothing to say."

"I don't want to marry Eliza."

Or maybe there *was* something to say. Sophie sat with a thud on the kitchen bench. And in an instant, he was on his knees on the floor in front of her.

"Oh, no," Sophie said, looking down at her lap. "No, no, no, no."

He took her hands again. "Sophie, please listen."

She wanted to stick her fingers in her ears like a small child and sing loudly to block him out.

"No, Riley. Don't do this to her. Not because of me."

"Sophie." He raised her chin to look at him. "Listen to me."

"No, no, no," she said again.

"Sophie, don't misunderstand me. I *will* marry Eliza. I have to."

She ought to feel only relief she hadn't caused the division of a betrothed couple—and she did feel it—but she couldn't deny she also felt a sense of loss.

"I always thought it would be fine marrying her. There wasn't any pressing reason not to, and many reasons why I ought to. We have an agreement and . . . it's complicated. She helped me out, and I owe her."

"Wait," Sophie said. "You're marrying her because you are beholden to her?"

"It's a little more than that." He ran a hand through his hair. "It doesn't matter why, does it? An arrangement exists. But neither of us is in a hurry to marry. She knew I was going away to school, and she wants to stay with her father. And I'll be back here soon enough."

"None of that has changed," Sophie stated flatly.

"Everything has changed," he said, his voice rough. "From the first moment I saw you, I wanted to *know* you."

She understood completely, but it didn't make it right.

"And when we kissed," he said, "you felt it, too. How can we live without that feeling?"

Sophie, who'd had her heart stomped flat, disagreed.

"You know something, Riley, you would be surprised what you can live without. You don't want to hurt her," she pointed out.

"No, I don't. But how can I explain this to you, so I don't sound like a heel. You already know I'm engaged to a woman I don't love. She's my long-time friend, and for that alone, you're right. I absolutely don't want to hurt her. But I will never love her. That sounds terrible, and it would be, if she didn't feel the same. She does, and I know it."

"She told you that?" Sophie asked, wondering how any woman wouldn't want to hold onto Riley with both hands and not let go. How could Eliza not have fallen in love with this mesmerizing man?

"No, but she doesn't . . . that is, we don't—"

"I saw you kiss her," Sophie interrupted him.

He looked astounded. "How . . . ? Never mind. Yes, I kissed her. Because of you."

Sophie's eyes widened at that.

"Eliza and I haven't done more than hold hands in a long time, and I thought maybe, when I kissed you and felt like lightning had struck me, it was merely due to being all pent up."

He brushed his thumb across her lips, and their gazes locked.

She parted her lips, not sure what she was going to say, but as his gaze fixed on her mouth, all her words died. He was going to try to kiss her again, and she was going to have to stop him.

But he didn't kiss her. He groaned instead. "I kissed Eliza and she kissed me back, and it was only a kiss. She knows it, I know it." He looked chagrined. "I really tried, too."

Sophie cringed, not sure she wanted to hear about his attempts at ardor with Eliza.

"I held her a long time, waiting for that feeling. But it didn't come. Right now, sitting here with you, I'm dying to kiss you again."

"You're engaged, Riley."

"I want you to know I don't go around trifling with women," he said.

"I didn't think you did," she told him, but it was nice to hear.

He sat back on his heels. "I have to be honest, though, I'm no angel. I mean, men have needs."

She bit her lip, shaking her head slightly to stop him. She knew her brother had kept company with a widow for three years before he met Charlotte, and it was obvious they were more than platonic. But knowing about Reed was one thing. He was family. Having the man who made her sizzle tell her of his escapades was quite another.

"There've been times, in San Francisco . . . Anyway, Eliza doesn't know about any of that. You know she's rather territorial. It's a pride issue."

"Why tell me?" Sophie asked, as she brushed aside a feeling of jealousy that wasn't, by rights, hers to feel. However, it was too easy, looking at him, to picture his strong, healthy body atop some beautiful harlot willing to do his bidding.

"I'm telling you because when I think of you, I imagine what we could have. And it would be so much better than the life I've got coming."

He should be having this heartfelt discussion with Eliza, not her. Sophie reached out and touched his face, wiping a speck of dirt from his jaw. He caught her hand, turned his head, and kissed her palm.

"Sophie," he said, his voice husky. He leaned closer, merely the tiniest bit, and she leaned forward. It was inevitable.

His lips brushed hers, and a spark flared to life between them once more. This time he smelled like grass, and she breathed it in. His hands went around her, grasping hold of her low under her small bustle. She gasped as he pulled her forward, to the edge of the bench, until she was pressed against him where he remained nestled between her legs.

After a moment, his lips nibbled their way from her lips to her throat. "My knees are starting to kill me on this floor," he said against her neck.

She giggled, feeling a little hysterical at the feelings flooding through her but reveling in the heated sensations where their bodies touched. She let him pull her to a standing position.

"That's better," he said. And they didn't speak again as his arms went around her, and hers encircled his neck.

She raised her face to him, and when his lips met hers, it seemed to her the entire world fell away. He kissed like a man who knew what he was doing, she thought. *Had they taught him in medical school some special way that lips liked to be touched by other lips?* Now, his hand was on her hip. *Yes, he was clearly a man who'd done this before.*

He said he hadn't done anything more than hold Eliza's hand *in a while.*

When they broke for air, Sophie opened her eyes. "Riley, have you and Eliza . . . that is . . . ?" She broke off, feeling like a strumpet for even asking about his fiancée while locked in his embrace.

He leaned his forehead against hers and took a breath. "No, never with Eliza."

But certainly with somebody. He had mentioned someone in San Francisco, but a man as winsome as Riley Dalcourt most likely had his pick of girls growing up. Maybe even . . .

"Charlotte?" she asked suddenly, pulling back. That would be too terrible to contemplate.

"No," he was quick to assure her. "She and I were never even friends. We went to school together for a while, but she kept to herself, especially after her parents died, and then I went away."

"My brother worships her." Sophie wasn't sure why she was telling Riley. She'd believed she had the same relationship with Philip, although he'd never looked at her the way Reed looked at Charlotte. In fact, she didn't think he'd ever quite looked at her the way Riley was.

"I'm glad she found love," Riley said, tucking behind her ear a lock of hair that had escaped her bun. He was still talking, but Sophie found it hard to concentrate as he ran his finger along the shell of her ear and down her neck. "I knew Charlotte's brother better. Thaddeus was my age, and we got into some trouble together, just hijinks, playing in the mines, that sort of thing. Then later, having a drink behind the saloon. Whatever we could think of to amuse ourselves."

Including girls, Sophie imagined, having met Thaddeus and knowing he was nearly as good looking as Riley. She sighed. She was not perfectly pure herself. She'd let Philip do more than he should, although not as much as he had wanted, thank goodness. Or she could have found herself in a whole heap of trouble when he'd left her.

Wickedly, resting now in Riley's arms, she found herself imagining him doing the same things she'd forbidden Philip.

Riley bent low again, and she yielded her mouth to his lips and opened herself to his tongue. She could feel his thudding heartbeat, along with her own, and the pulsing low in her body was becoming insistent, nearly unbearable.

"I want to touch your bare skin," he whispered, voicing her own thoughts.

The kitchen door flew open and they jumped apart. Too late.

Sophie looked into Sarah's shocked face, and the color drained from her own. She had no excuse, nothing she could say.

"I should have knocked," Sarah said, clutching a basket with a pretty blue cloth over it.

Riley looked shaken but was the first to recover.

"We, that is, I—Sophie and I—shoot, Sarah, please don't say anything to anyone. You hear?"

"Of course," Sarah said, one hand fluttering to her throat, perhaps already choking on the words that threatened to spill out. Sophie knew Sarah would, at the very least, tell Doc, and he would think badly of her. She couldn't bear it.

"Sophie." Riley shot her a glance as intense and bewildered as she felt. "I'll talk to you later," he said. "It'll be all right."

She had no idea how it could be all right, but watched him nod to Sarah, grab up his hat, and flee through the back door.

Wishing she could run away as well, Sophie stood stock still, blinking for another moment, unable to think of anything to say to this woman to make her predicament seem less damning.

"I didn't mean to . . . ," Sophie began. "That is, Riley . . . uh . . . ," she trailed off.

Sarah put the basket down on the table. "Riley is about the most handsome young man this side of the Mississippi River, I warrant. Something about that dimple."

Sophie nodded miserably. Sarah had her hands on her hips, looking Sophie up and down. "You got dirt all over you, girl."

"Oh." She put her hands up to her face and then brushed them down her dress.

"He's going to marry Eliza Prentice. You know that?"

"Yes, he told me."

"She might get her pride pricked if she finds out Riley's sweet on you, but you're the one who's going to get really hurt here. And I wouldn't want to see that."

Sophie lowered her head.

"Maybe it's time you moved on to where you're going next," Sarah said, her voice had gentled, but that only increased Sophie's anguish. Beforehand, Sarah had been urging her to stay. Sophie knew she was going to cry and desperately wanted to be alone.

"I'd better get upstairs and wash up."

"Some things can't be washed away," Sarah said, turning for the door. She left the basket of food, which made Sophie feel even worse.

CHAPTER EIGHT

Sophie hurried along the street toward the clang of the cable car's bell. Charlotte's friend, the editor, had opened a number of doors for her. She'd had one audition already at the opera house and was headed to another at the San Francisco Symphony that afternoon.

So far, Sophie didn't like two things about San Francisco—that she hadn't come sooner and that she wasn't there with Riley. Most days, she longed to see him, just leaning in a doorway, as he did at Doc's practice, a smile on his devastatingly attractive face. He haunted her thoughts, an apparition of the man whom she would probably always wonder about, the man who had somehow crept into her heart and soul in such a very short time.

"Watch your step, ma'am," said the car's conductor, and Sophie handed him a nickel.

The city was everything she'd hoped. Boston was larger, but maybe because she was so familiar with everything back home,

San Francisco seemed infinitely more exciting. And she'd never seen so many foreigners within her country's borders.

She hadn't ventured out at night as yet, and had seen nothing of the Barbary Coast Riley had mentioned. She knew she would have to have a companion to venture there.

At her stop, she jumped off and got her bearings. Up ahead was the concert hall. She stretched her fingers out and curled them a few times and went inside.

"What'll it be, miss?" Sophie sat in The Ladies Grill at The Palace Hotel and ordered herself a meal. Her audition hadn't gone well. She'd performed at her best, but she could see by the bored look on the conductor's face, he was only doing it as a favor to Charlotte's friend. Herr Becker seemed to be barely listening and was writing on a piece of paper through her whole performance.

The orchestra had no open positions in any case. Becker had said she was gifted, as if he ran into gifted people every day, which perhaps he did. He took her address on Green Street, and that was the end of it.

She hoped the director of the opera house called her back from her first audition, but for the first time, she felt unsure. She'd already asked Charlotte to return the favor and pack more of her gowns in a trunk and send them along. Without the right wardrobe for the city, she would seem like an untutored country girl.

How well did Riley clean up for the city? Sophie wondered idly. But then she remembered when he did arrive for school, he might be married to Eliza.

The last time she'd seen him, he'd been running from the kitchen to escape Sarah's condemning gaze. Sophie had hardly slept that night. She'd thanked her good fortune the envelope Riley delivered contained her letters of introduction to the symphony orchestra's conductor and the opera house's director. She'd packed up and stopped at the Cuthins' house to say goodbye the following day. Despite her embarrassment and shame, Doc and Sarah had seemed as warm as ever. Then she'd left on the northern-bound train without ever seeing Riley again. After all, what was there to say?

Deciding to write to Sarah when she got back to her room and let her know how she was faring, meanwhile, Sophie was going to have a proper walk around The Palace. Less than a decade earlier, when it opened, it was the largest hotel in the world and was certainly the most opulent she'd ever stayed in.

In the Grand Court, carriages could enter the building and circle around to drop off their passengers. Traversing it, she couldn't help walking with her eyes lifted to the ceiling that stretched up for miles, it seemed, but was actually seven floors. Marking each floor was a columned balcony from where guests could gaze down at the interior courtyard.

Sophie glanced at the hotel's brochure in her hand, seven hundred and fifty-five rooms, each with a bathroom and a parlor. Sophie couldn't imagine that many people needing a place to sleep on any given night.

"Can I help you, miss?" A young woman dressed in the hotel's uniform had approached her, with brown hair neatly pinned up, regarding her with kind hazel eyes.

"I'm just looking," Sophie said. "That's all right, isn't it?"

"Many do," the girl said, then smiled. "Are you new to the city?"

"A week, so far."

"Carling." The girl spun around as a man approached, also in uniform. "Room 4008 has a question about The Oakdale." He sighed and his nostrils flared, as if with distaste over the establishment in question. "Go tell them it isn't nearly as nice as our bar. But if they must go, we'll provide them transport."

And the tall young man with his slicked down black hair and patrician good looks was off without a glance at Sophie.

Carling turned to Sophie with a raised eyebrow and half a smile. Then they both laughed.

"Sorry about Egbert. He was a bit rude. He runs the reception, and he knows every single guest at any given moment, so he knew you weren't staying here."

"Yet," Sophie offered. "I mean, perhaps I *was* thinking about it, and he's put me off."

"And *are* you thinking about it?"

"No," Sophie admitted, and they laughed again. "I've a room on Green Street."

"Oh, I'm on Russian Hill, too, on Lincoln. That's the next street up. Kind of cat-a-corner to yours."

"Carling," she heard Egbert's voice again.

"I've got to get on with it. What's your house number? I'll find you later."

"1039, and my name's Sophie," she called after the girl whom she hoped would become her new friend.

"You didn't even tell him goodbye," Carling said, shaking her head in wonder. "Good God!"

Sophie shrugged and poured another cup of coffee. They sat at Carling's table in her small flat on Lincoln Lane, in a white stucco building that seemed to have sprung up in an alley overgrown with trees and plants and accessible only by a cobblestoned walkway. Sophie had jumped at the invitation when Carling had come knocking at her door the day before. Another day had passed, and she was unsure how to continue in her job pursuit.

Carling was more interested in other aspects of Sophie's life.

"Still," she said, with a jaunty wave of her hand, "you did good to get away as you did. No harm, so to speak. Not used and sent packing."

Sophie agreed, although at the time, she hadn't felt used by Riley. Rather, she'd been a willing and equal participant. Carling was right, though. She'd had to get away. The path they had been on was clear to Sophie. And being someone's mistress was not exactly her heart's dream.

"I'll go mad," Sophie said, "if I can't touch a piano soon."

Carling, who'd been working at The Palace for two years, seemed to know everyone and everything that went on in the heart of the city, but she was in no way connected to the classical music enthusiasts.

"Hey," she said, thumping her forehead with her palm. "Have you tried The Grand?"

Sophie furrowed her brow, "A grand piano?"

"No, silly. The Grand Hotel. You know, the gingerbread structure, next door to The Palace."

"I saw it," Sophie said. "But what would I do there?"

"They've got a lovely bar. My fellow—well, when he *was* my fellow, before he caught sight of my landlady's daughter, that cheating cur," she paused, rolling her eyes. "Anyway, he took me there once. They've got a lovely piano and all. I know it's not the opera house, but you could at least play, and maybe they'd pay you. Just get on with it."

Sophie tapped her chin. It was worth a try. The next day, she wandered into The Grand Hotel, which sat on the corner, like a squat, showy, even gaudy aunt compared to The Palace next door.

At ten in the morning, the bar was empty. It was also quite lovely, Sophie thought, even more so when she spied the piano, which, as luck would have it, was a beautifully carved, square grand situated in the dark corner of the room. She was drawn to it like a moth to the flame. Without asking, she sat on the stool. Taking a deep breath, she started to play, and it was like sinking into a comforting, warm bath. The sounds were rich and full and true. Someone had tuned it recently, it seemed.

And then she let herself drift into the music with no other thoughts at all.

"Hey there!"

She jumped, brought out of her Chopin reverie by a loud but friendly voice. However, she didn't get up. She simply couldn't bear to take her fingers from the keys. Looking up at the man who appeared by her side, she noted both his sharp-looking suit and his kind smile.

"Don't stop," he said, leaning on the piano. "Obviously, you know what you're doing."

Sophie nodded. *Yes, at least here, with these 85 keys, she did.*

"I'm sorry, I couldn't resist."

"That's all right. Stay as long as you like, until eleven that is," he winked at her. "Then this place'll start to fill up. Say, what's your name?"

"Miss Malloy. Sophie Malloy."

He leaned closer and she could tell immediately he was interested in her person. That was nothing new. And her feeling nothing in return, that wasn't new either.

"I'm Freddie Vern. I manage the bar and the dining room."

She smiled. She was sure it was an important job, particularly by the way he said it with pride.

"How wonderful for you," Sophie said. He seemed pleased with her response. Should she ask him if he wanted a pianist? She knew what Carling would say. *Get on with it.* So she did.

"Your piano looks a little dusty."

He nodded. "We haven't had a player for a while. And I'm not certain it matters, profit-wise."

"Maybe you didn't have the right . . . player." She preferred the word *pianist,* but she could certainly adapt.

"Come to think of it, the last one was ugly, short, and bald. And played like he was using his feet. Didn't exactly draw a crowd." Now his flirting was unmistakable as he rested his hand on his chin and gazed at her openly. "Any suggestions, Miss Malloy?"

"I do believe I know a talented pianist who is neither short, nor bald."

"And definitely not ugly," he added, treating her to another wink.

"Thank you, Mr. Vern."

"Please, call me Freddie. And would this talented player be interested in our humble establishment?"

"For the right remuneration. Yes, she would."

He chuckled. "Why don't you come to my office and we'll talk more. I have a feeling you could charm my customers into staying for a few more drinks."

"In such a lovely hotel as The Grand," Sophie said, standing up to find she was looking at him eye to eye, "why wouldn't they?"

Dear Charlotte and dearest brother, Reed, for I know you share everything including my letters,

I will write separately to Mama. I have found employment playing the piano for a fine establishment. While not a professional orchestra or opera house, as I'd hoped, it is a revered institution, with well-behaved, upstanding patrons. They are also generous tippers.

She crossed the last line out as it sounded crass, although she'd been particularly pleased at the end of her first evening to discover the jar Freddie had set out for her was stuffed full of bills. The pay was poor but now, as the days had turned to weeks, she understood she could, in fact, pay for her room and all her monthly necessities on the wages plus the tips, if she were careful with her money. Still, she saw no reason to let her brother, a distinguished Boston attorney, know his sister was working in a barroom.

She sighed and grabbed another piece of stationery to begin again, but her mind drifted as it often did to Riley. It was going on two months since she'd seen him, but she hadn't forgotten a thing about how he looked or how he tasted or his warm vanilla scent. More importantly, she hadn't forgotten how he made her feel.

Freddie Vern had tried on more than one occasion to get her to agree to a dinner or even a walk. She'd turned him down as kindly as she could. She didn't feel any spark, and she simply didn't have the patience to pretend.

Letter finished and mailed, she stopped in at The Palace to see Carling. Sophie could usually find her positioned near Egbert Hull's concierge station in the large room they called the "office." Here two hundred attachés worked, mostly dark-skinned men recruited by The Palace from the eastern resort hotels. Their one job was to make guests supremely happy. Among this elite group of dignified, gracious staff, Carling was one of only a few females. She wore the same jacket as the rest of them but sported a matching skirt instead of the crisp, pressed trousers of the men.

Many of the guests preferred having a lively young woman help them with sightseeing or dining information.

"It's understandable, isn't it?" Carling speculated one evening over a glass of wine at one of the hotels' bars. "Anyone's gonna prefer me to humorless Egbert and the rest of his gnarled staff, especially now, when we've got more single women travelling than ever before."

Sophie could tell Carling actually liked Egbert immensely by the way she talked about him incessantly.

"Aw, he's not so bad," Carling admitted one evening, "not when you get to know him."

"He seems to be a hard worker," Sophie put in.

"Yeah, but a bit prissy," Carling said, "and he seems to think he's better than most."

"Maybe he thinks his job is a bit beneath him. Didn't you say he's been to university?"

Sophie knew her mother and brother would be mortified to discover after she'd attended the finest music schools in Boston and Europe, she was playing piano for tips.

"He is awfully smart," Carling agreed. "Sometimes, if we get a quiet moment, I bring him a cup of coffee and we talk. He knows a lot about a lot, and he doesn't seem to mind when I ask him questions."

"Maybe you could find out if he has aspirations for something more," Sophie suggested.

"I might," Carling said, and Sophie thought maybe her friend didn't know the word aspirations, but then Carling added, "I'm happy with my job as it is and having him working here, too. If he followed his dreams or what have you, I might never see him again."

Sophie smiled at the wistful statement. She'd been right about Carling's feelings for Mr. Hull. She wasn't going to interfere, but she did think it would be a shame if Egbert liked Carling, too, and didn't declare for her.

"Maybe you could ask him to join us for one of our get-togethers."

Carling looked astounded. "What? Ask Egbert to have a drink with us? Are you mad?"

Sophie laughed at her expression. "Think on it. It might be fun. Anyway, dear, I'll see you later." She left with one backward glance to Carling that showed the girl was musing on the idea at any rate.

Walking the single block that separated The Palace from The Grand, she drew her pelisse tightly around her. There was talk of a bridge to connect the second floors of each hotel, and Sophie hoped they built it. It would not only look sophisticated, but people could cross from one to the other without getting damp, which she was starting to do because of the heavy fog that day. Ducking into the bar's entrance, she hurried to hang her coat and hat in the closet for staff belongings and approached the bartender.

"Please, Percy, may I have a glass of water?"

He didn't guffaw at her after the first time. Now, he just accepted her strange ways.

"Water," he chuckled. "Here you go, Miss Malloy. It's a good strong one." And he set the glass on the bar before giving his moustache a twirl on either side.

Sitting at the piano, she took a sip before placing her glass on the opposite side from her tip jar on the piano's top. She couldn't explain to anyone how truly hard work it was to play for hours, especially as she played "real" music, not that saloon stuff she'd heard coming out of Ada's in Spring City or any number of drinking establishments in San Francisco.

Sophie played classical music and the customers loved it. Some had heard about her and started to come to hear her play. Freddie told her of the compliments he'd received on her behalf. And she was bemused to receive applause after each song, proving people in the bar were actually listening and not ignoring her as background noise. All in all, she was quite satisfied with her audience over the past few weeks.

Stretching out her fingers and curled them in a few times, she considered what she felt like playing. At some point, she knew she would have to avail herself of some sheet music. She'd only memorized so much, and even then, sometimes she cut a long piece short or threw in one of her own works. No one minded or noticed.

Something lively today, she decided. Something *vivacissimo*. She began a Scarlatti sonata and let everything fall away. Nothing penetrated her musical castle, as she'd come to think of it. As she played, she built it up, note by note, stone by stone. She'd first used it to keep the heartbreak over Philip at bay, and now it kept the loneliness and the longing for Riley waiting outside the drawbridge until her final piece each night.

Occasionally, Sophie would smile and nod her thanks, as a patron came forward to put money in the jar, although she never spoke while playing and rarely heard the noise around her.

However, out of the blue, Riley's voice sliced through her concentration and breached her musical fortress like a knight-errant on his steed with a particularly powerful lance. Her fingers faltered, and she looked up to see him, dressed for the city, quite improbably standing in her barroom where he ought not to be.

CHAPTER NINE

Blocking Sophie's clear view of him, Eliza stood, poised at the entrance. Whatever Riley had said to her, Eliza now turned to answer before she scanned the room and locked eyes with Sophie's horrified gaze. *Why hadn't she put her head down?* But Eliza looked right through, and, except for the briefest of hesitations, pretended not to see her. The petite blond murmured something to Riley, and they left the bar.

Sophie realized she'd stopped playing only when she suddenly could hear the din of voices and glassware clinking where, normally, she heard nothing but the music. She had no idea how she'd heard Riley over the crowd. Her heart was racing. *Had she just seen Mr. and Mrs. Riley Dalcourt?*

"Something wrong, lass?" she heard Percy say behind her. Shaking her head, she started to play again, not even caring what it was, so long as her fingers kept moving.

Finally, it was her dinner break. As part of their agreement, Freddie allowed her to take a meal in their dining room each evening, without charge. Tonight, she had no appetite, but instead, wanted to escape the bar for as long as she could. Craving San Francisco's damp, moist air, she hoped it would clear her head of what still seemed an unlikely apparition—Riley in a hat utterly unlike what he wore in Colorado and a tailored dark suit. Eliza wore a gray dress, perhaps traveling clothes.

Maybe they'd only just arrived. Maybe they were on their honeymoon.

They'd pledged their troth and joined as man and wife. They could now enjoy themselves in the marriage bed. Sophie could imagine Riley's lips on Eliza's skin, his hands undressing her. Hurrying to The Palace, she ran right through the courtyard and passed between the large glass doors, held open by staff. Then she headed for the employees-only office. Egbert was at his desk, an imperious clock perched on a grand structure behind it and with all sorts of drawers and cubbies. He was stuffing mail into a cubby and turned at her footsteps.

"Is Carling nearby?" she asked without preamble.

Egbert frowned. "Miss Malloy, she is working, and her duty demands—"

"Please, Mr. Hull, I need to speak with her."

He sighed. "You may try The Tapestry Room. She might still be showing it to a prospective renter. Do you know where it is?"

"Yes," she said, "thank you." Ignoring the curious look on his face, she turned away. The Tapestry Room, she murmured to herself, recalling a large chamber as lovely as it sounded. Carling had taken her on a private tour of the hotel, and they'd stopped in to the exquisitely furnished, private dining area that wealthy San Franciscans rented for what they considered small dinner parties.

Practically running to one of the five richly carpeted staircases, eschewing the nine elevators as being too slow, she desperately needed to talk to Carling.

"Sophie?"

All the blood drained out of her head at the sound of Riley's voice, uncertain and loud in the echoing space. Too late to discuss this turn of events with the only friend she had in the city, Sophie gripped the banister.

"Sophie!" His voice was certain now. Turning slowly, she inwardly cursed herself, for the sight of him literally made her knees go weak. *What a ninny!*

"Riley," she said, acknowledging him with a tilt of her head, as if they were the most casual of acquaintances.

He took a couple hurried steps toward her, and for a moment, she feared he was going to catch her up in a hug. At last, he slowed.

"I can't believe it's you. What are you doing here?" he asked, plainly flummoxed.

She couldn't tell if he was happy or simply shocked. "I live here."

"In San Francisco?" A grin spread over his face, ushering in his enchanting dimple. *Oh, Lord, don't let him smile like that at me.*

"I take it congratulations are in order," Sophie offered.

He frowned.

She rushed on, "I saw you and Eliza earlier. I assume you're staying here at The Palace?"

"You saw us, where?"

She ignored his question. "Is she here, now, at The Palace?" She regretted how her voice was rising, but she couldn't seem to breathe deeply.

"Yes, she's here. Eliza's father wanted her to have the best. She's upstairs, but I—"

"I have to go back to work," she blurted. Carling had shown Sophie a sampling of the rooms. They were elegant with beautiful beds. Instantly, she pictured Riley and Eliza in one of them that very night. She certainly didn't want to hear about it.

Starting to step around him, she startled when he grabbed her arm.

"Sophie—"

"I have to go."

But he was so close, and his hand on her arm was like a firebrand.

"Please, Sophie," he said. "I can't let you disappear again. Sarah wouldn't tell me where you went. It was torture not to know."

She paused. She couldn't live in San Francisco and not see him, could she? Was she that strong?

"I . . . ," she looked up into his soft brown eyes and melted. "I work at The Grand, next door. I'm the piano player," she confessed.

Wrenching her arm free from his grip, she walked away without looking back. But she knew he would come.

Less than twenty minutes later, he was there. She felt him before she saw him. He sat down at a table against the wall, ordered two drinks and when they were placed in front of him, he walked over to the piano.

"Will you join me for a drink?"

"I'm working," she said, without looking up. *What would Freddie think if he walked into his bar to find her sitting with a man?*

"When do you get a break? I'll wait."

Blast! How was she supposed to focus on playing, with Riley seated a few feet away? If she had a drink with him, perhaps he would go back to Eliza at The Palace.

"I'll be over in a minute," she told him and finished up the piece, fairly certain she'd flubbed the ending and missed out an entire measure. Riley and a few others clapped anyway.

She curled and uncurled her fingers and went over to his table.

"That was lovely," he said as she sat down.

"It was not." Sophie felt immensely resentful. All her hard work at not thinking about him and at putting the image of his tawny eyes, sensual lips, and saucy smile out of her mind was undone in an instant.

"Where's Eliza?" she heard herself snap.

"In her room, getting freshened up."

She had looked perfectly fresh earlier, Sophie thought. "I think she saw me earlier."

Riley nodded and sipped his drink. "That's why she hustled me out of here so quickly, I guess."

"Did you tell her? That we kissed, I mean?"

"Yup."

"Oh, God," Sophie muttered, lowering her head into her hands. She'd be branded a harlot in the entire state of Colorado and now in California, too.

He reached across and touched her arm, causing Sophie to jerk her head up, the feel of his warm hand both welcome and disconcerting.

"I didn't have to offer the information, actually. When you skedaddled from Spring the way you did, Eliza came right out and asked what was up. Particularly after she heard me pressing Sarah for information. Eliza's a smart woman, and I guess she saw something between us."

Something between them. Eliza had been right. *And was she already Riley's wife?*

"So, why are you sitting here with me while on your honeymoon?" She could barely get out the last word.

Riley looked stunned. "Oh, Sophie, is that what you think? We didn't get married yet."

Sophie couldn't deny the immediate sense of relief.

"You must really believe I'm a first-class cad if you think I'd be on my honeymoon and having a drink with you. I tried to tell you at The Palace, but you ran off so fast. Eliza's staying there, but I'm not. I've got my old rooms that I've had ever since I started medical school."

"She came away with you unmarried and unchaperoned?"

Riley shrugged. "She told her father we'd be in separate accommodations, and it's true. Who else does she have to explain herself to?"

"But why not simply get married?" Even Sophie was getting tired of their games and she'd been witness only to the tail end of over two years of pussyfooting around.

"She didn't want to. She wanted to see San Francisco. That's all. Also, she's still a bit sore about you."

Sophie nodded. "And now she knows I'm here."

He rubbed the back of his neck and then downed his drink. "She didn't mention it. I guess she didn't think I would run into you standing in the lobby of The Palace. But it's probably going to eat at her. Even though we have a solid agreement, she doesn't want to be made a fool of, and I can't blame her. If she were publicly eyeing another man while engaged to me, I'd feel betrayed." He looked thoughtful. "Why *were* you in the lobby?"

"My friend works at The Palace," Sophie said. No need to tell him she'd gone half-crazy at seeing him and needed some advice. "How long is Eliza staying?"

"She's booked in for a week. She won't leave her father longer than that. I'll put her on the train home."

"Then what?" Sophie asked, ignoring the horribly matter-of-fact way he discussed his fiancée, not to mention the grim look on his face. She wondered what he would do if he could pay Eliza back whatever he owed her.

"Then I finish up and become a doctor. Doc's plan was always that I'd take over for him."

Sophie didn't miss Riley's lack of enthusiasm.

"Is that what you want? To go back to Spring City?"

"The one thing I've always wanted to do was practice medicine. I never thought it would matter where. But truthfully, now that I've lived here and been in the hospitals—they're magnificent. And the new techniques are amazing, not to mention the scope of the work. Why, I've seen more interesting cases in one week at City-County Hospital than Doc has seen in ten years in Spring."

He was quiet a moment, spinning his empty glass around and around on the table. "But I owe him."

It seemed to Sophie that Riley's problem was he felt he owed too many people too much for him to make his own decisions and have a life that made him happy.

Luckily, that wasn't her problem or her concern.

"I have to get back to work." She pushed her chair back. "Thank you for the drink." Even though she hadn't touched it.

"Sophie, will you . . . that is, do you mind if I come back and listen to you again?"

She tried to shrug nonchalantly yet she felt anything but.

"The Grand Hotel Bar is open to the public," she remarked. "Even if I wanted to, I couldn't stop you."

He stood up, next to her, too close. She was sure he could hear her heart beating fast and furious.

"But you don't want to, do you?" His eyes locked on hers, and if they'd been alone, she was sure it would have ended in an ardent embrace, so strong was the connection.

She cleared her throat and looked away a moment, glancing at the boxy-shaped piano she'd come to think of as hers. She would not answer his question. It was pointless.

"Goodbye, Riley." Just a few steps and she sat down and surrounded herself with music. She didn't watch him leave.

CHAPTER TEN

"Oh, my God! And I missed it! Stupid Egbert! If only he'd sent someone else to The Tapestry Room, I would've seen your Riley. It was the first time I was off the floor all day."

Sophie sat in Carling's kitchen. Her friend was taking a bit too much delight in the drama of the situation, perhaps forgetting Sophie's heart was involved, not to mention Eliza's.

"I don't understand the woman," Sophie said, pausing to sip her second drink in the last half hour. "She has eyes, doesn't she? Riley Dalcourt is the easiest thing on a woman's eyes ever, I swear. And Eliza strings him along as if men ask her to marry them every day."

Carling snorted. They were drinking something stronger than coffee, and it was starting to take its toll. "Maybe they do."

"Well, she is about the prettiest woman I've ever seen," Sophie confessed. "Tomorrow, you can see her, too. Find out what room she's in and—"

"And what? Spy on her?" Carling asked. "See if your Riley does spend his nights in her room?"

Sophie blanched. Actually, she didn't want to know that. For some reason, it was easier to imagine him taking his release with a paid prostitute than with a woman to whom he could become emotionally tied. Why the hell wasn't he in love with the blond, blue-eyed, petite Miss Prentice? What was wrong with the man, anyway?

"No, don't spy. Just take a look if you want to."

"I'd rather take a look at your Riley."

"Stop calling him that. And what about Egbert? You know, if you overlook his humorlessness and his snotty manners, he's quite dishy."

"That's a lot to overlook," Carling said, beginning with a small giggle. Then she laughed so hard the tears pricked her eyes. "But I have thought the same thing, if we're being honest. Under his starched uniform, there seems to be quite a strapping man."

Sophie started to laugh, too, then covered her glass when Carling tried to pour her more wine. Her thoughts lurched from Egbert to Riley to one of her early conversations with him.

"You know what we should do?" She moved her hand and let Carling fill her glass after all. "We should head to the Barbary Coast area."

Carling's hazel eyes became large as doorstops. "Are you serious?"

Sophie nodded. Ever since Riley told her about the wonders of the place, while sitting in bucolic Fuller's restaurant, she'd been dying to see it.

"What? You mean now?" Carling's eyes darted to the window and the darkness beyond.

"No better time," Sophie said, standing up a little wobbly. "After all, from what I know, they're just getting started over there. It doesn't get into full swing until the wee hours."

"Full swing," Carling echoed. "Jesus, Mary, and Joseph!"

In half an hour, they were stepping off the Presidio trolley on the corner of Union and Columbus with still a few blocks to walk toward the water. Sophie was right, no one was settling in for the night. Rather, the streets were busy and getting more crowded with each passing moment, everyone seemingly good-humored, jostling each other, moving in a general tide from one building to the next.

Sophie and Carling held hands and moved determinedly forward. At first, they dared not slow down for fear of being swept into one of the seedier looking establishments, each with a barker calling out the evening's entertainment. Finally, Sophie grabbed Carling into the nearest doorway.

"What are you doing?" Carling hissed, as a man bumped into her, paused, eyed her up and down, and then tipped his hat. "Get on with you." Carling turned her back on him.

"I decided we'd better jump in somewhere or we'd end up in the bay. Besides, I hear music."

Gripping each other more closely, they went inside, astonished at the paintings of naked women adorning the walls. There was music, indeed, a small orchestra, but it was definitely not the main attraction. Most of the patrons were men, and they were staring at a stage that contained dancing girls in various stages of undress.

"Good God," Sophie murmured.

"Too right," Carling said. "I think we should leave."

"Wait," Sophie murmured as the audience burst into applause, cheers, and loud whistling. On the stage appeared a woman in a large headdress, a spangle-covered short corset above which her nipples protruded, and see-though Turkish pants. A barker on the street behind them yelled, "Just in time, folks, step in. See Little Egypt and her exotic dance."

"Hey, you." They both turned as one to the nearest table. A man their own age sat there, his tie undone, his eyes glazed with alcohol. "Pretty girls. Take it off."

"I beg your pardon." Carling had her hands on her hips.

"No begging, darling. Take off your clothes."

"Why, you!" Carling started to swing her purse at the man's head.

Grabbing her hand, Sophie pulled her back outside. The pleasant effect of their earlier glasses of wine had left her, and she was starting to feel a needling of fear.

"Have you noticed we're the only women on the street?"

"Yes," Carling agreed. "The only women are *inside* these places." She lowered her voice, "And I'm not sure, but I think most of them are ladies of the night."

"I think you can be sure," Sophie said as she was inadvertently elbowed by a large man, clutching a whiskey bottle. "Riley said I couldn't see the Barbary Coast because I was a woman, but I didn't know he meant it literally."

Carling stared at her, and Sophie shrugged.

"We're here now. We might as well see a little more before we go home. At least, we'll have a story to tell."

The next place they peeked in was more of a gambling den, but still, scantily clad women were everywhere. This time, it was Sophie who was accosted, as a young man, evidently in his cups, tried to pull her toward a staircase, with the offer of an "extra 50 cents" if she spanked him.

Carling dragged her out of his clutches right before he passed out on the stairs.

"Are you ready to go home?" she demanded.

"It sounded better when Riley described it," Sophie confessed, as they moved along the street, "with music everywhere. I thought it would be more the atmosphere of a fair."

Right then, Sophie got jostled again. "I think I've had a man's hand on about every part of my body," she said. "Let's cross over."

Across the street, from inside the blatantly titled Ye Olde Whore Shop, music blared out.

"A steam piano," Sophie said, wanting to poke her head inside to see it, but Carling held her back. Next door was The Living Flea, equally loud. But as they approached The Dew Drop Inn and saw the vulgarly erotic signs and the naked women hanging out of the upper stories, Sophie's footsteps faltered.

"I give up," she said to Carling. "If we're not extremely careful, we'll end up in an opium den. This is definitely men's entertainment."

With that, she was grabbed from behind, hauled off her feet, and dragged inside the open door beside her. Her last view of Carling was her horrified face as two men blocked the entrance so she couldn't get past.

"Unhand me, at once." Sophie was surprised her voice came out as steadily as it did when she was awash in fear.

"Virgin or not, senorita?" a man behind her asked.

"How dare you!" Sophie stamped her foot for good measure even though she was trembling from head to toe. At last, she was released and turned to see a Mexican man with a gold tooth, smiling broadly.

"We don't have to discuss anything. Strip and I'll see if you're worth keeping."

"I'm leaving."

"I pay top dollar. Twenty of 'em a week, and I provide clothing." He gestured over his shoulder, and Sophie couldn't help but look, staring in fascinated horror at five women dressed in red jackets and black stockings, and nothing else. Each was with a man. Some sat on a man's lap and some were pressed against the wall. Each had the man's hands or mouth on them in some fashion. One couple was in the middle of the act, itself, lying across a round table.

She edged backward, coming up against one of the men who blocked the entrance. Was Carling still outside trying to get in?

Gold-Tooth was laughing. "You'd look good like that, senorita." He crossed his arms, considering her. Then he reached out, slid his hand into her short coat, and palmed her breast through the bodice of her dress.

Gasping, she smacked his hand away, pulling her dolman tightly around her and crossing her arms. It was then she realized her purse was gone, no longer dangling from her wrist. She felt a tendril of despair curl through her. *How had this night gone so terribly wrong?*

"So, virgin or not? I have a special room if you're a virgin. You can service customers in there for a few weeks, then come back down here."

Sophie didn't even try to understand how anyone could service men and be in the "virgin" room for a few weeks.

"I'm leaving," she said again firmly. "If you don't let me go, I'll . . . I'll . . . My brother is a lawyer," she finished lamely.

The man considered her, not appearing too worried, but then he shrugged.

"Fine, but maybe you regret it sometime soon, eh? I pay better than the rest." He looked past her. "Pedro, Juan, let the 'lady' leave. Give her some help."

They parted in front of her. "No, that's not necess—"

With a hard shove against her back, she was flying out into the darkness. The last thing she remembered was throwing her hands out in front of her as she crashed onto the street.

Sophie came to in a strange place. It was very bright, causing her to close her eyes again. She could hear the echoing voices of people who seemed far away. Confused and hurt, both her head and her hands and even her knees, she had no idea where she was or why. She didn't want to speak because her mouth felt bone-dry, so she settled for making a sound, somewhere between a moan and a sigh.

Immediately, she heard a scuffling sound and opened her eyes again. To her astonishment, Riley Dalcourt was looking down at her.

"Hey, beautiful," he said, showing her his dimple.

She was too confused to answer. Maybe she was dreaming, but she didn't usually feel such discomfort in her dreams.

"Water," she whispered.

He turned away and then back in an instant, holding a glass of water. He lifted her head slightly off the pillow with one large hand and helped her to take a sip. It wasn't very cold, but she was extremely grateful. From this position, she could see two nurses with their long white aprons covering their puffy-sleeved gowns, walking the length of the long room. They hardly made a sound on the spotless wooden floor.

Sophie was sure, after her thirst was quenched, she would be able to think clearly again. Lifting her right hand to take the glass from him, she saw bandages.

"Oh," she gasped in distress, swiftly lifting her other hand, which wasn't bandaged but showed a few scrapes on the palm. She curled and uncurled her fingers, relieved it felt perfectly normal. Her right hand, however, was completely immobilized. Her pulse raced as panic whipped her heartbeat to a rapid trot.

"What happened?" she asked, hearing her own high tone of fear.

Riley pulled up a chair beside the bed. It was strange to see him there, with his smoothly combed hair, his clothes spotless, looking every bit the city doctor. And no trace of a cowboy at all.

He was calm and professional when he told her, "I think you were robbed."

Breathing deeply, she attempted to calm down. Then she frowned, vaguely recollecting the feeling of flying toward the sidewalk, and a flash of pain. Or was it the other way around?

"I was pushed," she said, after a moment's consideration.

"Your friend, Miss Rilkers, brought you in."

"When?"

"Last night," he told her.

No wonder everything ached. "Is Carling all right?" Their evening was coming back to her, beginning with too much wine and ending with her in a . . .

"Miss Rilkers was unhurt, but she's very worried. I'll let her know in a minute that you've awakened."

She was awake, all right, and everything was coming back to her as fast as Mercury's winged feet. Did Riley know where she'd been? Why did that matter? After all, she was not his business. She went to brush her hair off her face and froze at the sight of her bandaged hand. *God her wits were dim today.*

If Carling was fine, then the next most important thing was her hand. But the question she wanted to ask was sticking in her throat. Instead, she formed the next most reasonable question.

"Where am I exactly?" Obviously, she was in a ward, with beds lining two walls and many large windows. She could see a white-painted brick fireplace near her, but it wasn't lit. She couldn't see the other patients, only one of the nurses who'd stopped at a bed farther down the room. And she wrinkled her nose at the smell of some disinfectant cleaner.

"You're at City-County Hospital. It's the best hospital in San Francisco. We use surgical gloves," he paused and pulled a pair out of his coat pocket and waggled them at her before shoving them away, "and carbolic acid as antiseptic. We even have our own nursing school, and you might be impressed to know there are women doctors here. Dr. Finley, one of my professors, worked on your hand, but he's a he."

She jumped at the mention of her hand and irrationally felt tears well up in her eyes. She had to ask him.

"What's wrong with it?" Her voice came out as a croaking whisper.

"Nothing too bad," he said, seeing her distress. Then, gently, he added, "But two fingers are broken."

The blood drained from her head, causing the room to tilt. She was glad she was already lying down.

"And my head?" She heard her voice quiver.

"You had quite a knock on it, but your pupils are dilating and constricting correctly, and you're speaking quite normally to me. All signs are good, although I'd like to see you on your feet and taking a few steps."

Sophie didn't feel like standing up. But she realized she had to use the bathroom and told him so, parsing her words for modesty's sake.

"Nurse," Riley called out to one of the women to assist her.

Minutes later, Sophie was looking at herself in a small mirror in a bathroom in one corner of the ward, with the nurse holding her arm and Riley right outside the door. Her forehead was bandaged, her chin was scraped, and her face was pale. Her hair looked like a bird's nest. All in all, not good, she thought, not with the man she . . . she *cared about* seeing her in all her hideous glory.

With her good hand, she felt her forehead under the white bandage. Apparently, an egg was in the nest, though a small one.

"Don't touch it, dear," the nurse said.

Sophie sighed. She wanted to lie down again. She wanted to sleep and wake up to find this was all a dream.

"How are you doing in there?" came Riley's voice through the door.

She ought to be embarrassed, but after all, he was almost a doctor. Sophie smiled at the nurse. "I'm ready."

"We're coming out," the nurse said, then more quietly to Sophie, "That young man hasn't left your side for hours. Mr. Dalcourt is very popular here, not to mention skilled, and we're looking forward to his becoming a full-time attending physician."

With her good hand, Sophie wrapped the hospital robe around the white unfamiliar nightshirt she wore, wondering fleetingly who had removed the gown she'd been wearing the night before. Then she allowed the nurse to tie the belt at her waist.

"Feeling steady?" Riley asked as they emerged.

"Enough, I suppose." Sophie said.

After he dismissed the nurse with a word of gratitude, he held her elbow for the walk back down the ward to her bed.

With extreme gentleness, he helped her to recline before making her comfortable against the pillows. All the while, she couldn't help gazing at the planes of his handsome face and noticing the way his shirt stretched over his chest, while he made the smallest of movements. She was certain he was doing the nurse's job and not the usual practice of a medical student. Then he caught her watching him, and he smiled.

"Do you want to tell me what happened?"

"Not really," she said truthfully. "Didn't Carling tell you?"

"Just that you were out on the town." He narrowed his eyes. "What is it that neither of you want to say? Sophie, what were you doing?"

"Exploring the city," she hedged.

"At nearly midnight!" His brown eyes darkened with understanding. "Why, the only places open are gambling dens and brothels."

"*Mm.*" She feigned interest in the ceiling.

"Damn it all, Sophie! Tell me what you were doing."

"I wanted to see the Barbary Coast, all right?"

He made a sound that was a cross between anger and exasperation.

"To be precise," she said, "I believe I ended up in the red-light district."

He looked at her as though she had lost her wits entirely. "Don't you know women have gone missing from that area? Don't you read the papers? Kidnapped for the purpose of enforced prostitution."

"For your information, I was approached with such a proposition and, as you can see, I made it out alive." She spread her hands and caught sight of her bandages again, promptly bursting into tears.

Suddenly, all the fear she'd felt the night before rose up and choked her throat. She was so lucky to be lying in a clean hospital bed with Riley by her side. She could be held captive in the virgin room.

The horridness came flooding back, but now Riley was putting his arms around her.

He gave her the briefest of consoling hugs, then pulled back to look at her, his gaze hard and direct, while she used the bedsheet to wipe her tears with her good hand.

"I'm not going to lie to you, Sophie. What you did last night is about the stupidest thing I've ever heard of. I think you realize that now, and will never, ever go there again. Am I correct?"

She didn't appreciate the tone of his voice. She was not a child. "I ought to be able to walk around this city like anyone else," she said mulishly. "That man with the gold tooth—"

"Gold tooth! You're talking about Carlos Perez Alonso."

"How would you know?" She had a disturbing image of him lying back on the brothel table with one of the red-jacketed women draped over him, long legs in black stockings wrapped around his lean hips.

"He's as infamous as his Dew Drop Inn."

"Have *you* ever been there?"

His eyebrows shot up and he looked like thunder. "That's beside the point. Do you realize you could have disappeared, never to be seen again?"

She did, in fact, have precisely such a realization, and it scared her to death, but she wasn't letting Riley know it. "Carling wouldn't let that happen."

He swore again and ran a hand over his eyes. She thought it was shaking slightly.

"Riley, I know now that I shouldn't have gone to the Barbary Coast, and I won't go again."

He looked at her with a level gaze.

"At least, not without a male escort," she added truthfully.

He flushed red, apparently angry once more. "What? No, you ridiculous woman. You will never go there again. Ever!"

"I only wanted to hear the music you'd mentioned." She tried a winning smile, but he didn't thaw. "And I wanted to experience a bit of the excitement."

His nostrils flared a moment, and she watched his jaw working, until at last, he asked, "And did you?"

"I heard some dreadful music actually, and then . . . ," she trailed off, thinking of her "bit of excitement."

Riley brushed the wayward hair from her forehead. She wanted to turn her cheek against his palm, wishing especially here, under these circumstances, his touch didn't affect her. She dragged her thoughts together into something cohesive.

"I guess my purse is gone." What had been in it? Some cash, but not a lot, enough for a meal and cable car fare, and her favorite ivory comb.

He shook his head. "You didn't have it when you arrived. Sophie, will you tell me what happened?"

She pursed her lips, feeling torn. "It will most likely make you angry again."

"Most likely," he agreed. But this time he gave her a wry smile.

"I wasn't trying to go into the Dew Drop Inn. We'd gone into some dance hall." She watched him roll his eyes. "And then into a gambling den, where a man . . . Well, never mind that."

Riley's jaw tightened once more.

"Then I was pulled into that horrible Dew Drop by Gold-Tooth, or Carlos whatshisname, and held against my will while he—"

"While he what?" If ever a man looked like he was going to explode, it was Riley. She swallowed.

"While he offered me a job," she mumbled, mortified.

"Offered you a . . . I'll fucking kill him." His voice was too loud and his eyes were blazing.

"Riley!" She was shocked beyond measure, not only by his language, which was certainly not befitting a physician in a hospital, but also by the vehemence of his words. "You'll do no such thing. Not on my account."

She pictured the two large men who guarded the gates of that particular hell. She'd better bring Riley back around to medical matters before he decided to bring out his six-shooter.

"When can I leave?" She fluttered her eyelashes, trying to distract him. He didn't answer at first, but slowly, he uncurled his fists.

"I know what you're doing," he ground out, "so you can stop with the eyes. Do you have any idea how dangerous—? I mean, of all the ludicrous, outrageous ideas—" He didn't seem able to finish a sentence, looking as though he could throttle her at any moment.

"When will I be discharged?" Sophie tried again, desperately wanting to move beyond her serious breach of good judgment. Thank goodness she hadn't mentioned the wine, or Riley would be demanding she become a teetotaler.

She could see he was trying to regain his composure by the way he closed his eyes and sighed. At last, he looked at her.

"The ward doctor will come in and check you over. Head injuries are considered serious stuff around here. I would think, though, by tomorrow, or at the very latest, the next day, you can be released."

He paused, then asked, "Do you live alone?"

She stared hard at him, until he amended, "I mean, no roommate, such as Miss Rilkers?"

"No."

"*Hm.*" He looked worried.

"I'll be fine," she assured him. "Next thing you'll do is demand I bring Sarah to San Francisco to cook for me."

At last, he nodded. "That's not a bad idea."

She made a face at him. "No. She already thinks . . . ," she stopped.

"Thinks what?"

Her cheeks flushed scarlet, remembering the look on Sarah's face when she caught them kissing. "Nothing. I can't imagine she's thinking too highly of me at the moment."

"You're wrong, but no matter." He frowned. "I'll look after you."

She sighed with exasperation. "Yes, Riley, why don't you move in to my little set of rooms and wait on me hand and foot. I'm sure that will be perfectly acceptable to Eliza."

He ran his hand through his hair. "You could go back to Spring City or to Boston, until your hand heals."

He would probably be married by the time she got back from the East Coast. "Maybe. I'll wait and talk to Carling."

"She's here somewhere. I'll go find her." He hesitated. "Shall I send word to your family? Your brother, perhaps, and Charlotte?"

"God no!" Reed would be on the next train and he'd take her home whether she willed it or not. "I mean, I'll send them a telegram when I'm out of the hospital. I think I need to rest now," Sophie said, dismissing Riley because she felt close to tears again at the thought of her hand. She'd lost her livelihood and her joy, as well as her respite from the world, all in one fell swoop. Not to mention her purse.

He was looking at her so intently, she closed her eyes, but as she did, the first tear rolled down her cheek.

"Sophie," he murmured, "please don't cry." She felt his lips brush against her forehead. He smelled so good, like fresh vanilla, and she wished he could lie down next to her and hold her. "Your fingers will heal quickly. I promise you."

Her eyes popped open to see him still leaning over her, as he stroked her tussled hair. "Can you truly promise me that?"

"Yes," Riley said, and the way his eyes bore into hers, she decided to believe him. "I had better let you sleep now." But his gaze had moved down to her lips.

She couldn't speak as she watched him lower his head. Unable to stop herself, she curled her good arm around his neck and waited for him to kiss her.

"Well, hello," came Carling's delighted voice.

He'd nearly kissed her. Smack in the middle of the women's ward, with two nurses and a host of patients and the possibility of an attending physician walking in at any minute, and Riley had nearly kissed her.

Taking the steps in the stairwell two at a time, in moments he was outside in the fresh salty air. *Damn!* What was wrong with him? He'd never acted unprofessionally before. But his head had been swimming ever since he'd walked into The Palace and seen her. Like a miracle! He'd told himself it couldn't possibly be Sophie Malloy, but there she was nonetheless.

Right then and there, he'd had to reengage in the monumental battle with himself to keep his hands off of her, to keep away from her entirely.

But to find her in a hospital bed! A haze of red blurred his vision merely recalling the moment he'd done his rounds the night before, discovering her pale and unconscious, with her precious hand injured! Even then, he was shaken deep down by tremors of possessiveness and rage. He clenched his fists again. Thank the good Lord she hadn't been hurt worse, but at least he had a way to vent his anger—all over the infamous Carlos Alonso's face.

He headed for the cable car stop outside the hospital. To find Sophie against all odds in San Francisco and then to have her snatched away again by the likes of such scum, it would have sent him insane, he was sure of it, even if she could never be his.

As it was, he would find it excruciating to leave her behind when he graduated and left the city. *How was he going to do it?* He wasn't sure he was strong enough. However, for Eliza's sake and for Sophie's, when the time came, Heaven help him, he hoped he was.

CHAPTER ELEVEN

"You should be staying with me," Carling said, after bringing Sophie her evening meal for the third night in a row and staying to eat with her.

"No, I'm all right. Except for taking forever to dress, I can do almost everything myself," Sophie assured her. "I just wish I had something to do all day. I miss my career, such as it was."

"I can't say the same," Carling said and laughed. "Though Egbert would miss me, I think." She winked. "He's all worried about us living alone after what happened to you."

Sophie didn't want to admit to Carling she felt the same as Egbert. She jumped at every noise and definitely didn't want to go out at night. She was even worried for Carling walking home two blocks.

"I've been on Russian Hill for two years now," Carling said, hands on hips. "If some bloke comes near me, I'll clobber him."

Sophie had no doubt Carling meant it, too, and she had to remind herself it was her own foolhardy idea to venture to the Barbary Coast.

"So besides me, any other visitors?" Carling asked, cleaning up the dishes.

Sophie blushed. She knew what her friend meant. Carling had been teasing her mercilessly since coming upon her and Riley in the hospital, and interrupting what surely would have been a kiss.

"No one. But Freddie Vern sent me a note yesterday with some flowers and said he'd stop by this evening. In all likelihood, he means to sack me in person."

"He wouldn't. He's never had such a busy bar."

"Pshaw," Sophie said. "People go for a drink, don't they, not for the music?"

"Not just any music. I'm sure Mr. Vern—"

As if conjuring him, there was a knock on the door. They looked at each other, eyes large until, with relief, Carling ushered in Freddie.

"We were just talking about you," Carling offered, making Freddie redden in the cheeks.

"Oh, yes?" He eyed Sophie. "You don't look as bad as I expected."

Sophie smiled. "What did you imagine? That I'd be bandaged from head to foot?" Then she held up her hand. "Isn't this enough?"

He sobered. "Yes, it's more than enough." He looked at Carling then back at Sophie. "I'm simply going to say this, even in front of your friend. I don't like the idea of your living alone here. I'd like to offer you a room at The Grand."

Sophie saw Carling's jaw drop, mirroring her own.

"I don't understand," Sophie said.

"Gratis, complimentary, free," Freddie said, coming forward and taking a seat. "The Grand has some rooms that hardly ever get rented out. They're smaller, at the back side of the building, on the third floor. You can have one for free."

"Until my hand is better?" Sophie asked.

"No, even after, until you don't need it anymore."

"Get on with you," Carling said, leaning her chin on her hand. "Living at The Grand! What about me, then?"

"What *about* you?" Freddie shot her a smile. "Are you my star piano player?"

"No, but I'm currently her best friend."

He cocked his head. "Sorry, sweets. You'll have to ask someone at The Palace for a room."

Carling made a face. "Phooey, they're not giving rooms away for free. I can tell you that. Not by half."

Sophie had stayed silent. *Did she want to live at The Grand?* She'd learned from Riley that he lived near the hospital, on Mission Street. She would be closer, but she brushed the thought away. Obviously, when he married Eliza, it wouldn't matter how close she lived.

"Let me think about it, Freddie, will you? I'm not sure. And I hate leaving Carling on the hill by herself."

Freddie shrugged. "I wish I could offer you both something, but I can't, and the rooms are too small for two beds. You can't swing a cat in there."

"The Palace doesn't have any small rooms. Only big ones and bigger ones," Carling said dreamily. "Still, it's rather luxurious, I think, hotel living, even if it's a small room at The Grand."

"I'm grateful, Freddie. I truly am. Just let me consider." Sophie frowned. She would have no kitchen of her own, but she'd also have no rent to pay. "How are you managing at the bar?" She had to ask.

"My cousin is filling in."

A male pianist! What if he was more respected? What if he played better than she did?

"Don't worry," Freddie added, seeing her concern. "He knows two songs, and they're maudlin at best."

"Ooh, that'll drive customers away," Carling said. She looked at Sophie and winked. "Maybe you better ask for a raise when you get back."

What if she couldn't go back?

"Hey, what's that look for?" Carling asked.

Sophie bit her lip. "What if my fingers don't work correctly again? I mean, I need to spread this wide," she said, holding up her other hand for them to see, "to reach across an octave."

"Your Riley said you'll be fine in no time, didn't he?"

My Riley. Eliza's Riley.

"*Your* Riley?" asked Freddie, eyes narrowing. "Who's that?"

"She means the doctor," Sophie put in. She knew men could be strange and competitive, for no reason at all. And she didn't want Freddie to withdraw his offer before she even had a chance to accept it. "How long will you hold my position?"

"Don't worry about that, sweets. Just get better. And let me know if you want the room. Remember, it's tiny, but you won't have to worry about rent." Freddie got up and went to the door. "Righty-o. I won't keep you ladies."

"Freddie," Sophie stopped him before he could leave. "Would you please escort Carling home? It's only a street away, but I worry about her."

Carling started to protest, but Sophie interrupted, "Dearest, I would feel so much better knowing you were home safely. Anyway, after that lovely meal you made me, I'm going straight to sleep."

Carling frowned.

"I'm happy to do it," Freddie offered.

"Please," Sophie said, "I don't want to worry about you."

"All right. If you insist. I'll let this handsome gentleman *escort* me home."

"Better not tell Egbert," Sophie teased.

"Oh, tell me all about Egbert," Freddie said as he closed the door behind them, leaving Sophie alone.

She sat with her thoughts a moment, feeling beyond distracted. She hadn't yet told her family about "the little incident," as she'd come to think of it. She didn't want to upset her mother or Reed. Besides, the man who took her purse probably needed the money more than she did, and she should count herself lucky she didn't have to share the fate of the red-jacketed women who worked for Gold-Tooth.

Besides, she could always go home and live with her mother in the lap of luxury if all else failed. But she didn't want to fail! She wanted to be successful. She wanted to play piano and make people happy simply by listening to her.

Sighing, Sophie stood, wishing it were a few hours earlier and still light out so she could go for a long walk.

"Blast it!" she swore aloud. She'd never felt fearful before, not even in Rome, and she was sure this feeling would pass, but her bandage was a reminder of how everything could change in an instant. She might as well go to bed as she'd told Carling. Besides, since she'd sent her friend home, it would take her ages to get out of her—

Another knock. Sophie froze, then relaxed. *Stop being ridiculous!* A criminal wouldn't knock.

Still, she lifted the curtain and peered cautiously out the window onto the step. *Riley!*

Her heart started hammering.

He knocked again. Taking a steadying breath, she opened the door, thinking he might be more dangerous than a criminal.

His eyes seemed to take all of her in with one sweeping glance before fixing on her own dark-blue gaze. "Good evening, Sophie. I was—" he stopped short, offering a rueful shake of his head.

"I was going to say I was in the area, but I can't lie to you. You are the one person with whom I feel compelled to be utterly stripped, so to speak."

"That's quite a greeting," she said—never mind he was already five kinds of inappropriate.

"May I come in?" He held up his doctor's bag. "Official medical visit."

"Then I guess you may," Sophie said, stepping aside to let him pass. When she turned, she realized two things in short order. One, he filled the room. This wasn't like Charlotte's homestead where she could run down the hall to the kitchen to try to gain a little distance from her involuntary attraction. This was a small apartment, and Riley Dalcourt was not a small man. And two, he had the remnants of a split lip and a black eye.

"What in God's name happened to you?"

He had the gall to shrug as if walking around looking like a thug were an everyday occurrence. "I'm fine."

"That's not what I asked. I can see you'll live to tell the tale. How did you get your face in that condition?" She glanced over the rest of him, to see if he had any other injuries, and noticed the knuckles of his right hand, curled around his bag, were scraped.

"You were in a fight," she guessed.

"Apparently."

"Are you going to tell me or do I have to keep asking? Remember, you said you can't lie to me."

"I paid a visit to Alonso."

She frowned, and then it dawned on her. "Gold-Tooth?" She felt scared all over again. And yet Riley stood in front of her, whole and safe. "You went to that awful place?"

"It's not that awful in broad daylight, at least if you're a man."

"Why? What could you possibly hope to accomplish?"

"Justice," Riley stated.

"Oh, please. That's for a court of law. You went for revenge."

"Payback, then." He smiled. "And it felt great."

"You shouldn't have gone there. It's not your place to defend me."

"Who then? Does your brother even know about your hand?"

She didn't answer him. The fact she hadn't yet written to her family was not his business.

"Tell me what happened," she urged, thinking of the brutes she'd seen. "How did you escape alive?"

"Have a little faith, woman. I didn't simply walk in and ask to wrestle with Carlos Alonso and his gooneys."

"Gooneys?" A strange word. Was that what he called the prostitutes?

"Yes, those big guys who guard the doors."

She was sure her face had gone three shades whiter, and immediately, she had to sit, which she did, upon one of her kitchen chairs since there was no place else other than the bed. The thought of Riley up against three men, particularly those three dangerous men, made her blood run cold. She almost wished he'd been wrestling a harlot instead.

At the look on her face, his own expression became sheepish. "Sophie, I'm fine. I merely wanted to make sure Alonso understood he'd made a mistake. I informed him he'd accosted a lady the other night."

"And?" Her voice sounded strange to her ears.

"And when he didn't apologize, I punched him in the mouth. Split my hand open on his stupid gold tooth."

She winced.

"Then one of his men tried to grab me from behind, but I was quicker. I kicked Alonso in the stomach and then the face before I turned to address the others."

"I'm not sure I need a blow-by-blow report." In fact, she knew she didn't. "Just tell me how it is you're still alive."

He grinned. "Honestly?"

"Yes, please."

"One of the guys was about to take my head off with his fist, when a customer came in. He was distracted long enough for me to get my hands around his neck and squeeze."

"Squeeze?"

"Yes, I cut off the blood supply to his head by pressing here and here." He pointed to his own neck. "He got a strange look on his face and dropped like a stone. Then the other guy spun me around and socked me in the eye before I could knock him out with a blow to his chin, which I did. If you land your fist right here," he pointed under his chin, "you can knock a man out almost every time."

"Good to know," she murmured, thinking she could easily be sick, thinking of Riley in the middle of such an altercation.

"That left Alonso, who held his hands up in surrender. The coward! I'm actually a little surprised he didn't have a gun."

Her stomach heaved at the idea, and she took a deep breath to quell it.

"What about your lip?" she asked.

He shrugged again. "One of the whores did it. Caught me by surprise. At that point, I decided I'd done enough."

"More than enough." She looked at her bandaged hand and held it up to him. "After your heroic effort, at least I'm completely healed." She ought to be grateful instead of sarcastic, but the thought of what could have happened to him . . .

"Oh, no, wait. My hand is *exactly* the same, proving what a stupid risk you took. In fact, now you're injured, too. Men!" she said with disgust.

"I know, I know." He smiled ruefully. "But maybe Alonso will think twice before he grabs a woman off the street."

"Doubtful. I bet he'll forget about me and you in the time it takes his face to heal."

"I think losing this will remind him." He reached into his trouser pocket and pulled out something small. Holding his left hand out to her, he uncurled his fingers. Lying on his broad palm was a gold tooth.

Sophie gasped, then her eyes flashed up to Riley's twinkling gaze.

"Sweet mother," she exclaimed. "How did you get that?"

"Came out when I kicked him in the face. It went in a perfect arc over my head. I caught it and pocketed it right before I had to put my hands around the gooney's throat."

"I've changed my mind. I'm glad you went." She couldn't help grinning. "You *are* my hero," she said, and she meant it. "But don't do anything like that again."

"That's what *I'm* telling *you*, Sophie. No more forays like that one."

"I promise." Suddenly, the room had closed in again. With her sitting and him standing over her, she felt the unwelcome desire to kiss him. She watched him place the tooth on her table.

"A memento," he said, his voice gone quietly serious.

"Is that why you came? To give me his head on a platter, so to speak?"

He gestured to his medical bag again. "I told you this was a medical visit. Dr. Finley said you'd have to go back for a follow-up appointment, and I thought to save you a trip."

She stood up again, wanting to be on even ground with him, although all this did was bring her closer to him.

"Are house calls standard procedure for medical students?" Now, why had her voice gone all husky?

"No."

She cleared her throat with a little cough before she asked, "And did you ask me if I wanted you to save me a trip?"

"No, but—"

"It's not like I have much else to do right now," Sophie added, feeling as though she needed to keep her tone practical and even a little cold. Riley was in her room. At night. They were alone. Every nerve ending in her body was clamoring. "The hospital was rather an exciting place. And I think it might take me three trolley car changes to reach it."

"Only two, in fact," he said. "Look, I'm sorry." He gazed directly into her eyes. "I overstepped my bounds coming here. I'll leave. Dr. Finley will want to see you in the next day or so. He will look in your eyes—stunningly gorgeous eyes, by the way—and listen to your heart. He'll examine the bump on your head. That type of thing. He won't open the bandage and touch your hand, Sophie. Not yet."

He turned to leave, and all she could think was how she loved to hear him say her name. He had the slightest of drawls, and her name sounded nothing like it did on the lips of any man on the East Coast.

"So, this *is* purely a medical visit?" She didn't know why she pushed him to admit anything. He was almost out the door. She'd nearly escaped this wildly perilous situation unscathed. Yet somehow, she'd asked him a question, the answer to which could make their circumstances end badly.

He turned but looked down at his shoes, at his bag, at the wall behind her head, then finally at her. "I really can't lie to you."

She stared at him, frozen, as Riley stepped closer, putting the bag on the floor before taking her face in his hands and looking ever so deeply into her eyes.

"But I'm going to look into your lovely eyes, like this."

She swallowed, waiting for his next words.

"And I'm going to listen to your steady warm heart, like this." Shockingly, he bent low and turned his face, pressing his ear to her chest in which she knew her heart was thumping like a trapped rabbit. He stayed like that a moment, while she barely breathed, then he raised his head.

"And I'm going to give you my best diagnosis."

She nodded, mesmerized.

"I'm a man who desperately needs to kiss you."

She very nearly laughed. He had diagnosed himself instead of her. She was grateful, for he could have said it the other way and he would have been right—she was a woman who desperately needed him to kiss her. Yet to have heard him say it would have been a tad embarrassing. Instead, she was downright terrified. Sarah was not going to barge in and stop them, and Carling was safely back at her own apartment.

There were only the two of them and neither of them had proved to be very good at restraint.

He took her composure as encouragement, she supposed, for he tilted up her chin. She breathed in his scent of vanilla soap for a moment. When his mouth touched hers, his kiss sent a surge of warmth all the way down to her toes. She let him explore, reveled in feeling his tongue slip between her lips to touch hers. It was wicked and blissful, and she didn't want him to stop.

But stop he must.

With her good hand, she pressed against his suit coat, in the vicinity of his chest. Straightaway, he released her.

"You can't keep doing that," she told him exasperatedly. Her legs felt wobbly and her lips were tingling.

"You didn't tell me not to," he pointed out.

"I shouldn't have to tell you. You're engaged. Are you going to marry Eliza Prentice?"

"Yes," he ground out.

"You have to leave. I'm not going to be your *chère amie*."

"My what?"

"Fancy term for someone to warm your bed after you're married."

He cringed. "That wasn't what I intended."

"What did you intend?"

He ran a hand through his hair. "I'm an ass."

"Agreed," she quipped.

He grinned.

"Don't smile at me like that. You're a doctor and a good one from what I saw in Spring City. How can you be so good at that and not have it carry into other areas of your life?"

He frowned slightly. "I don't follow you."

"Just be a faithful fiancé and, after that, a supportive husband."

"To a woman who has no real feelings for me, nor I her."

Sophie wanted to knock his and Eliza's heads together. "Then you shouldn't marry."

"I have to," he said quietly.

"Yes, you said that before. You owe her, I believe. Medical school tuition, is that it?"

"More than that."

"Do you want to tell me?" Sophie asked, relaxing a little now that the immediate danger had passed.

He sighed. "She convinced her father not to take my parents' house and land when they couldn't pay. I never even explained to my father why the threatening letters from the bank stopped."

"And why did Eliza do that for you?" Sophie could imagine the payment she might extract from Riley when she looked at his firm generous mouth and his long lean body. Yes, payment wouldn't be so hard to accept.

"We agreed to get married. Her father wanted to know she'd be taken care of after he died, and there wasn't anyone else in town who . . . ," he trailed off.

"Who what?" she prompted him.

He shrugged, looking embarrassed.

"Who looks as good as you?" Sophie suggested. "Who measures up to Eliza's level of attractiveness?"

Riley blushed. "That's not what I was going to say. Jesus, woman! There are plenty of good-looking folks in Spring City."

Perhaps he really had no idea of his own draw, but Sarah had been right—he was the most handsome man in the United States. Or, at least, Sophie remembered her saying something to that effect. In his denims or his city clothes, when Riley was near her, Sophie felt hot all over. She almost missed the fact he was speaking again.

"Eliza couldn't see herself married to a farmer or a rancher or a storeowner. That left me, I suppose. Or Thaddeus Sanborn, but he was never around."

"A doctor or a drifter? I guess she made the right choice." Riley would have been Sophie's choice, too, but for reasons other than his becoming a doctor.

"When I'm so close to earning my degree, I can't leave her high and dry."

"A highly developed sense of honor," Sophie mused, knowing she ought not to be mocking him. "And Eliza is willing to settle for this match, without love and without passion?"

"I suppose so. She's a good woman despite her temper."

"You admire her. Well, that's something to base a marriage on, I guess." She couldn't believe she was advising the man for whom she had such strong feelings on how to make his upcoming marriage work. Next, she'd be offering to help Eliza choose her wedding dress!

He shook his head. "We already know we can be kind to one another. We even understand each other to a degree. Our marriage will be a real one, I imagine, with children."

Sophie wanted to scream, thinking of Eliza growing big with Riley's child one day. How fondly he would look at his beautiful wife. Yes, Sophie wanted to have a full-blown tantrum.

"Knowing all this, why do you persist in dallying with me?"

He groaned. "Why, indeed! You're like a fascination, Sophie. Or like opium. Once addicted to it, it's nearly impossible to break the habit. When you disappeared from Spring, I went mad for a few days, and then, after getting stymied by the Cuthins, I resigned myself. Or I thought I had."

He shook his head, looking perplexed. "You left my life as abruptly as you entered it, and I convinced myself your disappearance was for the best. But I've found you again, and my feelings for you haven't changed."

Taking hold of her undamaged hand, he added, "I need to see you and touch you. I want to breathe in the fragrance of your skin. Damn it, you're mine."

He brought her hand to his lips and lingeringly kissed her knuckles before turning over her hand and placing a searing kiss in the middle of her palm.

Sophie's breath hitched, and she felt her toes curl inside her leather slip-ons, while her stomach seemed to drop away as if she were on a swing. She stared, enthralled, at her hand held in his.

"You were meant to be mine," he stated plainly. "I know it as surely as I knew I was meant to be a doctor. I knew it when you opened your mouth and apologized after I'd knocked you into the street. I wanted you more than I ever wanted any woman, especially after I saw your purple drawers."

"They were lavender," she corrected him without any hint of humor, for certainly two hearts were breaking in that one small apartment. She'd known this desperate feeling before but had suffered alone, when Philip had let her go the way a child thoughtlessly captures and releases a butterfly. She tugged her hand free.

Thank God Riley hadn't gone so far as to say he loved her, although he'd danced around it. Throwing away love was much worse than throwing away their intense physical attraction. It was downright wicked to waste love. That's how she'd felt with Philip, too. In honesty, however, her blood had never stirred like this when he was near, nor when he touched her. While she'd imagined herself in love with the cool, ideological man— used to his ways, entranced by his thoughts, comfortable as a couple—he'd hardly made her feel anything in comparison to Riley.

Exhausted with the strain of wanting him and knowing she couldn't, or shouldn't, have him, Sophie's tone was harsh.

"If we gave in to this 'fascination,' what then? My bed is right there." They both looked at it. She saw him swallow, then his jaw tightened.

"You could persuade me to lie down with you," she continued, "or I could entice you, I suppose. Either way. But after we went to bed together, what would happen? Do you think after we make love once or twice, we'll be done with each other? Will it be easier, then, to marry Eliza?"

He looked stricken. "I think after I have touched you in all the ways I want to, I'd never be able to let you go."

Her mind flitted to the tempting thought of his hands on her bare skin. She let her breath out slowly. Their relationship was like a piece of music. They were stuck in the chorus, even though she could well imagine the verse, beginning to end, and her heart felt tight and heavy with the futility of loving him.

"You might not intend it," she said quietly, "but perhaps you're using me to get out of your engagement. I think you're an honorable man, terribly torn right now. I think if we end up in that bed, you won't go through with marrying Eliza, but it will be my fault. You'll be able to place the blame at my feet, rather than making the decision on your own."

"I would never blame you," he vowed.

"You misunderstand me. I don't think you would resent me, but I would still be the catalyst, the reason you *had* to tell Eliza—finally—you won't marry her. She could blame me, too, of course."

Sophie went to her door, walking a little stiffly to keep her legs from shaking. "I decline to be the tool for either of you to disentangle yourselves from your passionless business-arrangement of a marriage." She heard his footsteps.

"How did you get to be so smart?" he asked, standing closely behind her.

She turned, letting him pull her into his embrace. If she hadn't had one hand in bandages, she would have moved his coat aside and started to unbutton his shirt, simply so she could press her face against his chest and feel his warm skin. She swallowed and his gaze darted to her throat.

"I won't drag you to that bed," he assured her, "I promise." The words were barely out of his mouth before his lips were on the pulse point of her throat. He kissed her skin and then flicked his tongue over the same spot. She shuddered.

"I've wanted to taste you forever, it seems," he said, his voice husky.

As close as they were, she could feel his manhood firm against her stomach and she pressed closer, making him shudder slightly. She longed to touch him everywhere. Now they'd decided they wouldn't act on this white-hot desire, they were teasing each other beyond reason.

"What were you doing before I arrived?" he asked against her neck.

"I was about to undress." She couldn't believe the whispery voice was her own.

"You might hurt your hand. Let me help you."

She started to protest.

"I've never broken a promise. That's why I'm in the pickle I'm in now," he added, referring to his engagement. "I won't make love to you. Not tonight. I told you that."

Without another word, he began to undo her buttons, then her laces, until her layers were pooled at her feet and she stood in only her cotton shift. His hungry gaze lingered on her dusky nipples, tantalizingly visible through the fine fabric.

Swallowing, she let him hold her good hand as she stepped over her clothes, and he kept holding it as he led her toward her bed. Sitting upon it, trembling at the intimacy, Sophie fervently wished things were different, that Riley could raise her shift and explore all her womanly places already warm and damp for him.

Wordlessly, he unpinned her hair, until her long, dark braid hung over her shoulder, loose tendrils everywhere.

"Shall I brush it out?" he asked, his voice thick.

She shook her head, unable to speak.

Returning to the pile of clothing, he picked up each piece in turn and placed it over the back of one of the kitchen chairs. The last garment, he buried his face in for a moment, then tossed it from him onto the end of her bed.

"I'm going to do the hardest thing I've ever had to do. I'm going to leave you, just as you are. Your eyes are huge, blue sapphires, and you are the epitome of any man's desire. A goddess, except for the bandaged hand," he added, perhaps in an attempt at levity.

She tried to smile, but her lower lip wobbled. This was the closest they would ever get to her heart's yearning. She knew she had only to open her arms to tempt him back to her side. In that case, the blame truly would be hers.

Instead, she bit her lip and remained silent, except to say, "Goodbye, Riley," as he slipped out her door.

Without a piano to soothe her, or even the ability to play if she had one, Sophie curled up on her bed and cried, not solely for herself, but also for the honor-bound young doctor who owed too much.

CHAPTER TWELVE

Riley walked the streets a long time, breathing in the damp night air. What a snake he was! Sophie must hate him. He wished he had his horse so he could ride right through Golden Gate Park, then up the Twin Peaks and back to the harbor. But no amount of galloping was going to let him ride away from what he'd done that night. *Hell!* He would probably gallop straight into the bay and have done with it.

Sophie was here, in San Francisco, which both gladdened him and tormented him. *Was the good Lord trying to drive him insane?* He stopped and leaned his back against a chilled brick wall, dropping his medical bag at his feet.

He'd told her the truth. Weeks earlier, he'd made peace with losing her when he thought she'd walked out of his life forever, and he'd restrained himself from contacting Charlotte, who would certainly know where Sophie was. Whether she would have given him any information was debatable anyway. He had no idea what Sophie might have told Charlotte about their brief association in Spring, but she might have said he was a no-good cheat, and she would have been right.

Instead, he'd resigned himself to being a good husband to Eliza. Or, at least, as good as he could be, knowing there'd be times when he was going to imagine it was Sophie in his arms when he took his wife to bed.

But all that had changed. Sophie was there, and his gut twisted and his mind rebelled at losing her all over again. Eliza would return to Spring City in a few days, and he was not feeling nearly so resigned to losing Sophie as he'd imagined.

Damnation! He slapped the brick wall behind him with both hands. The stinging was a pathetic replica of the pain that felt like boulders crushing his chest.

He'd been so weak earlier. *Why had he gone to Sophie's home?* In his heart of hearts, he knew he'd intended to have relations with her. He couldn't lie to himself, as he couldn't lie to her. If she hadn't been so damned practical and honorable and decent, he would still be with her, spending the whole night pleasing her. He would have despised himself in the morning and, worse than that, Sophie would have despised him, too.

But for one night, *oh, Lord,* for one night, he would have made love to her with everything he had and made her feel like a queen.

Sophie used her head and took Freddie Vern up on his offer. After all, without a job, she'd have to start depending on her family to pay for her little bedsit. That meant she'd have to tell them she'd been attacked. If she did, she'd be back in Boston so fast her head would spin. With Carling's help, Sophie was soon ensconced on the third floor of The Grand, in the back of the building.

"I'm starting to regret this," Sophie said as Carling helped her put the last of her clothes in the second armoire Freddie had brought in for her.

"Whyever for?" Carling asked.

"You won't be a street away anymore."

Carling hugged her. "I'll be a block away during the day. Come over to The Palace and see me anytime."

"But our evening chats over that god-awful wine," Sophie persisted.

"We'll still have them, but we'll have them here instead. Not exactly the lap of luxury this room, but it's cozy, or we can sit in the lounge. Now that you're a resident, I bet you can take your own drink in there. Or maybe get it 'on the house,' as they say."

"I can't have you leaving here late at night. I'd be ever so worried," Sophie said. "No, I've gone and ruined our lovely arrangement. And if my hand heals completely—"

"*When* it heals completely," Carling interrupted.

"All right. *When* it heals, what happens if I do get my dream position at the opera house or the symphony orchestra? I'll have to look for a place to live again. I can't see Freddie letting me live here scot-free if I don't work for him."

"You are a sad Sue today, aren't you?" Carling sat down on the bed and then lay back. "*Hm*, this room might not be the best, but this bed is fabulously comfortable."

Sophie sighed and joined her, staring at the high ceiling. "Yes, it is."

Carling took Sophie's hand. "Anyway, don't borrow trouble. Let's see how it goes. I mean, Freddie is obviously mad for you. If you fall for him, then you can live wherever he lives."

"Carling!" Sophie scolded, but she had to laugh at her friend's romantic notions. Freddie held no more interest for her than Dan had.

"Anyway, maybe I'll move closer to you, instead. Egbert lives on Bush Street, near Mason. Just as you'd expect, he has scrimped and saved and bought a house, nearly on Nob Hill. He's ever so sensible."

"How do you know this?"

"We had coffee together the other day, and then we talked about . . . things."

"Things?" Sophie couldn't mask the hopefulness in her voice.

"Oh, don't you start." Carling said. "He's way too proper for me. Stuffy and pompous and—"

"Rather good looking and smart, not to mention clearly having the ability to take care of a wife."

Sophie knew Carling could see all those good points for herself, and sure enough, Carling added, "He *is* rather handsome, especially when he has that dreamy look in his eyes, talking about what he'd like to do with his life. He's got big ideas for his future."

Sophie tilted her head. "Oh? You mean scaring all the staff at The Palace isn't enough for him?"

Carling chuckled. "Truthfully, he's not so scary. He just likes to keep things under control. That's part of his job. But he'd rather grow grapes. Not in San Francisco. Maybe up the coast a bit. He thinks he'd like to have a winery, and perhaps open a little inn, too."

"Really? I never would have imagined he was dreaming all that."

"I know," Carling said, looking thoughtful. "But he's got a lot hidden under his suit."

They both shrieked with laughter as they realized what her words imported.

"Does he now?" Sophie asked, when she could breathe again. "And how would a nice girl like you know?"

"Get on with you." Carling was blushing profusely. "You know what I meant. Anyway, you're right. I don't believe he means to be stuffy or pompous. At least, not all the time. I'd like to get to know him better and I'm starting to think he feels the same about me." She hugged herself. "No word from your Riley?"

"I don't think I'll hear anything more from him." That blackest of black thoughts stole all the merriment she'd been feeling.

"If it's any consolation, Soph, I think you did the right thing. A man can't eat his cake and have it, too. Either one or the other, I say."

Sophie nodded. *A box of broken cake. A broken heart or two. What's the difference?*

"By now, Miss Prentice might've had her fill of San Francisco and gone back to Spring City to wait for her doctor to return," Carling mused.

Sophie couldn't imagine choosing Spring City over San Francisco. But if Riley were the deciding factor, then she would think again.

"Personally, I wouldn't care where Riley Dalcourt was, in Timbuktu or Mongolia, I'd want to be with him. I mean, if I loved him, that is. I'm not saying I do, mind you." She could see she wasn't fooling Carling one bit. "Honestly, I don't know what that woman's waiting for."

"Perhaps if *she* feels the way *he* does, meaning not much at all, then maybe she'd rather remain a single lady as long as she can."

"Oh, it makes my head spin," Sophie admitted. "Frankly, I'm glad I'm not in the middle of it anymore. Let them sort it out."

"Yes, get on with it, I say."

"I know you do, Carling. I know you do."

Sophie spied Egbert studying his clipboard and stopped. She observed him for a moment. His tall frame was on the thin side, but at least he carried no paunch. Perhaps a couple of years working a vineyard would fill him out nicely and give him a few hard muscles the way—

She stopped her thoughts from straying to a certain dusty cowboy doctor. Egbert would look after Carling, Sophie was sure. And her friend deserved a little looking after. Perhaps, he needed the tiniest of pushes in the right direction.

"Good day, Egbert."

"Sophie." He inclined his head. She was glad they were on a first-name basis as she now was with most of the staff at both the hotels. They were all starting to feel like friends. "What can I do for you?" he asked a bit stiffly, as, most likely, he was all kinds of busy and didn't have time to stop to help her.

"Oh, nothing. I was hoping Carling was on a break."

"Ten minutes, she will be. You can wait in the break room if you like, although I shouldn't let you."

"I appreciate it. Freddie doesn't let any non-Granders in *his* break room."

"Mr. Vern, the restaurant manager?"

"Yes, why I think Carling knows Freddie, too. I believe he went walking with her a couple weeks ago." She was stretching the truth a bit, but he had walked her home that one time at Sophie's request.

She saw Egbert frown. Just then, Carling appeared at one end of the lobby, walking briskly with a hotel guest. She flashed them both a grin and gave a little wave behind her back as she passed by. She looked vibrant, efficient, happy. And beautiful. What man wouldn't want her?

Egbert's eyes followed her progress until she was out of sight.

"Could you tell me one thing before I go, Egbert?"

Distracted, he mumbled, "I suppose so."

"Can you tell me if Miss Prentice has checked out?"

He gave her his full attention. "Guest information is strictly confidential."

She produced her warmest smile. "Oh, Egbert, I'm sorry. I understand if you don't know the answer. I'm sure some things are above your station."

He bristled. "I am obviously aware Miss Prentice has left The Palace. No guest information is *above my station*, as you so delicately put it."

"Obviously," Sophie said. "I'll wait for Carling in the break room. If you speak with her, please let her know I'm there. I wouldn't want her to go looking for me at The Grand by mistake. Though I'm sure Freddie would be happy to see her again."

Sophie hoped she hadn't gone too far with her last words. She would keep her fingers crossed Egbert did, indeed, talk to Carling and ask her out on a proper date before the day was through.

She wandered toward the break room. So, Eliza was gone. That told her almost nothing. Would they marry soon or wait? It was none of her business anyway.

After a cup of coffee with Carling, during which she tried hard not to mention Egbert, Sophie headed to The Grand's reception desk where her mail was being delivered. Once or twice a week, she checked it, hoping for a letter from home or an employment offer from the orchestra or the opera house. She waited patiently while the clerk searched.

"Miss Sophie Malloy," he confirmed, handing her a letter she could see at once was from Boston. Addressed in her younger sister's hand, she didn't doubt it would be full of news about their mother and how Reed was getting along as a proud new father. It made her heart ache with missing them all. And her youngest nephew would grow up without her. She stuffed it in her purse to read with her evening meal.

With no job to do, no friend to be with, no man to take her out, Sophie took a horse-drawn bob-tail car directly to Woodward's Gardens, not caring it was a long way. After all, what mattered the time when she was at such loose ends? She'd wanted to see the so-called "Central Park of the Pacific," although she would have dearly loved to experience it with . . . with Carling. *Yes, Carling, not Riley!*

At first, she thought the specter of Riley would hang over her entire visit to the park, but as she wandered the museum, looking at the collectibles, and then breathed the fragrant air of the conservatory with its exotic and tropical plants, she started to feel better.

Eventually, she ate a meal, listening to the pipe organ and nearly gathering up the courage to ask if she could play it. In the end, she decided not to. It was too early to try, and the bandages would hamper any attempt. Basically, she was scared to find out her career, and lifelong dream, was over before it had even begun.

By the time she made her way home, it was dusk. Her feet were tired and even her hand was aching under the bandages, which made her feel irritable. Even so, she let Stan, the evening elevator operator, tell her about a guest who was so terrified of the lift, she had to be held in place by her husband. Sophie liked his stories, but she knew from experience if she encouraged him, she'd spend the next ten minutes trapped listening to him before he opened the elevator's gate and doors. Thus, when they reached her floor, she moved to the front, thanked him, and bid him good day.

Blissfully, she sank onto her bed. But no sooner had she removed her bonnet and gloves and prepared to put her feet up than a brisk knock sounded on her door. She knew it wasn't Carling by the lack of a singsong voice calling her name.

Riley! Her mind leaped to the conclusion. It probably hadn't been difficult for him to find her new place of abode. Did his coming mean he'd called off his engagement to Eliza? He would have understood from their last encounter she didn't want to see him unless such were the case.

Patting her hair, she smoothed her shirtwaist, tugging on the sleeves. *Oh, how ridiculous of her!* He'd seen her in her shift. How could the appearance of her clothing matter?

Girding herself for the next onslaught of desire at his mere presence, she took a deep breath and opened the hotel room door.

"Sophie, I found you at last."

"Oh my God. Philip!"

CHAPTER THIRTEEN

His boyish face smiled at her. "Is that a happy greeting or are you very angry with me?"

Sophie was speechless for a moment. He was absolutely the last person she expected to see and seemed, thus, like an apparition.

Was she happy to see him? She was unsure through the tumult of feelings, but she thought, indeed, she was. He seemed like the part of her life that was stable and comfortable. He was the love of her university days and her travels in Europe. He was *her Philip.*

"No, I'm not angry. Just surprised beyond all measure."

"Is it too improper for me to enter your room?"

Sophie considered for a moment, then turned to survey her small domain. It was her entire home at the moment. The bed was neatly made, wrinkled only where she'd recently sat upon it, and her clothes and unmentionables were all tucked away. She gestured for him to enter.

"I suppose it's all right. You may sit on the bed if you like."

"After all," he said, striding in and filling the space, "we are not strangers to each other."

She blushed. No, not by half. This golden-haired man had kissed her many more times than Riley Dalcourt, and yet it was Riley's kisses that filled her dreams.

"How did you find me? Why are you in San Francisco? What about Oxford?"

He looked delighted. "So many questions. Before I answer any of them, I want to apologize. Frankly, I'm shocked you're even speaking to me. I used you horribly."

Sophie was shocked, too, but for a different reason. Searching her heart, she wondered at the lack of despair which used to rear its head at the mere thought of Philip, along with emptiness and anger. All three emotions had vanished, brushed away completely by Riley's scorching kisses and his heated touch.

How well her heart had healed! Philip expected her to still be crushed by the abrupt way he had forsaken her. But it was simply no longer the case.

She smiled benignly at him. "Philip, how can I hold you responsible for your true feelings? One can't force love, no matter how convenient." She'd learned that from Eliza and Riley.

"But we'd been a couple for a long while," he continued, seeming to want her to dredge up some semblance of grief.

"I accept your apology for leaving me for the famed halls of Oxford. I do."

He looked as if he wanted to pursue the subject of broken hearts, but after a moment, he let it go.

"You look wonderful."

She held up her bandaged hand, unable to believe he hadn't noticed it for himself. She'd been back to Dr. Finley and had the first bandages removed. Now, she wore a smaller white wrap. Still, her hand looked like an Egyptian mummy's.

"Blazes, Sophie! What happened?"

"I had a bit of an accident," she told him.

"Your family said nothing about it."

"They don't know," she admitted.

"Can you still play? What about your career?"

She shrugged. "Time will tell. It's only been a few weeks. But I have it on good authority my fingers will heal just fine." She thought of Riley's promise and smiled. "Still, it is rather inconvenient. Nerve-wracking, actually." Rather like having the former love of your life appear out of nowhere. "How did you find me, Philip? Why are you here?"

He didn't answer at once. Instead, he patted the bed. "Will you sit?"

She sat, keeping a good distance between them.

"I won't bite, you know?" He looked serious for a moment. "I've missed you."

She didn't know what to say. She *had* missed him, but not anymore. Sophie could remember the strong feelings she'd had for him, then the intense pain, but now, she had so many other feelings crowding her heart.

"I went to your mother's house first and learned you'd gone to Colorado, and then on to the west coast. I was flabbergasted. You were so far away. I think I supposed you would always be right where I could find you."

"When you wanted me," she pointed out.

"Touché." He looked down at his hands resting on his own knees. "So here I am. Your family had your address quite wrong, however."

"I moved here after my accident. This is temporary until my hand heals and I start to play again."

"Where were you playing? Your mother mentioned you had some prospects at the orchestra."

She was saved from answering by a second brisk knock on her door. Sophie found herself in a dilemma. Answer it and risk someone finding out she had a man in her room. Or ignore it and miss something important, a message from Carling, perhaps. Standing, she opened the door.

"Freddie," Sophie said, with false jocularity. There was no way to hide the presence of another person behind her in the small space, unless she somehow grew quite a bit wider.

"I was wondering if you'd like to join me—" He stopped dead as he saw the blond man on her bed, sitting very comfortably, arms crossed over his chest.

Sophie stepped to the side. "Freddie, this is Philip Wainright from back home. He's . . . an old friend."

Freddie looked uncertain, but Sophie ushered him in at the same time as Philip rose to his feet.

"Philip, this is Freddie Vern, a new friend," she said, giving Freddie an encouraging look. "He secured this lovely room for me." She didn't want to mention he was also her employer and hoped Freddie wouldn't bring it up either. Somehow, playing piano in a bar wasn't the great success she wanted Philip to hear about.

The two men shook hands, posturing a bit but saying how pleased each was to meet the other.

"I guess you can't come downstairs for a drink with me tonight?" Freddie said, looking from Sophie to Philip. "Can you?"

"Uh, *hm*. Philip, are you staying here at The Grand?" Sophie was stalling, still unsure what Philip was doing in San Francisco.

"No, I'm next door at The Palace. Naturally, if I'd known you were here, it would have been my first choice. Still, we have a lot to discuss," he said, eyeing Freddie.

Did they? Sophie wondered. She couldn't think of anything to talk to him about, even after all this time.

Another sharp rap came at her door, and Sophie didn't even hesitate. Puffing out her cheeks in disbelief, she smiled to each of the men before squeezing between them to open the door. Tentatively she peered out and her heart nearly stopped.

Riley!

"I know what you're thinking," he began, but she stepped to the side so he could see the other occupants of her room. He stopped mid-sentence.

"No," she said, "I don't think you do." Then she added, "Come in, Mr. Dalcourt. Meet my friends, Freddie Vern and Philip Wainright."

"Philip!" Riley repeated, his gaze locking on him as he stepped forward.

Sophie remembered then she'd mentioned him by name to Riley at least once.

"This is Mr. Riley Dalcourt . . . from Spring City," she said lamely to Philip, hoping Riley would take Philip's hand, which had been left hanging out like a limp flag.

Riley did take it finally, giving it a quick grasp and dropping it even faster, his eyes never leaving Philip's face. Then he shook hands with Freddie.

"Riley," Freddie repeated, thoughtfully, then obviously he remembered where he'd heard the name, adding with a frown, "Sophie's Riley?"

Sophie jumped when Freddie repeated what Carling had said, and she saw both Riley's and Philip's eyes widen at his remark.

"Sophie's Riley," Philip said loudly, staring from her to him and back again.

"He's my doctor," Sophie said. "I mean he's *a* doctor. Well, not quite, but almost."

Riley opened his mouth either to contradict or confirm, but before he could say anything, they all heard a female voice call out "Sophieeee," followed by a quick rap, rap, rap.

"Honestly," Sophie muttered, yanking the door open again to see both Carling *and* Egbert. Sophie stepped sideways so they could see. Carling burst out laughing. Sophie turned to her guests.

"Since the occupancy potential of my room has been quite surpassed, I suggest we take our little party downstairs."

"Oh, a party!" Carling exclaimed and clapped her hands. But Egbert cleared his throat.

"Actually, I was going to take Miss Rilkers to supper and we wondered if you might like to join us," he said, directing his invitation to Sophie alone. But the unwelcoming slope of his brow made it clear he'd been forced by Carling and would prefer to be alone with her.

"No, no, you two go on," she told them, knowing she would hear all about it the following day when she would also have to explain her room full of men. "Have a wonderful meal."

Closing the door on Carling's wicked grin and her wide, mischievous eye, Sophie turned back to the gentlemen. *Who was next to go?*

"Freddie, it was lovely of you to ask me for a drink. Perhaps another time?" He'd been a good friend, and she hated to put him out, but obviously, there were pressing issues.

Both Riley and Philip wore similar scowls on their faces regarding Freddie, but neither had the right to their jealousy, if that's what they were feeling.

Freddie looked dour but nodded curtly. "I'll be downstairs. Let me know if you need anything," he said pointedly.

"Thank you. I will." She gave him an extra warm smile when he left. Now, it might become a little harder.

Leaving the door open, she turned to the two men who were left, both staring directly at her. They were striking in their differences and their similarities. One blond and blue-eyed, the other all rich shades of brown. Both similarly tall, perhaps Philip a shade shorter, and Riley a tad broader of shoulder. Their mouths were entirely different.

Why Sophie should notice that, she didn't know. But Philip had a bow-shaped mouth, with a full lower lip, whereas Riley—her eyes darted to his lips. Riley's mouth was maybe a bit wider, his lips quick to curve into a generous grin. It was imminently kissable. She caught her breath.

"Mr. Dalcourt," she asked, "what are you doing here?"

She watched Philip's gaze swing over to Riley, who clearly wanted to ask the same of Philip, but it wasn't his place to do so.

"I came by to give you these." He pulled a small white, paper packet out of his pocket. He handed it to her. "Pain tablets. Dr. Finley wanted to make sure you had them in case you start to use your hand too soon. Your fingers will be sore and stiff when you begin moving them again."

She looked down at the envelope and shook it. It made a small rattling sound. "That's very kind of you to come all the way across the city."

"No trouble."

"So," Philip broke in, "you're a doctor?"

"No," Riley said.

Sophie waited for him to say more, but he looked unwilling to speak to Philip.

"Mr. Dalcourt is a medical student, nearly a doctor." She thought it best to enlighten Philip before he got other ideas. "He works at the hospital where my hand was treated."

"I see." Philip rocked lightly from foot to foot.

Riley crossed his arms. Silence.

"I say," Philip offered, "we're heading out, old chap. Do you mind?"

Riley barely glanced at him. Instead, his eyes bore into hers. "I'll leave you to your evening." At last, he moved toward the door. Stopping beside her, standing very close, he looked down into her eyes. "That is, if that's what you want."

She heard Philip let out an exasperated sigh. How could she possibly respond to such a remark?

"Yes, thank you."

Riley pursed his lips in disapproval, apparently not thinking much of her spending time with the man who'd broken her heart. But all he could do was nod and leave.

"Something's up with that fellow," Philip said as she closed the door, but she merely lifted her shoulders noncommittally. "I got the distinct feeling he had something more than pain tablets occupying his mind," he persisted.

"He's a friend. I met him in Colorado, and he goes to medical school here." What else could she say?

"*Hm*, you seem to have an abundance of friends here." Then he shrugged. "But what did I think? That you would be sitting alone, pining for me. You wouldn't be my lively Sophie Malloy if you were."

His Sophie? She looked down at her hands. She hadn't thought of herself that way in a long time. Did she even want to spend time with Philip? She certainly wanted to hear what he had to say, even if it was only news from abroad.

"I'm hungry. Would you like to get something to eat?"

Philip smiled. It was a very familiar sight, and she relaxed. She'd asked him that question a hundred times, hadn't she?

"I'd love to. The restaurant at my hotel—"

"You know, I've had enough of The Grand and The Palace. I'd love to go somewhere else in this city."

"Somewhere else it is, then," he said agreeably.

Sophie nodded. "Let me change my shoes."

"I was a numbskull, a jackass," Philip professed for the third time.

"Yes," Sophie said because she was tired of telling him he hadn't been. "You were."

He looked surprised, his fork halfway to his mouth. "But you said before I was correct to follow my heart."

"I did, but if you're going to keep stating your faults, I'm eventually going to agree. Look, Philip, if you want to be free and go to the university unencumbered, that's fine. It wasn't fine last year because I had expectations."

"I know you did, and I let you down."

Sophie thought it was rather more heart-wrenching than merely being "let down." One minute they were about to be engaged and the next she'd been on a vessel bound for Boston and the comfort of her mother. Still, her sentiments had entirely changed. With her hand still bandaged and Riley Dalcourt refusing to leave her alone, she had other issues to contend with.

"Philip, we've talked about Oxford and my family and your family and San Francisco. Why don't you tell me precisely why you're here?"

He steepled his fingers on the table in front of him and stared at them a moment.

"I think I have made a mistake."

"About?" she prompted.

"Us."

"Indeed." She took a sip of her wine.

"I thought you'd be more excited."

"I don't know as yet to what mistake you refer, so how do I know how I'm supposed to react?" Sophie could think of more than one mistake he'd made. Taking another sip of wine, she waited for him to explain.

"Frankly, I think we should go back to being a couple. Your expectations were entirely correct, and Oxford would have been infinitely better with you beside me. There's not a day I don't miss you, your face, all of you. I want to hear you play for me, and I want you to discuss life with me again, the way you used to."

Sophie couldn't deny she felt an immediate sense of satisfaction, even relief. She'd been dismissed rather summarily by this man whom she'd loved. He'd done so as if she had no value in his life. It had been a blow to her ego and her self-worth. Now, at least, by his words, she hadn't been inconsequential to him.

"Well?" he prompted, with a small upturn to his lips. "Have you nothing to say?"

Staring at his face, she was so accustomed to his moods and emotions, she knew how he would react. If she smiled sweetly back at him with agreement, he would respond in kind and take her hand. His lids would droop ever so slightly, and he'd look at her from under them in a come-hither way designed to stir her passions. It would end in a kiss.

However, if instead she remained impassive, as she felt at the moment she would, his tentative smile would disappear immediately, replaced by pursed lips and a slight frown of disapproval. Instead of a kiss, she'd receive a cold shoulder. She used to do nearly anything to avoid that.

"Philip, I *am* surprised. You seemed so very certain not too long ago that our paths had to separate. What has changed?"

"I told you, Sophie. I missed you at Oxford. I was lonely for you. I went out with other girls, but they weren't you."

She wondered at her own lack of jealousy. She felt no spike of emotion, nothing compared to how she felt when she saw Eliza and Riley kissing in the backyard—jealousy combined with a physical reaction, like a strong stomach cramp.

"Of course they weren't me, Philip. But you *had* me. You didn't *want* me. Perhaps you haven't found the right girl in Oxford. That doesn't mean, however, you want me any more than you did last year when you left."

He looked down at his plate and away from her dark eyes. "I remember how stunned and sad you were when I said I was going to Oxford alone. I expected you to be happy to see me." He was pouting.

"I *am* happy to see you, but I cannot give you my heart as if it were only yesterday we were last together. Surely, you understand that. A lot has happened since then. We would have to fall in love again."

Could she fall for Philip now she'd felt such ardent stirrings for Riley? Sophie didn't know. He looked the same, but she was far different. Philip smiled at her once more.

"Then I shall make you fall in love with me again."

She considered. She'd been content with what they had before, and she almost hoped he could do it. After all, Riley would never be hers.

"How long are you staying?"

"Until I have your promise to come back with me."

"Be serious, Philip. You didn't leave Oxford for an open-ended period of time. How long are you booked up at The Palace?"

"A week at the hotel, but that can be extended."

If he thought she'd melt in his arms in a week, he'd better think again.

"But I'm not going back to Oxford at all," he added. "It wasn't for me, as it turns out."

She sensed Philip was holding something back, but she didn't press him. He fiddled with his napkin for a moment before he spoke again.

"I'm considering Harvard, of course, but also Williams and Amherst."

"Is that so?" Sophie tried to keep her face neutral. Inside, though, she was cringing. *Good God!* Williams College was the last place she'd want to be, in the center of nothing. She needed a big city or at least a port town to feel as though she were somewhere alive. She could no more live in Williamstown than she could in Spring City. But then, Riley wasn't asking her to go back to Colorado with him anyway, to live as a small-town doctor's wife. Yet if he did . . .

"Sophie, let's go somewhere we can be alone to talk. Back to my room or yours."

They had spent many hours alone before, but she hesitated. They were so used to each other. When they sat close, they always used to kiss or hold hands. If he stayed late, they sometimes did a little more.

Now, however, she thought it not only inappropriate but . . . unwelcome. One thing could lead to another, and they currently had no understanding or arrangement between them. In truth, her mind was too full of Riley, anyway. Anything that happened with Philip would be merely to fill the loneliness, like a musician using a cadenza for a self-indulgent solo no one wanted to hear.

"I've caught you by surprise, Soph, I can tell. Come on. I'll get you home and you can think about what I've said."

In a few minutes, they were back at The Grand in front of her door.

"It has been very strange being with you again," she admitted, looking up into his familiar face with his pale skin and reddish cheeks. His blond hair was cut shorter than before and his blue eyes gazed at her becomingly.

"Strange in a good way?" he asked, leaning against her door jam.

"Yes, I suppose. You know, it seemed as if everything happened so fast last year. One minute, I was in Rome planning my move to England and the adjustment from sunshine to rain and pasta to pork pies. Then the next minute," she trailed off, picturing her small flat in Rome and how lonely it was after he'd left without her.

"It's good to see you, Philip, truly, and to know you still care for me," she admitted.

"Oh, I do." With that, he reached for her. She let him pull her into his arms, until her stomach and hips were snug against his. Her senses were assaulted by the familiar feel of him and his accustomed scent.

As she smelled the sweet orange aroma of his Florida Water aftershave, the image of the long-necked glass bottle with its pretty yellow, blue, and green label popped into her head. A spare bottle used to sit in her bathroom. She sighed as his hands settled at her waist.

"I'm so sorry I hurt you," he said.

She stared into his eyes. He hadn't seemed sorry when he'd left her. He'd been excited at his new start. That had hurt most of all, how easily he'd seemed to part with her.

"I'll never do it again." He lowered his lips to hers, his mouth pressing firmly, intimately against her own. She clasped her hands behind his neck.

It was exactly the same as it always had been.

It was so utterly different than kissing Riley.

She jumped back, feeling disloyal that Riley's name had popped into her head when her mouth was joined to another man's.

"I'll see you tomorrow, then," Philip said, wearing a bemused expression.

Perhaps he thought she was overcome with emotion due to his kiss. After closing the door, she sat on her bed, amazed by the past few hours. Then she flung herself back, as she'd wanted to do hours earlier, before everyone started knocking. And inevitably, as she knew she would, she considered Philip's kiss.

Sophie groaned. It was nothing like Riley's kiss. Her heart hadn't raced, her stomach hadn't fluttered, her female parts weren't tingling. It had been pleasant, nothing more. But

Philip's kiss had not changed—*she* had. She now knew how exciting a kiss could be.

Lying in the dim light of her room, she imagined Riley leaning over her, slanting his lips across hers, teasing her mouth open, biting her lower lip with a sensual nibble. Just thinking of him caused her womanly core to prickle with anticipation. He would rest his weight on her, and his tongue would move into her mouth and touch hers. And she would long for more.

She wanted to lift her own skirts and touch herself to ease the feeling of desire. She wanted to run to Riley and say to hell with his promise to Eliza. At that moment, she would let him take her, even if it was only for a night, even if he could never be hers.

She hummed, thinking over what she'd eaten that day, in accordance with the current idea of how certain foods, such as pork, eggs, salt-meat, candy, pies and cakes, pepper, pickles and condiments—*damnation, just about anything!*—could cause her to feel this fervent desire for release.

Balderdash! She simply wanted Riley, although she supposed she ought to long for the calmer affection she used to have for Philip.

But she wanted Riley.

CHAPTER FOURTEEN

When Sophie awoke the next morning, she forgot for an instant that Philip was in San Francisco, merely a block away at The Palace. Then she remembered his kiss.

Could she love someone yet experience only such a tepid sensation in his embrace? Stretching languorously, she thought of how she felt when Riley's mouth was upon her. Damn the man for tempting her with his perfect kisses!

She didn't want to go to Williamstown or to Amherst as Philip's wife. Still, she could almost see herself living back in Boston or in Cambridge while Philip attended Harvard. She would, perhaps, teach at the Conservatory and her life would be settled. She yawned widely.

Oh dear! She could imagine it, but she wasn't sure she liked it. Still, she remembered how warm and full her heart had once been at the notion of being Mrs. Philip Wainright. *She could feel that way again, couldn't she?*

Startled by the knock at her door, Sophie knew a moment later hearing her call out her name, "Sophieeee," it was Carling. Carling! Her first date with Egbert! Jumping up and grabbing her wrap, she threw open the door.

138

"Tell me everything!" they both said at once.

"You first," they both said again. Then they dissolved in laughter, with Sophie pulling Carling into the room where they sat upon the rumpled bed.

Carling eyed it mischievously until Sophie smacked her on the arm.

"What happened then?" Carling asked. "Go on, you first."

"Just dinner with my old friend, Philip."

"Just dinner," Carling mimicked. "And no hanky-panky?"

"Carling!" Sophie pretended to be shocked. "All right, if you must know, he kissed me goodnight. But that was all. He wants to take up where we left off, apparently."

Carling's eyes widened. "You mean he wants you back?"

Sophie nodded.

"And do you want him as your beau again, and maybe even as your husband?"

That was the question of the hour. Sophie shrugged. How could she answer when she didn't know?

"And your Riley?" Carling persisted.

"I've told you, he's not *my* Riley. Anyway, he came only to give me some tablets for my hand."

"Truly?" Carling's eyes narrowed slightly.

"Yes, truly. Now, tell me how it went with Egbert."

Her friend smiled shyly, an unusual occurrence for her. Sophie beamed back.

"Come on, tell me."

"He's very nice," Carling said. "Rather sweet. We had a lovely meal and . . ."

"And?"

"He said I was beautiful." She put her face in her hands and squealed. Then she looked up with her eyes shining. "He asked me to be his girl. Can you believe it?"

"Of course I can. Why not? And you are beautiful."

"He also said I was smart, and it wouldn't have mattered to him how pretty I was if I didn't have a brain and a bit of spunk." She hugged herself. "Oh, Sophie, I'm so happy."

"I can see that, dear one. You deserve it. And I think he's a good man and an excellent match. Imagine you at your own vineyard. Madame of all you survey." They smiled at each other.

"It's still a bit of a dream, but why not? I mean, we could do it as well as anyone, right?" Carling asked.

"Better, I should think," Sophie said. "Will it be strange to work for him now that you're his girl?"

"Nah, I never much obeyed him anyway, not that he'd know that, of course!"

They laughed harder. "I better get to work now though," Carling added. "We can't all be ladies of leisure like you."

Sophie sobered after she left. She didn't want to be a lady of leisure. She dressed and went downstairs. It was early. The bar was deserted. Seated at the piano, she rested her hands on the cover. Then slowly, she opened it. With her good hand, she played a few notes and tried to relax, but she felt like a one-handed juggler in the sideshow.

If she couldn't play anymore, then perhaps being Philip's wife was her next best option.

"The four of us? Out to dinner?"

"Carling, please stop repeating everything I say," Sophie admonished. "Yes, if you and Egbert want to, that is. Philip and I used to have a group of friends in Rome. And we can't just keep staring at each other while we eat every meal. It's been a week, and it's starting to get stale."

Carling giggled. "It will only be Egbert's and my second time out together."

"That's fine. We don't have to stick to you like tar. We can leave you to your after-dinner drinks if you're sick of our company and want to be alone with your fellow."

Carling blushed, something she did often when Egbert's name came up. Sophie was happy for her friend, and hoped the other couple's presence would alleviate a little of the strain between herself and Philip. He was courting her as if she were a duchess. Flowers, chocolates, dinners, and then kisses after dinner—and the constant pressure to do even more.

The previous evening, he'd pressed her against the wall and insinuated his thigh between her legs, pressing her skirts tight, his hands roaming up and down her body. They had done that numerous times before when they'd been a couple in Rome, their rooms so close they could practically climb from his balcony to hers, if he'd been the daring type.

Sometimes they'd touched each other lying down on his bed. More than once over the years, she'd pushed for him to go even further, driven to distraction by his caresses and uninhibited by too much Italian red wine. Back then, he'd been the one to put her off, saying he was a gentleman who could wait until they were married.

Sophie was not prudish, but now she had to be sure he represented her path in life—to be his wife—before she gave herself entirely to Philip. He'd hurt her badly before, and she couldn't help feeling he wanted to be intimate with her in order to seal their arrangement and lock her into accepting him.

She'd had no further contact from Riley. Even when she'd gone to the hospital for a checkup on her hand, hoping to glimpse him in such an innocent setting, she'd been disappointed. She knew she had to put him out of her mind.

"We'll see you at The Oakdale, at seven sharp."

Sophie was trying to look forward to it. At five o'clock, she was out of the bath and considering her choice of clothing when there was a knock on her door. One of the housekeepers had agreed to do her laundry in the hotel's washroom for a small fee. She opened the door and turned away to pick up her linen bag of soiled clothes.

"It's all ready," she said.

"Ready for what?"

Riley's voice stopped her in her tracks. Putting her hand to her throat, she could feel her pulse start to race. Looking at him, dressed in his traveling clothes, she had a sense of foreboding.

"What are you doing here?" Her voice sounded choked, and she coughed to clear it of the myriad emotions welling up inside her.

At this juncture, Sophie knew it would not look good if Philip, or anyone for that matter, came upon them. Riley shouldn't have come up to her room, certainly not after dusk and with her in only a dressing gown.

"I came to say goodbye."

As if struck, she took a step back. Her insides clenched, and she felt suddenly ill. It would take very little for her to scrunch up her face and cry. She'd left him behind in Spring City. That had been hard. However, if she were honest with herself, she'd felt hopeful she would meet him again in San Francisco, which she had.

Now, after being in and out of his life for weeks, it was even more difficult to let him go.

"You're going back to Colorado?"

"Tonight. It's an emergency. Eliza's father is waning."

"I see."

"I couldn't go without telling you goodbye." He ran a hand through his hair. "Honestly, I couldn't leave without seeing you again." He stepped closer, and she took another step back.

"Riley," she warned.

"I know," he said somewhat harshly, dropping his hands to his sides. "I know. I can't touch you. I have no right to touch you."

But, *oh God*, how she wanted him to, and she wanted to touch him back. Sophie wanted to put her hands on his arms and feel his strength. She wanted to run her fingers over his muscles the way she did the keys of her piano, and she wanted to rest her palms on his solid chest as he held her close.

Instead, clenching her injured hand in her good one, she kept them locked together. His eyes went to them.

"You should be getting the last wrap off soon. Did you take the pain tablets?"

"No, I didn't need them."

"I'm glad." Clearly, he was stalling.

Sophie had to get him out of her room. Before the maid came. Before Philip arrived. Before she threaded her fingers in his cocoa-colored hair and drew his mouth to hers. Before she begged him to kiss her.

"You had better go," she said, feeling grim. "You're taking the ferry to Alameda?"

"Yes." His eyes drifted to her mouth.

She saw no point in mentioning Philip had come to woo her and take her back East. It would change nothing. She would offer no ultimatum, no coercion or manipulation. They'd been honest with each other from the start.

She opened her mouth but didn't know what to say. This was so unlike when Philip left her in Rome. She'd been shocked and even a little hysterical, while he'd spouted platitudes about their separation being for the best.

With Riley, she'd known it was coming. There was no surprise, only bone-deep sadness. Plainly, he was as sadly resigned as she was. Regarding her own future, she was uncertain of anything except she couldn't be near Riley *after* he married Eliza. It would be torture at that point, more than it already was.

And now? Now, she had to get him out of her presence immediately. Something unthinkable would happen. They were like gunpowder and sparks.

He stepped closer again, and she had nowhere to go, with the backs of her legs touching the bed.

"Riley." Her voice was barely above a whisper. It sounded pleading to her own ears. *Please leave quickly. Please kiss me before you go.*

As if she'd spoken out loud, he leaned toward her, and in the next instant, their bodies were pressed together, their lips followed suit. His kiss seemed to steal all thought from her brain and send warmth flooding through her.

He groaned, bringing his hands up to cradle her face as their kiss deepened.

"Sophie," his voice was a sigh, and then he nibbled her lower lip before pulling away. "I hate leaving you," he said, his forehead against hers.

"Philip will be here shortly."

He stiffened but didn't release her. "I don't care for the man. He hurt you."

Apparently, men were good at doing that, she thought bitterly.

"He's sorry, and he wants me back. He wants to marry me." There, she'd told him anyway.

He made a sound, like a low growl before asking, "What do *you* want?"

Was she supposed to expose her heart to him, right before he got on a train to go home to Eliza? She didn't answer. It didn't matter. Surely, he could see it in her eyes.

"I want you, Sophie, but I know it's wrong." He touched her lips with his thumb. She flinched. "You were made for me, I think."

Riley was looking at her but seemed to be talking to himself. His hand went around and cupped the back of her head before he claimed his lips again. At the same time, she felt him kick out behind and heard the door close with a resounding slam. She jumped and pulled away.

"We can't do this, Riley."

"I can't remember why." His voice, low and tender, made her feel hot all over.

She started to cry, just a few tears that slid down her cheek before she could regain control.

"You know why." Her voice trembled because she, too, was finding it hard to think why it was wrong to be with this man who enveloped all her senses and to whom she was drawn so strongly she ached to touch him.

He wiped at a tear with the back of his finger. "I'm not sure any of those reasons are real. You're all that matters right now."

What if she never saw him again?
What if she agreed to marry Philip?

Could she take the memories made with Riley and let them sustain her over a lifetime? Dear God, what was she thinking?

He shook his head as though waking up from some enchantment.

"Christ! I'm sorry, Sophie. I didn't come here to upset you. I just wanted to look into your eyes again. I'll never forget your eyes or the way you look at me." He gave her a twisted smile that was more a grimace. "You *are* all that matters right now."

He stepped away from her. His jaw clenched. "I will always remember how you made me feel when you played piano."

That got to her. She closed her eyes. Riley understood it wasn't merely a gift of playing well. It was her soul she expressed through the music.

"Don't go." Two words that would change everything. They slipped from her without her thinking.

"Sophie, don't." It was his turn to plead, his voice gruff. "Please don't look at me that way. I'm trying to do the proper thing." He retreated farther, until his back was against the door.

"I'm tired of doing the proper thing," she said. "Here, in this room, there's only you and me. Correct?"

He nodded. She moved closer, until she was pressing *him* against the door. Still, his arms remained resolutely at his sides, his fists clenched, although she noted a bead of sweat break out on his forehead.

"And we're adults, yes?" she persisted, reaching up to kiss the skin at his neck as she had longed to do so many times. *Ah, vanilla.* Gently, she bit him just to the side of his Adam's apple. *Irresistible.*

"Sophie, you'll hate me later, and I couldn't stand it. I don't want to be someone who hurts you." He looked up at the ceiling away from her gaze.

"You already are." She said it matter-of-factly. It was true. But it wasn't Riley's fault. "I know my heart will ache tomorrow and I'll miss you terribly. But that's a price I'm willing to pay to have you make love to me." She touched his cheek and then rested her hand on his chest.

He swore, and she felt him tremble under her touch.

"Riley, I'll miss you anyway, so why not have this memory to take with us?"

His gaze locked with hers—a dark, fiery umber flickering in their mahogany depths—and she waited, heart thumping wildly. What would she do if he walked out the door? Then, he reached behind him and turned the lock.

Swiftly, he enclosed her in his arms and his mouth was on hers. She heard herself whimper and his answering groan. In two steps, he moved them to her bed where they tumbled together, and he began pushing her robe down her shoulders.

She wished she could tell him to slow down, that they could take their time. But they had so little of it. Instead, everything about this was urgent. Her desire, his need, the chance of being caught, the ferry's departure, then the connecting train. No, this wouldn't be slow and sweet. Rather than Schumann's *Träumerei*, this would be as fervent as the beginning of Chopin's *Fantasie Impromptu*, as their mouths and hands were everywhere at once.

His weight lifted and while she unbelted her robe, he tore off his jacket and tossed it to the floor, followed by his shoes, socks, and trousers. He came back to her still yanking at his tie, until he gave up and started working on his shirt buttons, but she knew he wouldn't make it in time and she'd never get to see him fully naked standing before her.

For her part, she was sinfully bare except for the sleeves of her robe, which spread out from under her along with the rest of it, the deepest midnight-blue silk.

"You're a luminous mermaid in the dark sea." He lowered himself gradually over her.

The weight of his strong body thrilled her, and she couldn't stop her hips from arching up to grind against him. She felt his answering thrust and then the smooth length of his shaft against her pelvis.

He kissed his way down her neck to the hollow of her throat, and she laughed. It was a desperate, joyful sound. At last, she could feel his muscles against her and breathe deeply the clean scent of him. *Her Riley at last!*

He nipped the skin at her neck as she had done his. Then his mouth moved over her collar bone, then lower between her swelling breasts. He brushed the side of his face against one nipple that beaded instantly, then he moved to the other to grasp it between his lips, his tongue circling it with precision. She arched against him again, but he was slipping lower. She wanted to experience all of these new wondrous sensations, but she needed the act of mating with him before their time ran out.

As his mouth continued to play across her skin, tasting her, he skimmed his hand down her flat stomach to her woman's core and cupped her. She bucked and spread her thighs for him. Having his large palm on her heated mound was far different than her own hand. He pressed her with the base of his palm, watching her face. She moaned out a sigh, then his finger slipped between the folds caressing the bud she'd only ever touched herself, and she sucked in her breath. Closing her eyes, she let her head fall back.

"God, Riley, I—"

"*Sh*, just let me touch you. You're perfect."

With his finger dipping inside her, she became damp with longing. Then he slipped a second finger inside her. She'd never done that, and it felt delightful. But why was he wasting time pleasuring her with his hands when he had the precise male part that would utterly complete her?

"Please," she murmured.

"Yes," he said, his voice rasping.

He drew back. In his hand was protection she'd only read about. Watching him put it on, how his thick protrusion seemed to move with a mind of its own, she yearned to encircle it with her hands.

This piece of his anatomy was magnificent, much more so in person than in the drawings she'd seen. It was also daunting. While she'd touched herself to extreme pleasure and knew her body, she couldn't imagine how his erect shaft would possibly fit.

Regardless, she aimed to find out.

He looked her in the eyes as he nudged her legs apart with his knee and settled between them. Then he fit his member to her damp opening. She was throbbing and, incredibly, she could feel his body throbbing, too.

"Sophie," he caressed her with her own name and started to press inside her.

She wanted to tell him she loved him, right then, but it wouldn't be right. It certainly wouldn't do any good to say it. Instead, she gave over to the sensation of him entering her. Yes, it burned, as she'd heard it would. But then the discomfort passed, and he was filling her.

"Are you all right?"

"Yes," she said, hardly able to breathe.

He moved, and she moved with him. He kissed her lips, and she kissed him back. It was as she'd hoped it would be. He was so hard and powerful, and she loved looking up at him, with his arms placed on either side of her shoulders while his body surged into hers, all his muscles rippling. He was the epitome of restrained strength and gentleness.

Yet as the heat grew between them, she had to close her eyes and focus on what was building inside her, the crescendo that seemed inevitable.

She was climbing a mountain of pleasure and knew, once she reached the peak with this man, she would be forever changed, forever linked to him. At the crest, she felt his hand slip between their bodies and touch her the apex of her desire. Gasping, her whole body shuddered, her muscles clenching around him until she felt lightheaded and breathless.

Crying out, she heard him seconds later releasing a guttural sound that mimicked the animal passion she felt.

Without thinking, she raked his back with her fingernails, and it didn't shock her. She reveled in the torrid release as she tumbled down the other side of the peak, holding onto him tightly before he collapsed beside her on her small bed.

"Sweet Jesus!" she muttered, her body limp, as if she'd rushed through Beethoven's entire *Sonata No. 21* in about three minutes.

He laughed dolefully and rolled to his side, facing her. But as he opened his mouth to speak, there came a knock on the door. They both froze, eyes wide open. She bit her lower lip, holding her breath.

"Miss Malloy," came the maid's voice. Sophie nodded her head indicating to Riley it was all right, and then they heard her footsteps as she left. "She came for my laundry," she said, nearly giggling at the nonsensical sentence, as well as from the sheer relief.

He let out a pent-up breath. "That was close."

She nodded. The surge of fear at nearly being caught had revived her from the after-lovemaking lethargy.

"You have to get out of here. Philip is coming to take me out."

Riley scowled. "Would you mind not mentioning another man while I'm lying naked next to you?"

Unbelievably, she found herself smiling. This was absurd. This could not be her life! But she'd been correct. Everything had changed. Riley was now her paramour, her confidant, the one person she felt closest to in all the world. And he had to leave.

"First of all, you're not naked. Not entirely, anyway." She touched his rumpled white shirt that hung open over his broad chest. "Second, you are not lying here another instant. You have to leave. Immediately."

He stared hard at her, with her practical persona firmly in place. She could see he was about to become tender, and she couldn't bear it. He took her face in his hands.

"Sophie, I—"

"No, don't say it. Whatever *it* is. You have a ferry and a train to catch, Riley Dalcourt. And I have . . . well, I have another path to take."

He gazed into her eyes for another long moment. "You're right." Still, he took the time to kiss her gently before getting up and dressing quickly.

As he did, she wrapped her gown around her and efficiently smoothed the covers on her bed, knowing later she'd have time to ponder and remember and maybe regret, although she doubted it.

After shrugging on his coat, he took her hand and drew her into his arms, leaning his chin atop her head. She tried to memorize the feeling of his unyielding body pressed against her soft, curvy one.

"Are you really giving Philip another chance?" he asked quietly.

How could he discuss it? She hadn't mentioned Eliza for decency's sake. At last, finding the strength, Sophie pushed him firmly away.

"As you said, you have no right, not even to ask me that." She unlocked the door and opened it, standing with her back pressed against the door trim.

Riley's eyes glinted with a myriad of emotions, but all he did was cinch the belt at her waist a little tighter and smooth her hair for her, running his thumb along her jawline one last time. Then he stepped out into the hallway.

Tilting her head to one side, she tried to look nonchalant while barely able to breathe. They stared at each other silently until Riley spoke.

"He's a lucky bastard."

"Who is?" asked Philip, coming upon them.

CHAPTER FIFTEEN

Sophie jumped, and Riley swiveled around. Neither had heard his approach.

"You are," Riley said, his voice challenging.

Philip stopped cold, his gaze wavering between pale-faced Sophie, barely dressed, and Riley, who was noticeably heated.

"What's going on here?" Philip narrowed his eyes, as he looked at them.

"Mr. Dalcourt was just saying goodbye—"

Riley cut her off. "You had better be good to her, Wainright. She's an extraordinary lady, and she deserves to be cherished."

"What business is that of yours?" Philip asked, moving to stand beside Sophie, taking hold of her trembling elbow.

Riley looked at Sophie then, and she saw her own sadness reflected in his glossy brown eyes. She could feel her heart beating in the base of her throat, along with a million unshed tears.

"It's not my business at all," he said, and with that, he left.

She took a single step forward, then stopped. Riley had looked so sorrowful, she wanted to run after him and comfort him.

"How odd!" Philip said, entering the room.

Sophie watched Riley disappear, and then, after a moment's pause, she turned to follow Philip. "Yes, wasn't he?" she said brightly.

Looking at Philip's face, she smiled tentatively and he smiled back. He moved to the bed and started to sit.

"No," she yelled, then scanned it for any telltale signs, but she'd tidied it well enough. Even she couldn't see the indentations of where she'd writhed only minutes earlier under another man.

Philip paused, half crouched, staring at her.

"I mean, it's getting late, and I still need to dress." She also needed to wash again. "You should wait downstairs."

He looked her up and down, and she blushed. He took a step toward her.

"Good thing you kept that man in the hall. That's certainly not appropriate attire for entertaining a man in your room. But your fiancé, that's another matter."

Her fiancé!

He encircled her in his arms, his hands smoothing up and down the silky material at her back. She tried to enjoy his familiar touch but, instead, it made her skin crawl. Not to mention that she felt like a harlot. She wanted to feel warm and loving and able to carry on normally. But, obviously, as she eased herself out of Philip's embrace, this was simply too soon.

"We don't want to be late," she reminded him, putting her hand on his arm and pushing him toward the door.

"Right," he agreed, "I'll be downstairs." He bent his head to kiss her, and she nearly gave him her cheek. Somehow, she forced herself to keep still as his lips touched hers. She felt no stomach-flipping thrill, no desire to rip his clothes off, but then, she also didn't feel the need to wipe her mouth, so that was something.

Perhaps if he smelled like Riley instead of like a cloying orange.

"More of that later," he promised, lifting his head and looking at her with what she could only describe as devotion.

Closing the door, she considered her future as pragmatically as possible, for it seemed romantic notions were not to play a part. She could live on the memories of her single passionate encounter with Riley and she could also be Philip's faithful wife.

Yes, she would be able to tolerate that, wouldn't she?

"I can see why you fell for him the first time and why you could easily do it again." Carling and Sophie were in the powder room of The Lick's gorgeous dining room, touching up their noses and smoothing their hair halfway through their meal.

Sophie's eyes met Carling's in the mirror. "You approve of him, then?"

"Yes," Carling said, "but he did break your heart, didn't he? Don't move too fast, Sophie. What's to stop him from doing it again?"

Yes, indeed. What if Philip took her back to Massachusetts and then changed his mind?

"If I marry him, I guess that seals the deal, so to speak."

Carling studied Sophie's face.

"What?" Sophie asked. "Do I have something stuck in my teeth?"

"Nah," Carling said, "I was wondering about your Riley. Have you heard from him?"

Sophie didn't know what to say. She couldn't spill the details of her intimate encounter with Riley from a few hours earlier. Such a conversation crossed the line from the usual female talk about letting a man kiss you for a moment too long or letting a man stroke your wrist. She had let Riley make love to her, knowing it was for one time only, with no future and no declaration of love. It was utterly shameless. And it had been utterly wonderful.

She would keep it to herself.

"You're smiling," Carling said, "so you have heard from him."

Sophie dodged the question. "He's not here anymore. He left for Colorado a short while ago." She imagined him on the Central Pacific, picturing the train she'd taken. He would switch to the Union Pacific and go as far as Cheyenne before heading south.

"*Hm.* Then it's a good thing you have Mr. Wainright. And quite a dishy, fair-haired fellow he is, too. Come on. They'll wonder what we're up to."

"I doubt it. Isn't discussing men what the powder room is for? Speaking of which, Egbert is so different away from the hotel, but also still so Egbert-ish."

Carling laughed. "Yes, he is. All the qualities I like about him are still there, but not the nasty hotel manager parts. I'm falling for him, you know?"

Walking arm-in-arm, they rejoined their escorts, and Sophie squashed any stray feeling of disappointment the man waiting for her at the table wasn't Riley. That wasn't fair to Philip.

"We've been discussing vineyards," announced Egbert.

Sophie arched an eyebrow as she looked at Philip. "And what would you know about growing grapes?"

"I know about drinking wine," he said lightly, raising his glass and taking a sip. They all laughed.

"He's a thoughtful fellow," Egbert added. "Helping me think quite clearly."

"Yes," Sophie agreed, "he's very thoughtful." After all, that's what a philosophy student specializes in. "And what are you thinking about?"

Egbert smiled. "Moving, taking a chance, speculating, all that exciting stuff."

"Oh, yes?" Carling asked, probably thinking of her future.

"Yes, and maybe some other exciting things," Egbert said with a wink to Carling.

Sophie was glad for her friend, the rest of her exciting life was all in front of her. Sitting next to Philip, she should feel the same way. So why did it seem as if the best part of her life was behind her or, at the very least, on a train to Colorado?

"Oh, Riley, I'm so glad you're here." Eliza threw herself into his arms as soon as she saw him. It was unusual for her to display that kind of need. She was not the clinging type, so he knew it was bad.

He held her, but the difference between comforting Eliza and embracing Sophie was immediate. Nothing stirred in him, except concern. Nothing urged him to hold her tighter or kiss her. He simply rubbed her back and murmured inanities, useless as he knew them to be, until she got ahold of herself and pulled away.

"You came so fast," she sniffed and took a handkerchief from her sleeve. "He's very poorly. Doc Cuthins is upstairs. He says it'll be over soon."

That was just like the Doc to tell it like it was. His patients appreciated it, and Riley intended to do the same in his own practice . . . right there in Spring.

"Would you like tea?" she offered.

He knew she needed something to do. "Yes, thanks," he accepted. "I'll go upstairs and check on your father, and I'll let you know what's happening. I know you'll want to be with him at the end."

She paled. "Of course."

Later, in the quiet hours between midnight and one in the morning, Elijah Prentice passed away, with his daughter and Riley on one side of him, the preacher on the other, and Doc Cuthins at the foot of the bed.

Riley slept in the guest room, so Eliza wouldn't be alone in the house for the first time in her life. At five in the morning, she came to his room, all pale skin in her white shift and silken golden hair, eyes so light blue they were nearly transparent. She climbed into his bed, and he welcomed her, putting his arms around her, feeling nothing but affection, knowing that was all he could expect from their marriage.

"Do you want to make love to me, Riley?"

He froze. If he was going to marry her, he'd have to, but right then, his sole thought was how he didn't want to betray Sophie. He swallowed.

"Do you want me to?"

She laughed softly until he realized she was crying.

"Eliza. Please don't cry. Any man would be honored to make love to you."

"Any man but you."

He couldn't lie, but sometime soon, after the vows, he would have to be intimate with her. "When we're married—"

"We're not getting married," she said. He could feel her wiping her face dry with the bedsheet.

"What are you saying? You're lying in bed with me."

"I'm free to do what I want. This is my house now. And don't tell me you've never lain with a woman before whom you didn't intend to marry."

That hit close to home and, again, his thoughts flew to Sophie. It hadn't been twenty-four hours since he'd made love to her, and now, he was in bed with Eliza. *What an absolute bastard!* But if he closed his eyes and kept his hands on her, he could almost pretend . . .

"Fine," her voice broke into his musings, "then we'll marry today. I'll talk to the justice of the peace."

Her emotions were bouncing faster than he could keep up. *Marry today?*

"Eliza, your father just passed. Give yourself some time to grieve."

"I am grieving, in here." She thumped her chest. "But Daddy's death wasn't a surprise. I'm not stricken and shocked. I loved him, even though I know most of the town didn't share my sentiment. And he loved me, unconditionally."

A few more silent tears rolled down her cheeks.

"Yes, he did. Anyone could see that." Elijah had been devoted to his daughter, and she deserved it. She deserved as much from a husband, as well. Hadn't Riley said the same thing to Wainright about Sophie?

He took a deep breath and held it a moment. He had to tell her what was in his heart.

"Eliza, I don't want to marry you."

"I know," she raised her hand and touched his cheek. "And I don't want to marry you, either. I only pushed you so you'd say it."

His brain was spinning.

What in the hell just happened? She didn't want to get married—not to him! She wasn't screaming or crying or throwing things. In fact, as he breathed a sigh of relief, he felt her do the same.

"I'm glad that's finally out in the open," she said, turning and snuggling closer, putting her head on his chest, as if they'd decided on what to eat for breakfast instead of breaking off a long-term engagement.

Nevertheless, he felt like dancing, so happy he hadn't hurt Eliza's feelings.

"Your hair smells good," he said, knowing it was a silly statement.

"I know."

He chuckled. "You've always been so sure. Even about us, I thought. I don't understand you."

"Men are so easily manipulated," she said, not unkindly. "I'm not so hard to figure out. I wanted to make my father happy. Making him think I was marrying a doctor made him so. He liked you, and it kept him untroubled. I'm sorry I held onto you so long, Riley, but I couldn't let our engagement end before he died, despite knowing you wanted it to."

"I see." So she was the one letting him down easy, "but now that he's gone, I can't just . . ."

"I know. How would it look? You'd be that horrible Dalcourt man who broke my grieving heart. Why, when you came back here to practice, you probably wouldn't even be welcomed. You'd be a pariah." She yawned. "I will make sure everyone knows I waited until my father died and then chucked you aside to gain my freedom."

Her hand drifted idly up and down his chest until he captured it and held it still. "I'm getting out of Spring, Riley."

"What? Why?" He lifted his head a little to look at her.

"I have been worse to you than you could imagine. In my heart of hearts, I love someone else. I always have." She paused. "You look surprised."

"I am." *He was!* "I had no idea."

"At times, I hoped you and I could marry and make a go of it, but I knew I couldn't be the wife you need. Not the way, say, Sophie Malloy could."

He started at the sound of her name.

"That's what I thought," Eliza said. "It's all right. I've learned we don't choose whom we love." She reached up and caressed his cheek. "And I appreciate you didn't abandon me for her when you so easily could have."

She pulled his head down and planted her lips on his. He held still as stone.

When she drew back, she snuggled against him again. "Nope, nothing there. To be honest, I was pretending for a moment you were him."

"You want to tell me who he is? I could beat the tar out of him for you."

"I wish you could. But he's not in Spring, and I have no idea where he is."

"Are you going to look for him?"

"No. That's unseemly in a woman, don't you think?" She yawned. "I'm going away for a while to see a little more of this world. That's all."

He smoothed her lovely flaxen hair. "I want you to be happy, Eliza. You sure as hell deserve it."

"You, too, Riley. You, too."

CHAPTER SIXTEEN

Within a week, Elijah Prentice was six feet under, his daughter had publicly broken off her engagement with Riley Dalcourt, and she had nearly finished packing up her trunks.

"I don't know Doc. She won't say where she's going." Riley sat in the surgery, drinking coffee, thinking about the many conversations he'd had with Eliza in the past few days, many of which centered on settling his debt with her. He wanted to pay her back, for the tuition and for his parents' mortgage.

At first, she'd waved any such discussion away with a flit of her hand, but in the end, she'd spoken plainly.

"Your monetary obligation never meant anything to me. I only set it up that way because I knew you were so damned honor bound, I could use it to hold onto you as long as I needed. Even with Sophie Malloy's unexpected arrival."

His cheeks heated. He didn't like talking about Sophie with Eliza. After all, he'd two-timed his fiancée, and he'd done wrong, terribly wrong, by Sophie. He hoped he could make it up to her now he was a free man. He was anticipating the moment when he returned to San Francisco, knocked on her door, and told her she was the sole woman in his life.

"What's that grin for, Riley? Just the mention of her name?" Eliza asked.

"I guess so." He squirmed on the porch seat, crossing his arms.

"I knew you'd fallen for her, even at the beginning. That's why I had her and Dan over. I had to make sure she was good enough for you when I let you go." Sitting on the railing, she swung her legs back and forth.

"Seriously, Eliza, you are a piece of work. Tell me what I can do for you?"

"First, become a great doctor, then be happy. If you choose to be happy with Sophie, that's all right by me."

"When I'm a doctor, I can pay you back everything I owe you, and I will."

"How about you set up some sort of fund in my name?" She tapped her cheek. "Yes, I rather like that idea. Something along the lines of The Eliza Prentice Poor People's Medical Care Fund."

Riley laughed. "It's rather a long name, but I think I can work on it. It's a great idea and generous, too." He stood up and took her hand. "I'm going to miss having you in my life, Eliza."

"I know."

And the next day, with a kiss on his cheek and a wave of her gloved hand, she was gone, her furniture all covered in cloth and a housekeeper left behind to tend to the rest.

"Wherever she's gone," Doc said, "she'll do all right. Don't you think?"

Riley shrugged. He had more respect for Eliza than he'd ever had before, and he hoped she found happiness. But she was not the woman uppermost in his mind. He was eager to get back to San Francisco and claim Sophie, and maybe punch Philip if he could think of any possible reason for doing so—perhaps because the man was breathing.

"What about you?" Doc asked.

"What *about* me?" Riley was glad Doc couldn't read his mind.

"I'm not getting any younger." Doc shook his head. "I can't believe I just said that." He scratched his chin. "I love what I do, but I can't do it forever."

Riley felt everything in him tighten. Eliza's freedom to jump on a train bound for anywhere was something he envied. He had a feeling his path was narrowing right back to Spring. And that, in itself, might cost him the woman he loved.

For love Sophie Malloy, he did, and now, at last, he could tell her. But drag her back to Spring City? That didn't sit well.

"You only have a few months left, right?" Doc already knew the answer.

"Yup," Riley agreed and sipped his coffee again. Less than that and he'd be a doctor.

"And then your plans are?"

Doc was going to make him say it.

"I'm going to come back here and work with you until you're ready to retire." The words were hardly out of his mouth yet Riley felt regret, tinged with fear that his destiny was not one Sophie would want to be a part of.

Doc exhaled a big breath. "I have to admit I was hoping you were headin' in that direction. Sarah wants to travel a bit, you know, before we get too old. And I would be sorely pained to leave my patients in the wrong hands."

"You brought a lot of them into this world."

"They're family, like you are."

Riley managed a thin smile although his gut was churning. "Then we're settled."

He was an absolutely unattached man for the first time in nearly three years, and all Riley wanted was to attach himself immediately to Sophie. However, as he arrived back in San Francisco, his head and his heart were conflicted.

Dropping off his bag at home, he stopped to wash up and dress in his good clothes. Riley was determined to put his best foot forward, considering his abominable behavior when he'd left Sophie weeks earlier.

His mind had gone back a hundred times to making love with Sophie, causing his body to react powerfully each time to the memory. Yet he knew it had been disgraceful to take her innocence and then leave her. If any other man had treated her such, he'd have taken his head off. But he loved her. He could admit it now. Better yet, he could tell her and without any sense of guilt or wrongdoing.

Except what if his loving her was not what was best for her?

He entered The Grand on quick feet and went up the stairs, two at a time. But a knock at her door brought no answer. He pulled out his pocket watch. Where would she be at three in the afternoon?

A few minutes later, he stood at the concierge desk at The Palace.

"Mr. Hull, may I see Carling Rilkers, please? Can you tell her Mr. Dalcourt needs a word?"

Egbert smiled politely, but it faltered and then disappeared entirely as he realized with whom he was speaking.

"Miss Rilkers? She's here and about somewhere. With a guest, I expect."

"Can you find her? I need her help. I'm looking for Miss Malloy."

Egbert looked pained. "Right. Miss Malloy. Yes, Miss Rilkers would know her whereabouts for certain." He shifted from one foot to the other. "So, you're back?"

Riley nodded then said, "Obviously."

"And your fiancée?" Egbert looked past Riley as if he thought she'd pop up behind him at any moment.

Riley's placid face clouded over. "Look, I need to find Sophie, and I would like to do it sooner rather than—"

"Riley Dalcourt," Carling's voice rang out across the lobby.

He turned. Finally, he'd get some answers. However, instead of her usual cheeky and welcoming smile, she looked thunderous as she stalked across the carpeted floor toward him.

"There you are, sniffing about here after over a fortnight's absence." She crossed her arms.

He ignored her animosity. "Can you tell me where Sophie is, please?"

"Why? Haven't you caused her enough heartache?"

He hesitated. Had Sophie told Carling about their tryst in her room? The women were good friends, but he somehow hadn't thought Sophie was the type to disclose her personal business, particularly when it didn't reflect well on either of them.

"Speechless now, eh?" Carling continued.

"Carling, please," Egbert broke in. "Perhaps you should tell Mr. Dalcourt—"

"Oh, I'll tell him all right. She's gone. My good friend has up and left San Francisco."

"Gone?" He felt his heart start to hammer. "Gone where?"

"Off on her *engagement* tour." Carling had a sour look on her face.

"Her engagement!" *Shit!* How could it be? He'd assumed wrongheadedly and with far too much pride she would be there, especially after what they'd shared. But of course she wouldn't be waiting for him. He had given her no reason to wait and many reasons not to.

Looking away from Carling's hostile gaze, he ran his hand through his hair. Then he shook his head.

"It won't do you any good. You can't shake it off," Carling scolded. "That ship has sailed."

"When did she leave?"

"Yesterday."

Almighty! That was another punch in the gut. "You're joking!" Had he really been so close to catching her? He could barely breathe.

"Nah, I wish I was. Easy as you please, since The Overland's ticket office is located in this hotel. Still, she's in good hands," Carling added. "That Mr. Wainright was smitten and ready to make her his wife."

Riley was reeling as if he was on a runaway coach with no one holding the reins. Turning on his heel, forgetting all his manners, he started to walk away. Then he heard Carling make a clucking sound behind him. Stopping, he swore under his breath before facing her and Egbert again.

"Where did they go?"

Carling's eyes narrowed. "Why would I tell you?"

"I need to talk to her."

"Talk to her," Carling spat out. "Why don't you talk to your fiancée? Go on with you. Leave Sophie alone."

Riley did not want to get into his personal feelings in the middle of the lobby of The Palace, but it seemed he had no choice.

"I . . . care for Sophie."

Carling expelled her breath in a big puff. "Too late," she muttered.

"She's engaged now," Egbert pointed out. "And she seemed very happy to go home."

Carling glared at Egbert.

"Home? They went back to Boston?"

"She has a diamond ring on her finger and all," Carling said.

"Carling," Egbert warned.

"Well, she will when she gets back to Boston."

"It seems I missed a lot." Riley paused, letting it sink in as he stared at the tiled floor. "I'm too late." He was back in San Francisco, and Sophie was lost to him.

"You won't do anything rash now, will you, chum?" Egbert asked.

Riley knew what the man was thinking. That he might jump on the next train and go after her, or simply jump off the nearest bridge. But she'd made a choice. Her old love who'd broken her heart had come back and redeemed himself, reclaiming her, removing the pain and humiliation. And apparently, she'd fallen for him again.

And, perhaps, when Sophie had let Riley make love to her, it had exorcised for her the tempting what-ifs that had been hanging between them since their first meeting in Spring City. Maybe their encounter hadn't been for her as incredible as it had been for him. By now, she might have already experienced the same with Philip.

Riley would never know. He'd made it clear to her she was none of his business. Now, he'd have to live with it.

CHAPTER SEVENTEEN

Sophie could not ignore the little voice inside of her one minute longer. Right after they pulled out of Chicago's Union Depot, she rose to her feet, made her excuses to Philip, and fairly ran the length of the train. Ignoring people's stares, she continued her flight until she opened the caboose door and stepped onto the metal platform. A cold wind struck her like a bucket of rousing ice water, which she needed.

Leaning back against the door, she clutched her mantle around her. The clackety-clack was so loud she could scream if she wanted and not hear her own voice.

She stared at the track stretching out behind her, all the way to San Francisco. How she loved that city! She'd fled Spring and welcomed her new start. Now, it was over and she was headed home. Not exactly triumphant, either. She'd managed to be no more than a piano player in a bar, but at least she'd done it on her own. Freddie Vern, dear Freddie, had seen something in her. She'd hated telling him she was leaving for good, as much as she'd hated breaking the news to Carling.

Beyond that, there was no one she would miss. She tried not to think of Riley at all. He was never hers to begin with and should have no influence on whether she renewed her relationship with Philip. Yet he was in her heart all the same. And he *had* influenced everything. They'd engaged in the most wondrously intimate act. For them, it had been brief but soul-shattering. What if it wasn't that way with Philip? Would it have been better not to know how perfect lovemaking could be?

A year ago, she would have gladly—ignorantly—married Philip. Then she'd witnessed Charlotte and Reed's connection. Despite the pain over her own broken heart, she'd seen for herself a different level of passion. All her brother had to do was look at Charlotte with his dark cerulean eyes so like Sophie's, and the auburn-haired woman stood transfixed. Some unspoken message would pass between them. At Charlotte's touch upon Reed's arm, he'd suck in his breath as though burned.

That was how Sophie felt with Riley.

I've made a mistake.

The thought rang in her ears as if she'd said it aloud, as though her truer self were finally speaking to her. She could not have Riley, but that didn't mean she had to start over with Philip. Despite weeks of his courting her, she had to acknowledge, at least to herself, she didn't love him anymore. He didn't make her tingle when he stood close. He never had. He'd been her comfortable, familiar friend, the man whom she'd assumed would become her husband.

The track continued to unravel behind her, taking her farther and farther from where she wanted to be. She had to tell Philip. Taking a fortifying breath of the frigid air, she went back inside.

Philip was looking out the window when she sank down beside him.

"Sophie, are you all right? I went looking for you."

She was wind-blown and red-nosed from the cold, knowing she appeared a frightful mess, but she felt more certain than she had in weeks.

"I don't want to go with you to Boston."

His mouth opened and remained so for a full five seconds before he closed it. Then he said, "The train is headed to Boston, Soph. I can't do anything about that."

Plainly, he was trying to make light of her words, but she saw the apprehension flare in his eyes. "What's the matter?" he asked.

"I've made a mistake." Her voice sounded precisely the way it had in her head. Positively certain. "I don't want to give up on San Francisco."

"Give up on it? What a queer way to put it! We don't have to live in Boston. In fact, we won't. We'll be in Cambridge. It's lovely there."

It *was* lovely there, but that wasn't what she wanted. "I don't want to live in Cambridge."

"But we talked all this out, many times." He took her hand. "You're simply getting a case of the nerves, going home where everyone will be waiting to see you."

He patted her hand and turned it over, raising the palm to his lips. He kissed it. She felt nothing, except the satisfaction of being with a man who loved her. And that was no small thing.

"After we're home," he continued, "it'll be like you never left."

That was what she most didn't like about going home. Carefully withdrawing from his grasp, she looked down at both her hands. They looked entirely normal again, but she had resisted playing, even after the last bandage came off.

After Riley left, feeling bruised by life, she hadn't wanted to know if she'd lost any mobility in her right fingers. Without Riley to tell her she would heal, she'd felt doubtful and cowardly. What if she put her fingers to the keys only to find she couldn't play properly, not ever again? Coming on the heels of his abrupt departure and imminent marriage to Eliza, such an outcome had been too much to bear.

Suddenly, though, she couldn't wait to play and see if her life could go on as it had before. Leaning her head back against the lace-covered leather rest, she closed her eyes. There was no point in talking to anymore Philip. He would philosophize away her reticence and offer persuasive reasons why she should accept how her life had come full circle.

No, she wouldn't debate with herself any longer, but rather, she would seek her brother's counsel as soon as she got to Boston.

Within minutes of entering the Malloy family home, Sophie escaped to the conservatory. The housekeeper was making coffee, Philip was speaking in hushed tones to her mother and younger sister as if she were a delicate invalid, and Sophie was plain exhausted. At the sight of her piano, however, with its fanciful inlaid walnut marquetry of flowers and leaves, she smiled and felt the tight band around her heart loosen.

When she was ten, Sophie had heard rumblings across the floor and had run downstairs to see what her father had bought. The Broadwood and Sons grand was still the most beautiful thing she'd ever seen. She knew its history—hers was made in 1846, very few of them were built, and Queen Victoria had requested its twin for her Masquerade Ball at Buckingham Palace in 1851. Indeed, when Sophie sat down at it, with its sturdy, richly carved legs and big solid pedals, she felt like a queen.

Placing her hands on the ivory keys, she relished their smooth, cool surface and felt instantly transformed, from a limp, fearful dishrag of a woman to a Titan. Her piano would not let her fail, even if she came to it blind and deaf. Closing her eyes, she struck a chord, then another. Then she began to play. It came out of her as easily as breathing.

Even so, she felt her hand cramp within a few minutes. After all, the muscles in her healing fingers were weak. Shaking it, she wiggled her fingers, ignoring the pangs, then briskly rubbed her palms together before starting again.

Yes, she was sore and out of practice, but her hand worked, and she played one of Bach's sonatas before her mother came up behind her.

"I've missed hearing you, my dear Sophie," Evelyn Malloy said.

Tears started to prick her eyes. How could she cause her mother more pain by leaving again?

"Coffee is ready, dear. Come sit with me and tell me everything."

Sophie nodded but didn't look up until she could get her emotions in check.

"I'll be right in, Mama. Has Mr. Wainright left?"

"Not yet. Don't you want to say goodbye?"

"Please tell him I'm tired and will see him another day."

Her mother hesitated and then walked away. Sophie closed her eyes and lingered another few minutes at the piano, fortifying herself before following to the parlor. Only her mother and her youngest sister, Rose, were there.

"Are you all right?" Evelyn asked, as Sophie went to the side board to pour herself a cup of coffee.

"Yes, Mama."

"You look wan," Rose said, scooting over on the velvet divan and patting the space beside her in invitation to her sister. "But the music was beautiful. I wish I could do that."

All three females smiled, knowing Rose didn't have the patience to practice music or needlepoint or drawing, for that matter. The fairer arts were not her forte.

"Will Reed be coming over?" Sophie hoped her big brother was intending to visit soon. Otherwise, she'd have to hunt him down at his house on the wharf.

My goodness! She sighed to herself, thinking how she must have matured if she wanted him to lecture her and tell her what to do. Moreover, as she sipped her coffee, she realized she did, in fact, want exactly that.

"Tell me why you had me show Mr. Wainright the door, dear, especially after he went such a long way to find you and bring you home."

"Oh, we've spent so much time in each other's company," Sophie professed. "I want to have you two to myself."

Her mother and Rose exchanged glances.

"That doesn't sound good," Rose said. "I mean, not if you're going to marry the man. Shouldn't you feel as comfy with him, like family, as you do with us?"

"*Mm*," Sophie agreed, noncommittally.

"Sophie?" her mother said, drawing out her name in query. "You traveled across the entire country alone with 'the man,' as your sister calls him. Do you intend to marry him, or not?"

Sophie shrugged. "First of all, Mama, we were not alone, not even for an instant. I have any number of passengers who can attest to that. Secondly, I don't know. I mean, I do know, but no one will like my answer, particularly Philip, so I shall keep it to myself at present."

Then she spent a long moment choosing a biscuit from the tray on the low table in front of her, so as to keep from viewing her mother's undoubtedly stricken expression. After eating it in silence, she leaned back.

"Let me tell you all about San Francisco, and then Martha can draw me a bath." Sophie launched into her remembrances, trying to make them see the city through her eyes. The ingenious cable cars, the steep hills all leading to the beautiful bay, and the people she'd met. She left out Riley, of course, uncertain whether she could even mention him without her emotions showing through.

"I think I want to see it for myself," Rose said, her eyes bright and wistful.

"Don't you get any ideas, young lady," their mother said. "I have one daughter back and I don't intend to lose another just yet." Then Evelyn stood up. "Come on, Sophie, have a bath and a rest. Maybe Reed will come for dinner with his family."

As it turned out, he didn't. The next morning, Sophie had to bear the interrogation of her sister and mother again until her older sister Elise arrived with her two children and started the whole questioning once more. Soon, they all knew of her job in the bar and about her accident. Her hand's unblemished appearance helped allay their initial alarm.

Whenever possible, Sophie escaped to her piano and wondered how she could ever leave it again. She was playing after lunch, lost in Mendelssohn's *Concerto No. 2* with all its sweetness and sadness when, a hand touched her shoulder.

"Reed," she exclaimed, jumping up to hug him. He lifted her and swung her in a circle.

He searched her face with his intelligent, dark-blue eyes and she moved a lock of hair, as black as her own, off his forehead. He smiled.

"I've missed you, dear sister."

"And I, you," she murmured. She might cry, so happy was she to be in his comforting presence. Pure familial love was a powerful balm. Her brother always understood her heart and made everything seem better, or at least, possible. And after her father passed away, he was the only male whose arms she could relax in entirely. Reed was also the one who made sure she'd been allowed to go to Rome to study music, easing their mother's worries.

"I would have come yesterday, but Emory had a runny nose, which is better now, but I didn't want to leave him. And Charlotte didn't want to bring him out of the house. She'll be by tomorrow to see you."

Secretly, Sophie was glad it was Reed alone. She loved Charlotte like a sister, but at that moment, she had enough of those.

Stepping away from him, she fixed Reed with a serious gaze. "I need to speak with you. I could use some advice."

"Uh-oh. It must be serious if you want to confide in me."

"It's certainly something I would have spoken about with Father." She ran her hand over the keys one more time and then closed the cover. Taking his arm in hers, they went to her favorite reading place, a window seat overlooking the back garden.

Sitting side-by-side, Sophie leaned against him, breathing in his familiar scent of sandalwood.

"I don't think I want to live here."

"You don't mean here in Mother's house, do you? You mean in Boston?"

"Actually, I meant on the East Coast." Sophie twiddled her skirt with her fingers.

"I see." He was quiet a moment. "And what of Mr. Wainright? I take it you don't want to marry him, either."

Bless Reed's heart, he was so astute. "Correct."

"Then why in blue blazes did you let him bring you over three thousand miles?"

She jumped at his tone, but had to defend herself.

"I didn't ask him to come looking for me in California. I was taken by surprise. And I had . . . I had other issues with which to contend."

Gently, he took her right hand in his and carefully examined it. "Mother let me know about the injury. You were very lucky. You should have sent me a telegram."

"You would have brought me back here straightaway if I had."

"True," he said, "and rightly so."

Sophie bit her lower lip. Her hand injury seemed far less important now than the emotional turmoil she storming inside of her.

Reed peered into her solemn face. "So, what's wrong between you and Mr. Wainright? You used to be smitten with him. I remember your long face when he went to Oxford."

"You know that electric feeling between you and Charlotte?"

He stiffened and she laughed. "I know you don't like to discuss your personal life, but Charlotte told me once how every time you look at her, she feels like she is sizzling."

A slow smiled spread across his handsome visage. "She said that?"

"See, even your reaction speaks volumes. I know you can't wait to leave me and get back to your wife's side and kiss her passionately."

"Sophie!"

"Well, true or not?" she demanded.

"True," he admitted, "but we were supposed to be talking about you."

"I want that feeling, that sizzle."

Reed coughed, clearly unsure of his footing with this delicate topic. "And you don't think you feel 'that sizzle' with Mr. Wainright?"

"I know I don't. I've felt it—" she broke off. Sophie had no intention of telling her brother about Riley, at least, not everything. After all, that was now over and done with. But the words had already slipped out, and Reed, being Reed, was not only her older sibling but the best lawyer in New England. He would get out of her what he wanted to know.

His face was impassive. "Have you, dear sister?"

"Oh, don't get your necktie in a twist. I'm old enough to know what I feel."

He ran a hand over his forehead and ended up pinching the bridge of his nose. "So, where's this man you sizzled with?"

She blushed but answered, "He's marrying someone else." Her breath caught, and she lowered her eyes. "Or he's already married by this time."

"Sophie." His quietly serious tone brought her gaze back to his. He scowled and Sophie watched his jaw tighten before he asked, "Do I need to settle matters with him?"

Good God. She could just imagine Reed heading across the country to give Riley a good thrashing. She had a feeling it would be evenly matched, except honorable Riley would most likely take a beating without throwing a punch in his own defense.

"No, please, Reed. It wasn't like that. We had feelings for each other, but I knew he was spoken for. He was honest with me from the start."

Reed studied her face for a moment. "I see. So, you came home, tail between your legs, hoping you could settle for Wainright."

"Something along those lines. But I can't."

"Nor should you. This other scoundrel—" He paused when she shook her head at his characterization of Riley. "This other fellow may be taken, but you don't have to make do. Nor do you have to live here under Mother's watchful eye if you don't want to. I admit, though, I like having you home."

She sighed. "I loved living in San Francisco."

"Because of the other man?"

She had asked herself that very same question. "I thought so at first, but, no, not because of him. I like making my own way in the world. Here, everyone knows our family. Everything is handed to us."

"I wouldn't say that, but I know what you mean. Here, you live under the Malloy shadow, not to mention the family's expectations."

"Exactly. In San Francisco, life is exciting. Even the air smells different, and the light is brighter somehow." She clapped her hands with uncontainable excitement. "And I made some wonderful friends in a short time. Besides, with train travel what it is, I could come visit at least twice a year."

He put his arm around her shoulders. "That doesn't seem like very much visiting, but we can negotiate. That is, if I put in a word with Mother to calm her down."

"Would you?"

He smiled. "I will. But what about Wainright?"

Sophie made a face. "I tried to tell him on the train, but he practically patted me on the head and as good as told me I would get used to my new life."

"Which he sees as?"

"As my being his wife, of course, while he is a professor at Harvard. That's after he finishes his philosophy degree."

"Sounds boring as dirt, probably similar to being a lawyer's wife," Reed remarked wryly. Sophie punched him playfully. "In all seriousness," Reed continued, "I'm sure Wainright's life would be perfectly suitable for some other lady, but not for you."

She had known Reed would understand. She hugged him fiercely.

He lifted her chin and looked her in the eyes. "I'm sorry if your heart got bruised by some blackguard out west."

"I promise you, that's not how it was. There was just something between us, so magical and inexplicable." Sophie knew her tone was wistful. "But all along, we knew we had no future."

"Sorry, pet. I hope you find it again."

"Find what again?" asked Philip.

CHAPTER EIGHTEEN

Sophie jumped. Philip had entered silently through the hall doorway beside them.

Reed gave his sister another hug then stood. "I think I will leave you two to talk." He patted Philip on the shoulder as he passed.

"Why did that feel like a condolence?" Philip's brow puckered with worry.

"Sit and talk with me," Sophie said, scooting over to give him room.

"All right, but I'm feeling less happy by the moment."

She steeled herself to keep from feeling sorry for him. "Philip, why did you choose to go to Oxford by yourself?"

He scowled. "I thought we'd been over this before."

"We have, but do you remember that last day in my apartment when you came to say goodbye?"

"Of course."

"You were so eager to start your new life, full of excitement for the future."

"Yes."

"And you didn't see me in your future," she reminded him.

"I believed you were part of my old life and I wanted everything new. But I was wrong."

"I don't think you were." She clasped her hands on her lap. "If you loved me as you think you did, you would have wanted to share that new life with me. You would have wanted to explore Oxford with me by your side. I don't think it was only a new town or university you wanted. I think you wanted to feel a passionate new love, too."

"Whatever I felt then is irrelevant. I want you now."

His words did nothing to soften her heart. "Why aren't you returning to Oxford? Tell me the truth now. I can tell when you're lying."

He pursed his lips for a moment. "I'm not allowed to go back, but it's not a pleasant story."

"I don't need a pleasant one. I'm not a child."

"All right." Still he hesitated, then blurted, "I had a liaison with the don's wife."

She gasped. "Your tutor's wife?"

He grimaced. "She was a minx. Always hanging around my dormitory. So wild and different." He looked past Sophie, and she could tell he was far away. "She professed herself very bored with her husband and admitted to being infatuated with me. I kept putting her off, but, in the end, the temptation was too much to overcome."

Sophie understood a thing or two about temptation. She couldn't blame Philip at all, except for his extreme lack of good judgment.

"She was looking for a way out of her marriage," Philip continued. "I thought we were falling in love, but after we'd, well, after we'd met together a few times," he explained, "she made sure we were caught *in flagrante delicto*, as it were."

Sophie pictured Philip and his ladylove in a dorm room with her husband walking in. It could as easily have been a hotel room. She swallowed. "What happened?"

"Exactly what she wanted to have happen. He sent her packing back to Portugal, with a sum of money so she wouldn't disgrace him any further amongst the university scholars. And he had me swiftly expelled for the same reason."

"Oh, Philip, I am sorry." But in her heart of hearts, she knew it was only then, after he returned to Boston, his thoughts had turned to her. She was safe and familiar, and he assumed, most likely, she would never, ever cheat on him. She felt as though she already had.

"You and I can make a go of it, Sophie," he beseeched, casting her a desperate look.

"No," she said firmly. "We can't. I'm leaving. I was wrong to come back with you."

Philip stood abruptly. "It's because of that Dalcourt fellow, isn't it?"

"No," she protested. "It isn't." She wished it were. She wished he were waiting for her.

"Then, perhaps, Mr. Vern, your boss?"

"No, Philip. It isn't anyone, except me. I simply can't see myself as your wife anymore." No need to be brutal and say how she could never love him with the passion she'd felt for another. "I'm sorry."

Rising to her feet, she purposefully linked her arm with his and walked him across the parquet floor of the conservatory.

"Will I see you again?" he asked, on a subdued note.

"Perhaps," she began, and then admitted, "but I don't think so. I wish you every happiness at Harvard."

He took her hand and brought it to his lips.

She smiled. "And, Philip, dear, stay away from other men's wives."

She was still in a Mendelssohn mood. The next day, it was her sister-in-law's brisk footsteps that nearly interrupted the concerto. However, at first Sophie didn't hear Charlotte or her companion. She finished the piece, then turned at the sound of applause, surprised to see Charlotte with a middle-aged man whom Sophie had never seen before.

"That was lovely." Reed's wife was the first to speak, and Sophie rose to greet her with a hug. "When I think how disgusted you must have been to see my old upright in Spring!"

"Oh, no! Far from it," Sophie said. "Your piano in the middle of nowhere was my salvation." Then she brought her hands up to her cheeks. "Oh, Charlotte, I didn't mean Spring City was in the middle of nowhere."

Charlotte grinned. "Yes, you did, and it is." She put her arm around Sophie's waist and turned her to the gentleman. "I'd like you to meet Mr. Hadley."

He took her hand and kissed it, looking at her benignly with intelligent eyes.

"Your playing surpassed my expectations, even from what Mrs. Malloy told me," he said, speaking matter-of-factly, with no hint of vacant flattery.

Sophie inclined her head. "Thank you. Your name is familiar, sir."

"It might be, young lady, I dare say."

Charlotte spoke up. "Mr. Henry Hadley is visiting family in Somerville. But you probably know him as a conductor and composer."

"Oh," said Sophie, looking at him now with professional interest, "*that* Mr. Hadley. You studied with Eusebius Mandyczewski in Vienna."

"I did." He bowed his head modestly.

Sophie was delighted. She gestured to her piano. "Would you care to play? It's a fine instrument."

"Yes, I heard." He ran his hand over the inlay. "Beautiful, too." Then he looked at Sophie. "But I didn't come to play. I came to listen. Will you play something else for me? Perhaps something from Lizst."

She looked curiously at him, then at Charlotte, who nodded.

"All right, I will." Sophie sat down and found her sheet music for *Liebestraum*, but after a few notes, she played from memory. After many minutes, she stopped, and as always when the last notes died out, she had the feeling she'd been away and had then returned.

Both her listeners clapped again, and Mr. Hadley said, "Bravo. Or *brava*, if you're a stickler."

"What's this all about, Charlotte?" Sophie asked, seeing the mischievous look on her sister-in-law's face. But it was Henry Hadley who answered.

"I'm going to conduct a symphony orchestra. I've a host of musicians already and found more at Ada Clement's Piano School."

"I've been there," Sophie said. "In San Francisco. I stopped in to practice the same day I auditioned for the orchestra." She wrinkled her nose when she recalled her cold reception.

"Ah, yes. For Herr Becker. How did it go?"

"He seemed unimpressed," Sophie said mildly, remembering the German's scowl and rude words in the middle of her audition. She spoke a little German, enough to know he'd thought she should not be trying to play "man's music" and that she would be better off using her breasts to feed babies. She kept both his sentiments to herself.

Henry sighed. "Becker's a misogynist and a fool. He wishes he were Bulow or Erdmannsdörfer, but they have more talent each in their little finger."

Sophie didn't know what to say to this apt assessment of the disagreeable conductor.

"In any case, it doesn't matter," Henry continued. "He's gone."

"Gone? Where?" Sophie asked.

"Back to Germany, I believe."

Sophie bit her lip thoughtfully as an idea sparked. "Perhaps I should audition again for the San Francisco Symphony."

"You just did," Hadley told her.

Charlotte clapped her hands, apparently delighted by the surprised look Sophie was certain she was wearing. "And how did my sister-in-law do?"

"Splendidly. She's in," he said, then smiled at Sophie. "That is, if I can pry you away from Boston to come west with me. It's hard to leave your family, I know. Mine's all here, too."

"Oh my goodness, yes! When do we leave?"

Thus, Sophie found herself on another long train trip heading west, this time in the delightful company of Henry Hadley, who was as eager as she to get to San Francisco, and his brother Arthur, an accomplished cellist, among other musicians rounded up by Henry. Sophie decided they were the merriest group of passengers on the train.

When not discussing music, she spent every waking moment reading *The Letters of Miska Hauser*, about all his music-related travels in San Francisco and was determined to look up all the places he mentioned. She kept track of the rails—New York Central, Michigan Central, Rock Island—until finally, they were back on the great Union Pacific Railway. Then, it seemed no time at all before she was stepping off the train in Alameda, California, and boarding El Capitan ferry.

She had telegrammed Carling and, bless her heart, she and Egbert met the ferry at the dock in San Francisco. The girls squealed in delight, and even Egbert threw his arms around them both.

"Sophie, Sophie, Sophie," Carling fairly sang her name. "I'm so happy you're back. Aren't I, Egbert?"

"She is. And so am I."

"Oh, smell it," Sophie says. "It smells like home to me now."

Carling laughed. "It smells like fish, but come on. Let's get you settled. Oh," she stopped short as a group of men gathered behind Sophie.

"These are my fellow travelers and orchestra musicians," Sophie proudly announced. "Henry Hadley, our conductor, and Walter, Septimus, Samuel, Seifert, Brooks, Adolph, Jean,

Edourd, and Arthur, Henry's brother." She paused. "Who are we missing?"

Another man wandered over carrying a trumpet case. "And Otto. These are my good friends, Carling and Egbert."

"Are you all staying at The Palace?" Egbert asked.

"No," said Henry firmly, amongst groans.

"Some flea-bag, then," muttered Samuel.

"The directors of the San Francisco Symphony are putting us all up in rooming houses near the hall."

Egbert wrinkled his nose. "I'm sorry to hear that. Maybe you can all come to The Palace for tea or coffee."

"Oh, yes," Sophie agreed. "We'll meet up again tomorrow. Perhaps around two in the afternoon?"

"Yes, ma'am," they all said in turn, except Henry.

"Sophie, this isn't all fun and games. We have hard work to do and fast."

"Oh, I know Henry. And I can't wait." They started walking to the trams. "We will be the best symphony orchestra the world has ever seen."

The one named Seifert chuckled.

"What? You don't think so?" Sophie asked him.

"Mayhap, Miss Sophie, but let's first try for the best that California has ever seen."

"Agreed."

As the sole female, she wasn't invited to the men's rooming house. Instead, she'd written ahead to Freddie Vern, begging for a week's stay, which he granted. After gingerly hugging her in the middle of the lobby in broad daylight, Freddie smiled.

"I shouldn't even let you have one free night, not after cutting out on me the way you did."

"Freddie," Sophie protested. She was so happy to get her room back at The Grand, she didn't even mind the disaster of her private life. "I thought I was getting married."

"Well, don't do it again," he said and laughed. But then he added, "You know, you'll have to find a place to rent soon. I can only let you have the room for a week, unless you want to start paying or playing piano for me again," he finished with a teasing look.

"You know I can't play in your barroom anymore." She tried to sound sad but couldn't contain the wide grin.

"I know, and I'm thrilled for you. I'll be there on opening night. Besides, I've found a replacement. From that piano school you told me about. Lovely girl."

"Really?" She raised her eyebrows at his enthusiasm.

"Not as lovely as you, Sophie," he amended, "nor half as good on the piano. Still, Catherine has a nice way about her, as you did. The customers are warming to her."

Sophie had an inkling the customers weren't the only ones warming to the lovely Catherine, by the look on Freddie's face.

"I shall come downstairs tonight and listen to her."

"It'll be my pleasure to sit with you," he said, leaving her at her door.

She hesitated, then turned the knob and pushed the door open slowly. At the familiar smell of the room, beeswax and lemon, and the vision of the small bed with its crisp white spread, certain memories, never far from the surface, flooded back. She caught her breath at their powerful hold on her. In an instant, she was back in Riley's arms, all fervent desire, demanding to be satisfied. She could almost feel his touch, his lips, his skin.

"Whew," she breathed out. It had been unforgettably wonderful, and she had to admit, she'd been beyond happy, downright relieved, to give the man her virginity.

If only she hadn't given him her heart!

CHAPTER NINETEEN

"Oh, my God!" Riley jumped up from the dining table, astonishing not only the other medical students with whom he was eating but the other occupants of the restaurant, as well. He didn't even notice their stares. Clutching the latest edition of the *San Francisco Chronicle* in his hand, he sprinted out of the restaurant.

It was already 6:45 on Friday night. He hopped onto the next Market Street cable car heading for The Embarcadero. Getting off directly before The Grand, Riley paused to glance at the building, thinking of his last time there and Sophie's incredible gift of herself. He'd taken it selfishly, never dreaming he would get a chance to make it up to her.

Turning onto Kearney Street, he ran the next four blocks until he stood in front of the Sherman Clay piano store. He rattled the door. Locked. *Of course it was locked!* He'd wasted precious time and was about to turn away when he spied a light on in the back.

Rattling the door again more forcefully, Riley saw some movement. A few moments later, an older gentleman with a moustache walking toward him. Slowly, he undid the locks and even more slowly opened the door.

"Sir, we are closed."

"Yes, yes, I'm sorry," Riley said, feeling desperate, "but I need a ticket, no, a season pass for the symphony, especially for tonight's show. And for all the rest."

"You should have gone directly to the box office at the hall."

"Right," Riley said, looking down at his shoes, then he looked back up. "But in the *Chronicle*, it said—"

"I know what it says in the *Chronicle*, young man, but that refers to the hours before closing time. Besides, it's opening night. Sold out, you know."

"But it can't be. I'll pay anything." Then he had an idea. "Wait, you must be going. I'll buy *your* seat. I'll pay you double what it's worth, triple, anything you want."

Riley marveled at his own rashness. After all, he had a limit to his funds, but the thought of seeing Sophie play at the concert hall had made him giddy. He still couldn't believe she was there, but it was printed in black and white. He opened the paper again.

Miss Sophie Malloy, pianist.

Not Sophie *Wainright!* She was most definitely not in Cambridge, nor the wife of a philosophy professor.

He realized he'd said her name out loud when the man smiled. "She's playing on one of our Weber's tonight. Concert grand, rosewood case." And the older gentleman stepped aside holding the door open. "Maybe you'd better come in."

Sophie decided on her pale cream gown. It would show well against the rich wood of the piano and her own dark hair. Her hands were steady as she smoothed the fabric and reached for her gloves. She'd prepared a lifetime for this moment, and no small amount of training had taken place in the last two months since returning to San Francisco. They'd rehearsed daily. Finally, tonight, they would show the patrons what they were capable of with Beethoven. Tomorrow, Wagner.

Backstage, Henry was everywhere at once, moving quickly, speaking faster, and delivering last-minute instructions to everyone. He looked dashing in his tailcoat but the effect was spoiled by the way he kept running his fingers through his hair, ruining its smoothness and making it stand straight up on top.

She put her hand on his arm at one point. He jumped.

"Fear not, Sophie, you'll be splendid."

She smiled. She was blessed with no stage fright at all, but didn't like to boast. She relied on the fact of being utterly prepared.

"Henry, we will all be splendid. Now, you must get in position. You're going to make a speech, remember?"

"My speech!" He patted down his pockets, then sighed. "Right here. Yes, I'm ready."

"Of course you are," she said and moved away to her side of the stage. Then she heard the applause begin as Henry walked onto the stage in front of the massive burgundy curtains. Behind it, they all took their places at their instruments. Those who weren't nervous gave smiles all around. She saw Otto run off stage to throw up, as he'd done during the dress rehearsals all week. James, the stage manager, kept a bucket ready, and Otto was back in his chair in less than thirty seconds.

A few minutes later, she heard the applause again and then, at last, the velvet curtains parted. The lights were already down in the theater, and Sophie could see nothing but the occasional glowing tip of a man's cigar. They began at once under Henry's magnificent conducting. After the first song, the lights came up and Henry introduced the principal musicians.

Sophie nodded when he said her name and looked toward the audience. Her slight smile froze.

In the front row, only feet away from her sat Riley. Then the house lights went out. She hadn't had time to see if Eliza sat beside him. As they started again, she nearly missed her first cue, which annoyed her tremendously.

When the lights came on at intermission, a single seat, his seat, was empty. Puzzled, she found herself scanning the aisles before going backstage to drink a cup of coffee with the rest of the orchestra. Later, after the performance, they would switch to champagne, but Sophie was already feeling lightheaded from the excitement of opening night combined with the surprise of seeing Riley.

That he should show up in the front row and then leave the seat vacant was beyond aggravating.

Another hour later, after they'd all stood and bowed, the curtain closed for the last time. Exhausted, the orchestra nonetheless was jubilant. If the insistent demand for an encore, which they'd happily given, was any indication, then the evening had been a rousing success. She'd noticed Riley's still-vacant seat and was starting to think she'd imagined seeing him.

Sophie ran to Henry as he came backstage.

"You were brilliant. We all were," she said, so proud to be part of this young orchestra.

"We were, weren't we? We had them! Could you feel it?" he asked referring to the audience.

"Ludwig had them," Sophie said, grabbing a glass of champagne that came by on a tray. "Tomorrow, Wagner will."

"Sophie," James said to her, "there's a man to see you, stage right."

"Thank you," she said, taking a gulp of champagne, then wishing she hadn't. Then she took another one and handed James her empty glass. She made her way to the side of the stage, hugging her fellow musicians along the way. It had been even better than she'd imagined. And now—

Riley.

He was watching her approach with a wide smile on his face. She hesitated, unsure how to greet this man who had been her lover but who could really be nothing to her socially, not in public. *Why was he there?*

"Sophie," he exclaimed with jubilance, immediately taking both her hands in his. She froze as he kissed them, both of them, twice, wholly inappropriate and sending shivers through her. Regaining her senses, she yanked them away.

"You're here," he said emphatically. "You're actually here."

"I am," she said.

"I thought you'd left."

"I had." She was having trouble putting her words together with the bubbly drink inside of her, but she added, "I came back."

"I see that. You were amazing. I couldn't take my eyes off you."

"Liar." She covered her mouth with her hand. She'd sounded angry when she meant to be teasing. "I mean, I saw you very briefly during the introductions, but you were gone by intermission."

"A woman had a baby," he smiled self-consciously.

"What? No! During the concert?" She felt a little giddy, and tried harder to be serious. "What woman in her right mind would be out if she was so far along?"

"She wasn't a patron. She was staff and apparently needed the wages, right up until the end."

"How did anyone know you were a doctor?"

"Almost a doctor," he amended. "It's a long story, but I got my ticket for tonight at the last minute and was speaking with Mr. Shepherd—"

"From the piano store?"

"Yes, we came here together, but apparently he prefers to watch from the back. I had mentioned about attending the medical college. When he heard the woman's distress, he sent for me."

Riley gave her another smile. "I missed only a little of the concert, right before intermission. Mother and child are safe at the hospital now. It was a boy. She's naming him Mozart."

"You're joking!"

"I am."

She giggled.

"I returned to the hall as you started to play again, but I couldn't return to my seat. You sounded equally stupendous from in the back as you did from up front." He took her hand again, this time to examine it. "It's superbly healed, don't you think?"

Sophie couldn't think, not with him holding her hand and running his thumb over her knuckles, his head bowed in concentration, his silky brown hair so close she nearly reached out to touch it.

His dear head, which she'd never thought to see up close again!

When he looked up, their eyes locked, and she would swear she felt a jolt.

"Why are you here?" she asked him. All at once, the champagne was making her feel a bit weepy. This was supposed to be a celebratory night. However, Riley's presence made her feel pain and remorse, as well as the desperate desire to be home in her new flat away from everyone.

"I was hoping you would let me take you to dinner."

She was so shocked she couldn't speak. Then Henry, his brother, Arthur, and Otto came over.

"We're heading to supper, Sophie. Are you coming?" Henry asked.

"Yes," she said at once. "I am. It was nice to see you, Mr. Dalcourt."

Although it hadn't been nice at all. It had been startling and disquieting. Seeing him made her feel all manner of unsettling sensations.

"Give my best to . . . ," she trailed off. *Blue blazes!* She couldn't even say the woman's name.

Instead, she took hold of one of Otto's arms and one of Henry's and urged them forward. When she turned away, Riley's face was not amused.

They'd taken three steps when she heard him say clearly, "I am not marrying Eliza. Ever."

She stopped, and the others stopped with her. Sophie closed her eyes. *Had she heard him correctly?*

"Would you do me the honor of having dinner with me, Miss Malloy?" Riley added.

She felt Otto pull away from her right side so she could turn and answer. Instead, opening her eyes, she turned to Henry on her left.

"I think I won't be having supper with you after all."

Henry nodded. "We'll see you tomorrow then." He released her arm and looked at Riley. "Sir, take care of our star pianist and make sure she gets to bed at a decent hour."

Sophie gasped, and Arthur coughed at his brother's indelicacy. Henry turned beet-red at what his words might convey. But Riley nodded seriously.

"I'll do that, sir. You may count on it."

They spoke very little on their way to dinner at a restaurant a block away. Sophie was hit with all the nerves she hadn't felt opening before a full house. Having just played her first concert, she was already over the moon. And now, going to dinner with Riley, she could barely stand her nervous excitement.

"You're humming," he said to her with laughter in his voice as he held the bistro door open for her. She blushed. It was late, early diners had all gone home. A few theater people remained, along with the concert-goers. They managed to get a private table away from the chilled street window, away from any noise. As soon as they sat, Riley took her hands again and merely stroked them.

"I am so happy to be touching you," he said, his voice low. "I've thought of nothing else since I saw your name in the newspaper."

She shivered. She'd dreamed of feeling his hands on her many times. That he was with her, sitting in a restaurant, sharing a mundane meal seemed a dream in itself. Smiling at him, she watched as a slow grin spread over his own face.

"Thinking you were three thousand miles away, I nearly fell off my chair when I read your name," he said. "How long have you been back?"

"A couple months," she admitted.

"You never tried to contact me." He sounded surprised.

"I saw little point in doing so," she admitted. "Not from how things were when you . . ."

"When I left you at The Grand."

She stared at him, and he stared back. She couldn't help but relive their last encounter, and Sophie felt her cheeks grow hot. He raised one of her hands to his lips and kissed it, then the other. She thought that it was a good idea they were in a public dining room. Besides, she still had questions.

"What happened with Eliza?"

"Her father died, and all she wanted was to be free."

"How convenient for you." She didn't mean to sound catty, did she? But she felt it, nonetheless.

Riley frowned. "What do you mean?"

"You would have gone through with it and married her, no matter how we felt about each other, isn't that true?" *No matter how much I loved you.* She pulled her hands out of his grasp. "It's convenient she let you go."

He skewered her with his gaze. "To be precise, I let *her* go. I told Eliza I couldn't marry her."

"Oh," Sophie said in a small voice.

"She gave us her approval, in her way."

Sophie tried to imagine how that conversation took place.

"Does Eliza know?" She blushed again. "What we did, I mean?"

"No, but she could tell how I felt about you. How I still feel about you." He picked up his glass of wine, then set it down without drinking it. "Sophie, can you forgive me?"

She was startled. "Forgive you? Whatever for?"

"I should never have let things happen as they did. If any other man had treated you such, I would shoot him."

"Then I guess we're both fortunate it was you."

He shook his head at her attempt at humor. "What happened with Wainright? Last I heard, you were heading east, ready to get a big, fat diamond and a marriage license."

"It sounds as though you spoke with Carling."

"The day after you left."

She gasped. "Oh my God."

He nodded. "That's how I felt. I thought I'd lost you by only a day. Can you imagine? And since you were heading all the way to Massachusetts with the man, I figured you must love him." He paused, looking at her intently. Obviously, the question was still on his mind.

"I didn't, and I don't," she said quietly. She watched him accept her words and relax.

"If Carling hadn't made it sound as though you were about to march down the aisle, Sophie, I would have come after you."

"Carling was trying to protect me."

"I know, but she could have told you two months ago I'd come looking for you."

"Did you tell her about Eliza and that you'd broken off your engagement?"

"No." He looked sheepish. "I was standing in The Palace, and I had an audience."

"Then she was right not to interfere. She didn't want to see me with a broken heart." *Again.*

They finished their meal on safer territory, talking about the last classes he was completing before graduation and his clinical work, and she told him stories of the crazy musicians that made up the orchestra.

When she was feeling truly exhausted and had lost the surge of energy from the performance, he escorted her home.

"Better than Russian Hill," Riley said, walking her up the steps of a massive mansion on Gough Street. Opposite was Jefferson Square Park, with its palm trees and open space.

"You haven't seen inside yet," she blurted, then realized that sounded as though she were inviting him in. "I feel safer here anyway," she added, thinking she might start talking nonsense with him so close.

"I definitely think it's a step up." He took her key and opened the door to the common entryway. He hesitated, as did she. Then he chuckled.

"What?" she asked.

"After all this time, this was our first date."

And despite all that had already passed between them, everything felt strangely new.

"It was a wonderful first date," she said, unsure what to do next.

He smiled and his dimple appeared. "I still can't believe you're here. And I'm here. And neither of us is attached."

"It does seem as if the fates are smiling on us at last," she offered tentatively.

"May I kiss you?" Riley asked without any further preamble.

She looked down the street, which was nearly deserted at that late hour.

"I think it would be all right," Sophie allowed. And then she held her breath as he bent low toward her. Seconds seemed to stretch to hours, and she was sure time was moving extra slowly. At last, she closed her eyes. Ever so lightly, he gave her a gentle, tender, welcome-back kiss.

"Sophie," he murmured against her mouth.

"Riley," she said back.

His arms came around her, and he pulled her closely against him. Right on the street!

She stepped back into the foyer, pulling him with her, away from the public eye. He deepened the kiss, slanting his mouth in such a way her lips opened slightly, and she felt his tongue touch hers. The single caress sent ripples of awareness right through her—this man was hers. Or she was his. Both, of course!

When he finally pulled away, she felt his teeth tug on her lower lip before he let her go. That small gesture made her knees go weak. Opening her eyes, she stared directly into his, the darkest brown orbs, shining in the lamplight. She wanted him to keep looking at her like that. She could take him up the stairs and along the hallway to her apartment. She wanted . . .

"I'd best go home," he said, shoving his hands into his pockets. "Right?" he asked, as if there might be some other option.

Feeling shaken at how entirely swept away by him she already was, Sophie nodded.

"I need to sleep," she pointed out, mumbling through tender lips.

He stroked her face. "I have no classes tomorrow, but I have rounds until early evening. Afterward, I'll be there, in the front row, tomorrow night."

"Will you?"

"Of course," he promised, "and the next, and every night after that, as long as you're playing."

"Ridiculous man," she said, but she was pleased. "You'll go broke."

"Can I take you to dinner again tomorrow night?"

She repeated his words, "You're here. And I'm here. And neither of us is attached."

"Until tomorrow, then." He moved rapidly down the stairs, walking backward a few steps along the sidewalk to watch her until she waved and started to close the door.

Then she heard him let out a loud whooping sound, and she might have imagined it, but she thought he yelled, "Purple!"

Back in his own set of rooms, Riley lay on his bed, legs crossed, hands behind his head, staring at the ceiling. He was not a drinking man or he might have a bottle of whiskey beside him, about half finished. Sleep evaded him, and in his mind, he was reliving the evening.

In the audience that night, waiting for the curtain to go up, his heart had been pounding so loudly he was sure the man next to him was going to complain. Then suddenly, Sophie was at the piano and looking so damned beautiful in her pale dress with her hair swept up that he couldn't breathe. *She belonged to him!* He wanted to stand up and shout it out to everyone in the concert hall.

From the first notes, however, it was as if she played every single listener's heartstrings right along with the piano keys. His mouth had opened in wonder at her talent, and he'd looked around him to see the audience all equally gripped by the majesty and magic of her talent. She didn't belong only to him, he realized. Her gift was so big, it belonged to the world.

And he was going to be a country doctor in Spring City, which was in no way a real city, not by any stretch of the imagination. He groaned and closed his eyes, blocking out the cracked ceiling overhead. It seemed to be mimicking his heart.

With his eyes closed, the haunting strains of Beethoven's *Allegretto*, the orchestra's final piece, played in his head, as it had on his walk home from Sophie's apartment. Unfortunately, it reminded him of a funeral dirge.

When Riley had passed the street leading to City-County Hospital, he'd stopped, and after a moment, he'd walked all the way there, although it was out of his way. He stared at the impressive building, but he was thinking of Doc's cozy office. That hospital building would be as out of place in Spring as . . . as Sophie Malloy, the concert pianist.

Rolling over, he punched his pillow, causing a down feather to waft into the air and land on his mattress. He couldn't deny the ecstasy he'd felt holding her in his arms again, nor discount how nearly impossible it had been to leave her at her door. He ought to be elated having her back in his life, unmarried as they both were. Yet, with every passing minute, his joy seemed to leak from him like a wounded patient losing blood. Now, he was feeling merely defeated.

In a matter of weeks, he would be a doctor, and moving back to Spring City. In a matter of weeks! It was ridiculous to consider her leaving the stage, depriving herself and her audience. Inconceivable!

For the life of him, try as he might, he couldn't picture his life in Colorado with Sophie at his side. He could offer her his whole heart, with no holding back and with all the love a man could give a woman. But he couldn't give her the future she deserved. And he was damned sure he wasn't going to steal it from her by asking her to be his wife.

CHAPTER TWENTY

Except for a midday rehearsal, which was filled with excited chatter after the previous night's success, Sophie thought the day dragged on endlessly. She wanted nothing more than to be back on the stage. Not only did she love performing, she was particularly thrilled knowing Riley would be in the audience to enjoy it and to meet her at the end.

And despite The Palace being a busy place on a Saturday night, Egbert and Carling both had managed to take the evening off and were coming to the concert. It made her happiness complete.

"I love Wagner," Otto said. "Tonight will be even better."

"Better than Beethoven?" Septimus asked. He stopped Sophie, who was walking backstage where they sat drinking coffee. "What do you think?"

"I would never presume to make such a judgment. If your bass—"

"Double bass," Septimus interrupted.

"Very well," Sophie amended, "if your *double* bass isn't tuned correctly, say tuned in fifths instead of fourths," Septimus shuddered at the thought, "or if Otto loses his trumpet altogether," both men chuckled, "then perhaps, we will think last night was better. Other than that, I believe we will give our audience a consistently superb performance every time we play."

"Glad to know you don't suffer any qualms, girly," Otto said and laughed. "If only I could be so arrogant, but I'm third chair, after all."

"Nonsense," Sophie said. "It's not arrogance, nor conceit, for that matter. It's self-assurance and more than that, it's confidence in our ensemble. We are in this together. So that had better be coffee you're drinking and you had best be ready when Henry says, 'Curtain.'"

"Yes, ma'am," Septimus said. "You hear that Otto. We'd best be ready. You should do your vomiting now and get it over with."

"Don't tease him," Sophie said, softening. "You'll be brilliant, and if you need to empty your stomach to play like a saint, then so be it."

She strode away, determined to get a little peace and to prepare her brain for a difficult solo that would come before intermission.

When the curtain came down on the San Francisco Symphony's second-ever performance, they received a standing ovation. Sophie knew she wanted to do this for the rest of her life. She couldn't help her dreamy smile, not even hours later, sitting with her three ardent admirers, having crab stew at Gobey's Saloon.

"Sophie!" came Carling's voice into her thoughts.

"*Hm,*" she murmured, reliving the last bars of the final piece of music when she'd experienced a cramp in her right hand and had played through it.

"Sophie, have you heard a word I've said?" Carling put down her spoon, exasperated.

Riley stroked her arm, sending shivers through her, and she came back to them.

"I'm sorry, it's hard to shake off the concert. I know it's over, but I still feel as though I have to work through the pieces."

"Carling wanted to know if you would ever get to play your own music," Egbert said. He had stood up with the rest of the audience, clapping in amazement. Not only was it his first time hearing Sophie play, but his first time at a classical music concert.

Glancing at Riley, Sophie recalled when he'd heard her own composition back in Spring City. She'd written nothing since then.

"I would need to write a whole concerto, and I'm far from that. Plus, I think I ought to be well-known first, so people will pay to see me."

"They paid at The Grand," Carling offered.

"They paid for their drinks," Sophie said with laughter in her voice.

"They came back for you," Riley insisted. "I know I did," he added under his breath so she alone could hear.

She'd heard the whole story from Carling, how Riley had come looking for her. Frankly, she was glad she'd already left with Philip. Without her trip back home, she would be lost— lost without Henry and his orchestra. She couldn't imagine her life in San Francisco if she'd returned to no more than her job in The Grand's barroom.

"We're going to look at some land for sale in Sonoma," Carling said, obviously trying to keep a conversation going with the four of them, even though Riley was quietly staring at Sophie, and she was now staring back at him. But that news brought her back to reality.

"This time of year? And so close to Thanksgiving?"

"It's not celebrated as widely here as I've heard it is in New England," Egbert explained.

Sophie frowned and looked at Riley who raised his eyebrows and shrugged.

"We never celebrated it in Spring City much," he admitted.

"The large hotels put on a big meal in their dining rooms," Carling said, "usually a roast beef dinner."

Sophie clucked. "But what about the raffle on Thanksgiving eve and the shooting match and the turkey and pigeon pie. And the pumpkin pie?"

Carling wrinkled up her nose. "Pumpkin pie?"

Sophie reached across the table and grabbed Carling's hand. "My God! Don't tell me you've never had it? And what about costumes?"

"You mean, like dressing up?" Riley asked. "Sophie, we don't do that out here."

"Fine, no costumes, but I will make you all a Thanksgiving meal. We shall meet at my apartment. I'll get some extra chairs, and we'll invite Freddie, too, with his new lady-friend, and of course, all the orchestra members from back East. Henry and Arthur will definitely want turkey and pie."

"I haven't seen inside your apartment," Riley said, making sure Egbert and Carling heard him, "but I imagine you'll need somewhere bigger if you're having all those people."

"Maybe one of the dining rooms at The Palace," Carling said, looking at Egbert, who shook his head wildly.

"Okay, then," Sophie said, "I'll ask Freddie about The Ladies Grill dining room. It'll probably be closed on Thanksgiving anyway."

She drifted away into planning mode, wishing she had her mother and sisters to help her. But Carling would have to do in a pinch, although she had no idea if her friend could make anything other than coffee and fish stew.

"There she goes again, her mind floating off," Carling said, as Sophie tapped her chin thoughtfully.

"I think we should retire," Riley said. "Our pianist here needs her sleep."

Riley unlocked the foyer door for her again and with his hand on the small of her back, he escorted her inside. This time, she let him come upstairs to her door on the first floor, a cheerful honeyed oak door on which she'd hung a sprig of dried flowers. He smiled at the homey touch.

"Are you free tomorrow?" he asked.

She responded with a wry smile.

"I mean in the morning, before the rehearsal," he clarified. "When does it start?"

"Two o'clock."

"I have no classes, no clinic, no rounds tomorrow. I'm free." And he wanted to spend all his time with her.

She leaned back against the door. "What do you have in mind?"

He couldn't help the slow grin that spread over his face. "I can't tell you what I have in my mind. You might slap me."

"Riley!" But she laughed.

"How about a stroll, then?" God knew he wanted to court this woman, to experience everything new with her, and to see her smile at him every day the rest of his life. When he was with her, all that seemed possible. "I know you've lived here a while now, but you can't have seen everything."

"No, of course I haven't. Not at all. I want to be like Miska Hauser. I read his book on the train."

He shrugged helplessly. He had no idea who she was talking about, but he loved to watch her mouth when she spoke.

"He's a violinist and a composer. But you must know, he wrote all about his travels here in San Francisco." She chuckled at his nonplussed expression. "Never mind Hauser. What time can we start?"

He was transfixed by her upturned lips. He wanted to kiss her. Maybe she would open her apartment door and let him in. *Was she as desperate to hold him as he was her?*

"I'll be here, on your step, at nine," he said. He had to escape right then or he would pounce. If he touched her, they'd end up in bed, and where would that leave her when he graduated in less than a month? He knew where. Alone, in San Francisco, with the impression he'd used her. Again.

He turned to go.

"Riley," she said.

He froze, his eyes fixed straight ahead of him, not looking at her.

"Riley," she repeated, more softly and he turned.

"Sophie, I'm trying to do the right thing. Last night, I nearly didn't." His voice sounded odd to his ears. But since he was trying, she could try, too, even if it felt harder to leave her than to recite in alphabetical order all the bones in the human body.

She sighed, and he watched her breasts lift gently, feeling heat shoot straight to his groin.

"Tomorrow, then." She slid her key into the lock and went inside. He kicked the wall viciously to relieve his tension, and her head popped back out.

"Are you all right?" She had a bemused look on her face, indicating she knew exactly how he was feeling—frustrated as hell.

"I'm fine. I . . . stumbled." And he hightailed it down the stairs before he changed his mind.

She really didn't seem to know he planned to take over for Doc. It had been mentioned, he remembered, at the dinner with Dan, but perhaps Sophie had been as distracted as he was that night. In any case, she was starting to make plans, for Thanksgiving and beyond.

He couldn't see beyond tomorrow, certainly not further into the future. At least, not a future with Sophie by his side.

CHAPTER TWENTY-ONE

For Sophie, it was an endless night. She had been ready and waiting and looking out the window for at least twenty minutes when she spied him coming up her front steps. She practically flew downstairs to meet him.

"Ready," she said, eager to take his arm in the bright daylight, where temptation wouldn't overcome them. It had been as difficult as playing Beethoven's *Hammerklavier* to stop herself from throwing her arms around him the night before. In the morning sunshine, cool as it was, she hoped to feel more even-keeled and less desperate to kiss him. They started to walk.

"This reminds me of walking with you along the boards in front of Dan's store, all the way to Fuller's."

"All the way, huh?" he said with a lopsided grin.

She laughed, thinking how small Spring City was. How did someone spend their whole life there, knowing every person in the town and perhaps not liking half of them? Or seeing the same faces day-in and day-out? In Boston, she could go weeks without seeing someone she knew or cared to see, for that matter. And there in San Francisco, nearly everyone was new to her, and she loved it.

"I don't think I've ever been happier," she said.

"Really?" His tone was strange.

"*Mm-hm*. Everything is beginning. My career, our relationship, your career, too."

He stiffened, and she felt him falter in his stride.

"What is it?"

He seemed to hesitate. "You reminded me about the exams. They're coming up soon. That's all."

"I'm sure you'll do fine. Doc's been preparing you all your life, hasn't he?"

"Yes, Doc's always been there for me."

Riley was quiet for while she chattered until Long Bridge stretched out before them across Mission Bay. It was still early enough, not to mention chilly, so the only people on the great span over the bay were fishermen, boys and men, who had arrived hours before to obtain a choice spot at the railing. Shoulder-to-shoulder, they stood, most with the bamboo poles rented from the bait shops on the bridge, and all of them were fishing for smelt.

Sophie and Riley strolled on the bridge beside the rail tracks until a horsecar traveled down the center, rattling the timbers. He pulled her close against his side as it passed, and she relished his warmth seeping into her. All too soon, for the sake of decorum, Riley released her, and she was assailed once more by the cold. A young boy eagerly showed them his catch of small silvery fish lying on a newspaper, and then they paused farther on the bridge to look out over the oyster beds.

"I love you," Riley said, without taking his eyes from the view and so quietly she almost missed it.

Her cowboy doctor loved her!

"I love you, too," Sophie told him, looking at his strong profile and wondering fleetingly why he didn't seem as joyful as she felt.

When he finally turned his face to hers, he claimed her lips instantly, his hand reaching out to hold her to him. With his mouth on hers, she ignored the November wind blowing, until her shivering was no longer concealable. He rested his forehead on hers as they reclaimed their breath, and then he took her gloved hand in his, starting back to the main land.

She thought he would take her straight home and make love to her. Instead, he pulled her inside a small café perched on the pilings next to the bridge.

"Coffee or tea?" he asked, settling her in a seat and walking to the counter.

Was the infernal man stalling or was he missing her obvious signals? Why, now, did he have to start courting her slowly?

"Coffee," Sophie said, "with cream. That would be lovely." Truthfully, she would rather warm up by kissing him somewhere private.

Riley came back with two coffees and some raisin cake for them to share.

In companionable silence, they ate until nothing was left, and Sophie moistened the end of her finger to pick up the last of the cake crumbs off the plate.

"It's the cold," Riley said. "It makes your body want to store up energy by eating more." He was speaking clinically, but she noticed he was staring at her finger she'd licked. Her insides did a funny flip. She pushed her chair out abruptly. No more stalling. She wanted to be in his arms at last.

"We'd better start walking back. I need time to change before rehearsal."

"You look lovely to me. You always do."

"You're sweet," she said, snugging her coat more tightly around her before they stepped outside. "But this is not the gown in which I want to appear in front of hundreds of people."

"Then we should get you out of it," he said.

Her eyes widened, as he grinned, but then he shook his head. "I mean, we'll get you home so you can change. What are you playing tonight?"

"Don't you know?" Her head was so full of Amadeus she could barely hear anything else. She imagined he could hear it, too.

"I have to admit I haven't looked at the program," he confessed. "After I saw your name in the paper, it didn't matter to me what you were playing."

She smiled radiantly. "Tonight is Mozart."

"You know, Sophie, most of us mere mortals do not know our Boccherini from our Bach, or our Mozart from our . . ."

"Mendelsohn," she supplied helpfully.

"Something like that."

"That doesn't matter, does it?" Her audience could enjoy the music without knowing anything behind it. Personally, she couldn't bear the thought of not knowing the history of the composers. Their stories brought the works to life for her.

"No," he took her hand in his and squeezed lightly. "When you start playing, you could be playing 'Mollie Darling' and we'd still be on our feet."

"I can't believe you're comparing Kinkel to Mozart."

"I'm not. I'm saying you can spin straw into gold, as the saying goes."

Instead of walking, Riley pulled her up onto the first cable car, and they were back at Sophie's apartment in minutes.

They entered silently, and he followed her upstairs to her front door. She put the key in the lock and turned it. Then she faced him, waiting for him to decide whether he was going to kiss her or keep his hands and lips to himself again and walk away.

At first, he did neither. He seemed to be studying her, a small frown in the middle of his forehead. Then, slowly, he reached up and took her face in his hands.

"Sophie?"

"Yes?"

"I—" But whatever he was going to say, he didn't. He took a step closer, and she tingled in anticipation. He pulled her toward him, and she fitted against his long muscular frame.

Exhaling slowly, she felt entirely at home in his arms as she did at her piano keys.

Kiss me, she begged him with her eyes. His eyebrows went up slightly, reading the message. Then he swallowed, looking serious, with no slow and sensual smile this time. As he bent closer, her arms slipped up his chest and her hands circled his shoulders to clasp together behind his neck.

When his lips touched hers, she sighed again. He groaned, causing something inside her to burst into flames. Immediately, she knew this was no gentle welcome-home kiss and no brief lovers' peck. This was a serious, feel-it-down-to-her-toes kiss.

Tugging on her lower lip, Riley then nibbled beside her mouth and down her tender throat while she clutched him. He reclaimed her lips and enticed them open to accept his tongue. At the same time, she felt his hips press against hers. Her knees softened even as she tried to raise up on tiptoe to better feel his hardness against her soft womanly places. Mostly, she wanted to lie down and feel him settle on top of her.

Freeing her hands, she reached behind her and turned the knob. With the pressure of them both against it, the door flew inward, and they nearly tumbled to the floor. Riley kept a hand on her waist as he grabbed at the door frame to keep them upright.

"Sorry," she muttered, "I should have warned you."

He half chuckled. "I was a bit lost in the moment anyway."

Walking her back a step in his arms, he made sure she was steady on her feet before he released her. They were both breathing heavily, and she could see his pupils had grown larger, filling his gleaming eyes with black desire. She felt the same. But he was hesitating as he had done at The Grand that fateful day, looking torn, even reluctant.

No Eliza stood between them, nor Philip on the horizon— nothing that could possibly stand in their way.

"Riley, I . . . I want you."

His jaw clenched, then he closed the door behind him, pulling her into his arms once again.

"You feel like heaven, Sophie."

He reached around and squeezed her buttocks, pulling her up against him, so she could feel the whole length of his shaft. Then he reached down and swept her off her feet entirely.

"I feel like an unwieldy cello," she grumbled, when he paused, not knowing where to take her.

"You're supposed to feel feminine. You're light as a butterfly." He walked through her small parlor into the kitchen and backed out, going to the next room and finding her bed.

"Bigger than at The Grand," he commented.

"I didn't complain at The Grand."

"Nor me." He lowered her gently to her bed and lay down beside her, resting on his elbow, looking down at her. "I thought that was going to be our one and only time ever." He touched her cheek. "And I wanted you so badly, like I do now. I hated to rush. I wanted it to last forever, but I also didn't want to do it at all."

She winced. "Because of Eliza."

"No. She didn't enter my head. I swear it."

He brushed his thumb over her lip, and she trembled. She was hot and prickly in all the right places, feeling as if she was wearing about a hundred layers too many of thick clothing.

"I didn't want to be the kind of man who could take your innocence from you with nothing to offer in return. But, as it turned out, I was that man."

His voice sounded so sad when all she felt was joy. Stroking his silken brown hair, she breathed in his familiar vanilla-soap scent.

Next, she touched his face, reveling in the roughness of his cheek against her palm. "I thought that one memory was going to have to carry me through a lifetime," she confessed.

Riley captured her hand, turned his head, and kissed her palm. "Instead, here we are." He settled closer and rested one leg over hers.

Lowering his mouth to hers, he kissed her. The pleasing weight of his thigh across hers made her arch against him. His arm brushed across her breasts, and she moaned with pleasure as he shifted his position until he was, finally, on top of her.

"We can go slowly this time," he said, breathless, as he nibbled her ear lobe.

"*Mm*," she murmured, not thinking they could go slowly at all. "Riley," she breathed against him. "We still have our shoes on."

She felt him kicking his off with some effort, but her own were ankle-highs, which she needed to sit up and unlace. Pushing against him, she tried to sit up, but he slid down the length of her body, kissing her through the layers of fabric, first her breasts and then her stomach, until he got off the bed and knelt down to start unlacing her boots.

She slipped off her coat and then her short-fitted jacket before undoing the buttons at her blouse's cuffs. Glancing at the clock that ticked relentlessly on her bureau, she hated the movement of the second hand. They still had time before rehearsal but not a tremendous amount. Their lovemaking would have to be a lively and spirited *capriccio* after all, and not the unhurried *adagio* she was hoping for.

However, after that night's performance, they would have all the time in the world.

Steadily undoing the buttons of her blouse, she glanced up to see him standing motionless, still wearing his trousers, staring at her.

"Riley?" she asked uncertainly.

"You're so beautiful. Even your hands. You have such lovely, capable, artistic hands."

She blushed and countered, "That's ridiculous. Your hands do far more important work than mine."

Sophie watched the frown appear on his face again and longed to smooth it away. Slipping her blouse from her shoulders, she paused. Immediately, he was beside her again. She let him remove her corset and then her shift before he pushed her gently back down on the bed.

Her nipples pebbled instantly under his gaze, and she started to cross her arms, but he held them away from her, leaning down to reverently kiss the underswell of each breast.

Then he blew on one rosy nipple making it tighten even further.

"I think I know what it's like to play a fine instrument," he said.

"Riley, stop teasing me." She closed her eyes as he plucked her nipple with his teeth.

"I'm not. I'm just learning what you like." One of his hands roamed down her naked torso to stroke her hip, then drifted over the short curls on her mound and stayed there. She arched against him.

"You know exactly," she panted, grabbing at his shoulders, "exactly what you're doing. You're nearly a doctor."

She felt him halt. Every movement stopped, including his breathing. Then he moved his lips to her other nipple and kissed her. But she writhed under him. He was still partially clothed, and she desperately needed him naked and settled between her legs.

"Riley, are you going to finish undressing?"

He didn't answer at first. He raised his head, his glittering eyes looking deeply into her own. Then he kissed her lips again before he lifted himself off her inflamed skin.

"I don't have any contraception," he said, not meeting her disappointed gaze. "Fancy word for protection," he added. Then, to her amazement, he grabbed the blanket that was folded at the bottom of her bed and tossed it over her naked, flushed body.

Closing her eyes, Sophie nearly cried in frustration. When she opened them, he was sitting up, watching her pensively. She wanted to feel Riley, all of him, inside her, to experience the *glissando* of one passionate movement sliding almost unnoticeably into the next, until they reached the final harmony when their bodies climaxed.

Why, she could practically play it for him on a piano. *Protection be damned!* She gave him, the man she loved, her most welcoming smile.

He jumped up. "I'd best be leaving."

What? Her pulse was racing, and she was trembling with expectation, but he was already gathering his clothes.

"Riley," she tried to call him back, hating the desperate sound of her voice.

"I have to let you go," he said, draping his tie haphazardly around his bare neck before slipping on his shirt. "I mean, so you can get ready."

Rising onto her knees in the middle of the bed, she held the blanket against her bare breasts. At first, he didn't look at her, and when he did, his eyes were sad once more. His tone, however, when he spoke, sounded angry—at what, or whom, she didn't know.

"I'm sorry, Sophie," he ground out.

Her eyes widened in confusion.

He shook his head. "I know you need time to prepare for tonight."

She wanted him to stay, nearly begged him to, so filled with longing as she was, except she knew it would be useless. He looked like a man who'd made up his mind to leave. She would let him go—for clearly, something was troubling him and being with her was only making it worse.

He finished dressing in silence, slipping his feet into his shoes and shrugging his shoulders into his coat. Then, he made for the door, moving as though his heels were on fire.

Grabbing her dressing gown from the chair beside the bed, she wrapped it around herself and followed him out of her bedroom, stunned by the rapid change in his attitude, wholly disappointed, and already missing him.

At the front door, he turned and took her in his arms.

"Will you do one thing for me?"

His manner filled her with trepidation, but she answered unhesitatingly, "Yes. Anything."

"Tonight, when you play, will you play only for me? The way you did in Spring City?"

She stroked his cheek, searching his earnest brown eyes for answers.

"Yes, of course." Crossing her hands behind his neck again, she breathed the scent of him. "I'll see you tonight?"

He didn't answer at once. "I'll be in the front row," he said at last, before kissing her again, taking care to ravage her mouth like a desperate man going to war. Then, while her knees were trembling, he slipped out of her arms and out of her apartment.

Sophie couldn't shake the feeling that, in a short span of time, something had shifted and was now dreadfully wrong. In a piece of music, she considered it *deceptive cadence*. One minute everything was flowing perfectly, and she had been assured of the ending. And the next, nothing seemed right.

True to his word, however, Riley was in the same seat owned by Mr. Shepherd in the front row when the house lights came on for the musician's introductions that night. And right before the lights went down after intermission, he waved to her. However, when the performance was over, he had disappeared.

CHAPTER TWENTY-TWO

"Riley," Sophie called out, knocking on his front door. At first, she chalked up his disappearance from the concert hall to his being called away for another ill patron or staff member during the performance. However, when he didn't contact her by Monday morning, she located his rooming house by the hospital.

Her knock was answered with silence.

Next, Sophie went to the City-County Hospital and asked at reception if he was in the building. He was, but he was doing rounds. She was told she could wait, and she did—over an hour—all the while getting more agitated and annoyed until, when she eventually saw him, she was ready to spit nails. Rather than the concern she initially felt and meant to convey, she knew she seemed like an angry, wet hen.

"How dare you run off and not contact me?"

Instead of looking apologetic, his expression proclaimed him unapproachable.

"I couldn't stay." His tone was clipped, even angry although she couldn't imagine what the cause was. He didn't explain why he couldn't remain at the concert hall until the end of the performance, and before she could ask, he continued, "And today, as you know, I have rounds."

She was not mollified. She had played only for him, as he'd requested. Apparently, he hadn't even noticed. Nevertheless, she took a deep, calming breath. After all, she didn't want to sound like a harridan.

"When are you finished?" She thought whatever was bothering him could be discussed over dinner.

He shook his head and raised his hands as if warding her off.

"Late. And I have to study. Tomorrow, too," he added.

"All right, then," she said, taking a step backward, away from his coldness. "I'll see you when next you're free."

Something was wrong, obviously, but she had no idea how to make him tell her. Turning on her heel, she got halfway across the lobby.

"Sophie," he called after her.

She halted and looked back.

"You played beautifully," he said. "I . . . I thank you."

She gave him a small smile, which he didn't return.

"I have to go." He disappeared down the hallway so swiftly she was left looking after the empty space.

"What the hell?" she muttered and retraced her steps home, feeling more confused than when she'd arrived.

Riley knew he was behaving atrociously. He couldn't even watch Sophie leave the hospital. He had to start walking in the other direction, or he would have gone after her and thrown himself at her feet. He distracted himself for the rest of the day on rounds, but that night, he gave up his futile attempts at studying to take a walk, a long, diverting walk.

From the moment he fled her apartment, on the verge of making love to her, he'd decided on a plan. He would make her hate him. It was a terrible plan, but one he was sure would be effective. And it would be easy to do, if the look on

Sophie's face when she confronted him at the hospital had been any indication. He had only to act as boorishly as possible and hurt the woman he loved more than anyone in the world. He could tell he was already accomplishing his goal, and it left him both irritable and depressed.

With luck, his plan would mean minimal contact with her, which was vital to his sanity and to sustaining his determination to let her go. For the first time in a long time, he headed to the corner bar and sat down for a drink.

"Get on with you," Carling said, setting down her cup. "That doesn't sound right."

"He was behaving very queerly," Sophie agreed. "And I have no idea why."

"The stress of his board exams," Carling offered. "Becoming a doctor can't be easy."

"True, but I've seen him in a crisis," Sophie said, thinking of the train accident in Spring City. "He is completely confident in his abilities. I have no doubt he'll make an outstanding doctor."

"Give him a little time, then," Carling suggested, pouring more coffee and adding milk. "I saw how he looked at you at dinner. He's a goner for you."

Sophie had thought so, too, but in her heart, she knew something had changed.

This was confirmed when Riley had not contacted her by week's end. The orchestra started rehearsals for the next series of concerts, and Sophie threw herself into them, heart and soul.

"You are positively driven, my girl," Henry said after she played through Brahms *Piano Concerto No. 1*. He'd halted the rest of the musicians when Walter's piccolo cracked from being left on a radiator and then Seifert missed his queue.

Looking around, she realized what had happened. They were all staring at her.

"I'm sorry," she offered while knowing she was about to cry. "I'll be right back." She fled the stage for the ladies' dressing room.

A few moments later, Arthur came looking for her. Wiping her tears hastily, she opened the door.

"Are you all right?" he asked, an awkward look on his face.

She was red with embarrassment. "I am. I just feel so stupid. To keep playing, making you all wait for me. And to ignore Henry's signal to stop. I'm mortified."

"No one minds, Sophie. You really are our star pianist, and if we get to sit back and listen once in a while, that's fine. Henry sent me, by the way. He didn't think it would look right for him to leave the stage."

"He is correct, as usual." *No one minded,* Arthur had said. Was that true?

"We're taking a little break, Sophie girl, and then we'll be ready to catch up to you." He gave her a reassuring look, and she watched him go. How sweet of him to say *they* needed the break, not her.

Taking a sip of water, she paced the room. She needed to focus on what she was doing and stop her mind from wandering to Riley. Yes, *merely* that! Yet it seemed as though, in the space of a week, the piano had ceased feeling like home and had become her personal battleground. Instead of getting lost in a song, she wanted to conquer it. And all the while she played, she longed for Riley's smile and Riley's warmth.

If she couldn't soothe herself with her music, then what was left to her?

Sophie did her finger exercises as she walked back onstage. The rest of the orchestra clapped. She hesitated then walked to the front of the stage beside Henry, and put her hands on her hips. So, they were teasing her now, applauding a performance she shouldn't have made. But it was as if her family were playfully ribbing her, so she bowed low and solemnly. Then Otto whistled loudly, and they all laughed. She took her seat back behind her instrument.

Thank God she had the orchestra, or she would truly be bereft.

On Saturday afternoon, Carling got off work and convinced Sophie to wander along Market Street for some shopping. They each had a bit of money and spent an enjoyable few hours trying on shoes and hats.

"You can never have too many hats," Sophie said.

Carling slapped a blue felt hat on her head and admired herself in the looking glass. She sighed and took it off. "I haven't asked, but any word from one Mr. Dalcourt?"

Sophie shook her head sadly.

"That's astonishing," Carling stated. "It beats all."

Sophie was equally flabbergasted. "Can you imagine if Egbert simply disappeared tomorrow and didn't tell you why?"

Carling's eyes flashed. "I'd murder him for leading me on." But she placed her hand over Sophie's. "I wish I could tell you I understood what's going on."

"It's all right," she said, although it wasn't. "I've decided to get on with it, as you say. I've got rehearsals to think about. And Riley's exams are next week. After that, I don't know what his plans are."

She tried to recall if their relationship had all been on her side. It seemed so long ago when he'd first kissed her in Spring City. He had certainly made the first move, unless he'd thought she was flirting by playing the piano for him.

And in San Francisco, had she led him on by allowing him into her room? At one point, after she'd been injured, he'd resisted her entirely and was able to undress her and leave her. Her cheeks burned. Hadn't she been the one to force him to her bed at The Grand?

Even after he'd sought her out a week ago, he hadn't pushed his way into her new apartment. And when given the chance, he hadn't made love to her. *No contraception*, he'd said, without much regret. Yet he'd told her he loved her. Why?

Her thoughts circled like a seagull over the bay.

Another week of rehearsals, this time including some of Henry's own compositions, and still nothing but silence from

Riley. On the eve of the first performance of their new series, Sophie had no illusions Riley would be in the front row or even in the concert hall. She could only be grateful he hadn't taken her offer of intimacy that day after their walk on the bridge. If he had, she would certainly feel soiled and discarded by his sudden and absolute abandonment.

The aromas, the tastes, and the lively flow of conversation, the laughter and the warmth in The Grand's dining room—all of it would have made Sophie feel as though she were home for Thanksgiving, except for the incessant ache over missing Riley. In another month, she would, indeed, be home for the long-anticipated visit over the Yuletide festivities. She had promised her mother, and while she couldn't wait to see her and her siblings, Sophie was most definitely not looking forward to traveling between the coasts.

She dreaded the long journey on the train, the hours during which she would do nothing but attempt to read while futilely pushing thoughts of Riley Dalcourt out of her head. At least, she could go home with copies of the orchestra's programs, her name prominently displayed with the other musicians, and feel proud of what she'd accomplished so far.

"You look pensive," Henry said, sitting beside her and handing her a glass of wine. "Good thoughts, I hope."

Dear Henry. In some ways he reminded her of her brother. The way he conducted the orchestra was similar to how Reed handled a case in court: No nonsense, fair, and with exacting standards.

"Yes, I was thinking of how lovely it will be to go home for Christmas." She told him her half-truth and then changed the subject. "It's a successful Thanksgiving, don't you—?"

The words died on her lips as, in the background, behind Henry, she saw Riley enter the room. Instantly, her pulse started to race. He was there! And he looked so handsome her heart hurt, dressed as he was in a gray suit, vest, and boiled white shirt. As she watched, he pulled at the collar as if it bothered him, and then he came to a stop in the middle of the room.

"Rivals the best I ever had in Massachusetts," Henry agreed.

She could see Riley was searching the room and helplessly, she rose as if pulled by a puppeteer. His gaze snapped instantly to her, his face remaining shuttered.

With supreme effort, she dragged her attention back to Henry, who had also stood.

"I'm afraid I have to get going. I've been asked to stop by a few homes," he said.

Sophie nodded, trying hard to follow their conversation when her brain was already imagining what Riley might say and what she might say back. But this was Henry, her friend.

"Bohemian Club members' homes?" she asked, not surprised by how promptly Henry had been welcomed into the elite group of San Francisco's professionals and patrons of the arts.

"Yes. You don't mind, do you?"

She could feel Riley approaching.

"Not at all. I think I have quite enough people here to keep me company. I had no idea this many would turn out. We have more displaced musicians away from their families than I imagined."

Henry smiled wryly. "I think it's more the case that most of the musicians prefer the people in this room to their actual families."

Riley had paused a few feet away, apparently not wanting to interrupt.

"And is Miss Barbour accompanying you on your visits this evening?" Sophie indicated the lovely young lady talking animatedly with Otto.

"Yes," Henry blushed. "I am very fond of Inez." The dark-haired soprano from Pennsylvania had been with them only a short time, but, plainly, Henry was head-over-heels for her.

"That's wonderful," Sophie said, meaning it with all her heart. "And you know, Henry, you are brilliant." She gave him a kiss on the cheek. "Get on with you, as my friend would say."

"I'll see you on Saturday for rehearsal, Sophie-girl."

She smiled absently at Henry, who slipped away, nodding at Riley as he passed him.

For a moment, Riley still didn't move, and Sophie couldn't help staring. Then, she swallowed the uneasy feeling as they walked toward each other through the crowd of revelers. For Sophie, everyone else disappeared.

"I didn't expect to see you here." *How could her voice sound so normal?*

"I know." He had the grace to look ashamed. "I would have come earlier, but we had an emergency at the hospital."

She nodded. "There's still plenty of food, and you're welcome to it. Let me get you a plate."

He put his hand on her arm to stop her, and she jumped at his touch, looking first at his large hand on her emerald green sleeve and then back to his face, more chiseled than she remembered.

"I didn't come to eat. I came to see you," he said quietly.

She shivered. He had dark circles below his eyes and a hollowed look under his cheekbones. "You can do both, eat and talk to me. You look rather as if you could use a good meal."

"I'm just tired," he said.

She wanted to lash out at him for his treatment of her, but she also wanted to kiss him. More than either, she wanted to take care of him, so forlorn and weary did he seem.

"Riley, sit down and I'll fill you up a plate. Look, there's a quiet spot." She pointed to the other end of The Ladies Grill, where two tables stood against the wall, empty but still littered with the remains of the Thanksgiving feast. Everyone else now stood in the center of the room or sat at tables pulled closely together.

He seemed to hesitate but then complied. She moved as fast as possible to the kitchen and filled him a plate, worried he would be gone when she returned.

As she hurriedly reentered the dining room, she nearly ran into Carling.

"Sorry," Carling said, "were you looking for me?" Sophie noticed her hair was disheveled.

"Where were you *and* Egbert?"

Carling blushed fiercely. "Oh, um . . . ," she trailed off, then noticed the plate.

"Still hungry?"

"No, it's for Riley." Sophie nodded her head to where he sat, his back against the wall, his head resting on the wall, too, his eyes closed.

"What in blue blazes is he doing here?" Carling had been almost as upset by his disappearance as Sophie.

"I don't know yet, but I intend to find out."

She started to move away when Carling added, "You let me know if you need help. I can give a good swift kick when necessary."

Sophie half-smiled. "I hope that won't be required, but I'll keep it in mind." Her smiled had died entirely by the time she reached him.

Riley looked as if he'd already been kicked. She stood by the table a moment, watching him, his eyes still shut, breathing evenly. He might be asleep. Deliberately, Sophie plunked the plate down in front of him, and his eyelids snapped open.

Sitting upright with a start, he didn't immediately look at the food. Instead, his gaze locked on her.

"Will you sit with me?" he asked.

She sat.

"I've been busy."

"*Hm,*" she murmured noncommittally.

"How are your rehearsals?" His polite question made her grind her teeth.

"Good," she said. "Performances, even better."

Suddenly, he looked down at the plate. Perhaps the aromas had finally tempted him. Picking up the fork, he took a bite of mashed potatoes and swallowed like a man who hadn't eaten for a while, savoring the taste and going back for more. He ate all the potato in silence and then the pigeon pie. When that was done, he put the fork down.

Sophie watched him, feeling as though she would be content to sit with him in silence forever, but she knew she couldn't.

"What's wrong?" she asked.

He stared at his plate. "I shouldn't have told you I loved you."

His words cut like a knife in her side. Instantly, she could barely breathe.

"Because you don't?" she asked, sounding choked.

Hesitation. "No," he said, cutting deeper.

She lowered her eyes to where her hands rested in her lap. Tears were pricking already, but she would be damned if she'd let them fall.

"Why did you, then?" Her voice came out in a gruff whisper.

"I wanted to spend time with you." He didn't say anything more for a moment.

She blinked again, and finally, she was able to look at him directly. He seemed to be about to take her hand but stopped himself.

"But I know you would have wanted more than I can give you. I've had a fiancée for a long time. I just want to be free now."

Was it possible she could feel her blood becoming colder? For it seemed her fingertips were suddenly chilled and then she felt shaky all over. Regardless, she had to speak to him levelly, as if her heart weren't shearing in two.

"You didn't have to lie to me, Riley. I was content to spend time with you." Perhaps he would grow to love her. "I still am."

She'd done it, offering herself to him, asking only for the gift of more time together.

He looked away, then back quickly, holding her gaze with his tawny brown one. "Are you supremely happy?"

"What do you mean?" At that moment, she felt anything but happiness.

"Being in the orchestra and living in San Francisco?"

Just hearing the words "being in the orchestra" still excited her. "Why, yes. It's everything I ever dreamed."

He nodded slowly. "That's good. That's what I thought you'd say, and I want you to know how glad I am for you, Sophie."

He didn't sound glad. She reached out and touched his arm, and he jumped. Then he grabbed her hand and clamped it down on his arm, so she couldn't remove it.

"I came to tell you goodbye."

She didn't know what to say.

"But I can't do it at this table." He stood abruptly and took her with him, out the side door into the hallway of The Grand and then beyond. He was moving fast, dragging her along behind him.

"Riley, stop." He did, but he didn't look at her. He was looking wildly around, searching.

"In here," she said, pulling him toward the employees' coat room.

Why did he hunger to be alone with her, even then, when he knew he had to be a wretched vile rogue and make her cut him from her life—and her heart—completely?

Once inside the closet, he pressed her back against the door, his face close to hers. She looked so kissable, and despite everything he'd said to her, he ached to kiss her.

"I can't see you anymore," he said.

"You don't have to love me," she whispered, then looked ashamed.

It broke his heart. She believed he didn't love her. That *was* the point, after all. Still, he had to let her know how wonderful she was.

"Don't say that," he said harshly. "Any man would be lucky to have you and to love you."

"But not you," her voice trembled slightly.

God, this was agony! He'd had nearly the same conversation with Eliza but for a vastly different reason and with opposite results.

He had to answer her. "No, not me."

Sophie closed her eyes, her beautiful, dark, shining eyes, but not before he saw her pain, mirroring his own. Lightly, he touched her chin, tilting her face toward his. She opened her eyes as his mouth came down on hers.

As soon as he felt her lips, he faltered. She was so easy to love. She was *his* woman, *his* Sophie. *Damn!* Grinding hard against her lips, he demanded she open her mouth for his tongue. The warmth encircling his heart turned to pure heat, tugging at his groin. With his hands on her shoulders, he pulled her up against him, crushing her to him.

Riley felt angrier than he had in his whole life. Not at her. Not even at himself. Why had he found this incredible woman to love when loving her would mean destroying her dreams? At the very moment when he must start fulfilling his lifelong promise to Doc, to whom he owed everything, Sophie was starting a career that promised to be dazzling, fulfilling, spectacular. Exactly what she deserved. And a thousand miles away from where he had to be.

Of their own accord, his hands were moving down her body, grasping, kneading, holding her firmly against him, his hips pressing into hers. It took a few moments for him to realize she was struggling to break free from his punishing kiss.

"Riley?" Her voice reached him, a little scared, confused, heartbroken. He was making it worse. He had to get it over with. He had to make her hate him.

"We can do this, right now," he said, hearing his own voice low and raspy. "Is that what you want? With a man who doesn't love?"

CHAPTER TWENTY-THREE

Sophie felt as though he'd slapped her, and in return, she raised her palm and struck him across the cheek. Then she gasped and buried her face in her hands. *Why was he being so horrible?* This wasn't her Riley!

Slowly, he released her and moved around her to the door. She felt his hand on her hair, stroking it ever so lightly.

"Good bye, Sophie Malloy. I will always remember you."

Just like that, he was gone. She burst into tears, sinking down onto the floor, and sobbing. She couldn't catch her breath for crying so hard, couldn't imagine ever moving from that spot, couldn't think beyond the last terrible moments.

She had believed Philip loved her and had been surprised when he'd cast her off. And now, Riley. This hurt so much more. She knew why. Because her whole heart and soul loved Riley dearly, unlike the comfortable affection she'd once felt for Philip. This was pure, devoted, passionate love, and it seemed impossibly cruel to learn it was one-sided.

After a few minutes, she quieted, trying to breathe deeply and evenly. Grabbing at the hem of the nearest coat, she wiped her face.

Damn him, she thought. How dare he offer to . . . to . . .

Sophie got off the floor.

Damn him—her heart ached so badly—*and damn her, too.*

The applause was deafening. It had been an absolutely successful night, and Sophie felt her heart grow lighter for the first time in weeks. Soon, she would be on a train, going home to see her family, and she could hardly wait.

It had been impossible to put Riley out of her mind as easily as he'd cut her out of his life, even though she'd spent less time *with* him than without him, and even less time thinking they had a chance together. Still, she'd firmly believed in their uncanny bond, a deep understanding of which she'd been certain. Now, forsaken, she wondered how she could have been so wrong.

Try as she might, her music career no long filled her with the utmost joy. It was her sole source of pleasure, but it was no longer nearly effortless. It was bloody hard work—hard to focus, hard to memorize, hard even to play the right notes consistently. And it took all of her remaining concentration to follow Henry and make sure she didn't let down the other musicians. For that, Sophie felt a spark of anger toward Riley.

Despite the strain experienced by its celebrated, primary pianist, the orchestra's audiences had grown, and the papers were filled with praise every time they performed. However, after the curtain closed each night, when Sophie lay alone in her bed, she thought of Riley and what might have been. Then, she was distraught as well as puzzled. She'd been so sure of his feelings for her, as strong as her own for him.

If he'd truly been using her, he could have had her a second time in her apartment, but he hadn't.

His words demanding freedom made sense, however. A man in a long, loveless relationship could only take so much, but he was the one who had come to find her backstage on opening night. *Why?* She'd asked herself that a hundred times.

It was as though she'd been carefully playing an intricate movement when someone removed a measure, maybe two, from the middle of the piece. She was lost, failing to grasp at something elemental and obvious, something she was overlooking.

Clutching her sheet, she tossed it up over her head, tired of the ache in her heart. But she no longer looked for him or even hoped to bump into him. That would be too painful.

"It's freezing. You're crazy," Sophie yelled at her younger sister, Rose, above the sound of the surf. The sand and rocks were covered in the previous night's snow. She'd allowed Rose to talk her into a midday train trip to the frigid beach, supposedly to look at the gulls and the breakers.

"I don't care. It's sunny and beautiful, and it looks like something out of a painting," her sister shouted back.

"I can hardly hear you!"

"When you play the piano, is it magic for you, like making love to a man?"

That, Sophie heard!

"Is there something you want to tell me?" she demanded.

Rose pointed along the isolated beach.

Standing on the boardwalk at the far end was a man in sailor's garb, evidently waiting for them. Rose gave her older sister a quick smile and started running toward him.

Sophie sighed, hugging her thick wool cloak around her while the December wind tried to whip it away. Rose was in love. Again. It was going to be an interesting Christmas.

Luckily, her sister's latest earth-shattering passion became everyone's focus over the holidays, leaving Sophie out of the spotlight. She welcomed congratulations from her family and friends on her success, but she didn't want to answer questions about why she'd given Philip the mitten earlier in the year, nor whether another prospect waited in the wings.

None of them knew about Riley Dalcourt or how her heart was in a deep-freeze as chilled as the Atlantic Ocean. Still, she was grateful for her new life.

When she had a quiet moment alone with Charlotte, she thanked her.

"My life would be so empty if you hadn't brought Henry Hadley to listen to me."

Charlotte arched a delicate eyebrow.

Sophie laughed. "No, nothing like that. Henry is quite smitten with our visiting soprano, and I couldn't be happier for him. But the orchestra has become my family away from home."

"Speaking of home," her sister-in-law said, "I forgot to tell you, I had a lovely Christmas card with a letter from Sarah Cuthins."

Simply the name, so unexpected, was like a sharp pinch. Sarah and Doc and Riley were irrevocably entangled in her mind, and Sophie's thoughts flew from one to the other to the next, until she was picturing Riley's last terrible kiss and his harsh words.

"I think your thoughts hopped a train," Charlotte said softly.

"Sorry, you're right," Sophie confessed. "I was miles away." *In a coat closet in San Francisco.*

"Thinking of Spring City? I know I was. Sarah said they're getting ready to travel as soon as the snows let up and the seasons change again. Most likely, by April or May, at the latest, they'll be able to leave."

"Dr. Cuthins is retiring?" Sophie asked.

"Yes, he can now. I don't know if you ever met Riley Dalcourt?" Charlotte asked.

Another sharp pinch from the past. Sophie blushed but lowered her head to hide it, feigning interest in her own hands. She started absentmindedly doing finger exercises while Charlotte continued.

"He was probably away when you were in Spring, although I'm sure you met his fiancée, or rather ex-fiancée, Eliza. Bane of my existence, that girl, and for the life of me, I never knew what I did to annoy her, but she loved to tease me."

Sophie wrinkled up her nose. She saw no reason to lie to Charlotte. "Yes, I met her. And Mr. Dalcourt, actually. Why do you ask?"

"Sarah said Eliza ended their engagement. It was the talk of Spring, more so when she up and left town. So strange! You saw for yourself how handsome Riley is." She tapped her foot. "And of course, you must have met Mr. Webster? His granddaughter, Anna, is getting married. And someone played a prank and put piglets in the general store overnight."

Charlotte had a faraway look, and Sophie waited, feeling anything but patient. *What was the news about Riley?*

"Anyway, Riley became a full-fledged doctor at last and is working with Doc." Charlotte laughed. "I guess they'll be calling them both 'Doc' now."

Sophie couldn't say she was surprised exactly. She remembered Riley's words about owing Doc Cuthins, for helping him and setting him on the right path. But somehow, after seeing him in San Francisco and having been in the modern hospital, she found it difficult to picture Riley back in Doc's small, rustic practice.

"With Riley able to take over, Sarah can finally come visit me," Charlotte prattled on. "She said she and Doc will stop here on their way to Europe."

"How lovely for them," Sophie murmured, but her mind was on Riley being back in Colorado. How long had he known he was going back? He'd never said anything about it, never discussed his plans with her.

She remembered thinking she would go anywhere if he asked her, wondering why Eliza had even hesitated. But now, staring at her fingers, she reconsidered. Riley was going to stay in Spring City, taking over as the town doctor. No doubt he would find a local lady to marry, and with any luck, someone as good and patient as Sarah, if that was possible.

In twenty years, would he have a wife who was dying to get out of Spring City and travel?

Sophie swallowed, admitting to herself, at that moment, she couldn't imagine giving up her place in the orchestra. In all likelihood, though, if he'd asked her, she would have done so. Yes, feeling the way she felt about him even before he'd declared his love so softly on the bridge, if he'd asked her, she would have gone with him.

And she would have hated it!

And Riley knew that.

At last, there was the missing measure of the music she'd been going over in her head. Riley knew she loved him, knew she would go with him to the ends of the earth, and knew she'd be utterly miserable. Could it be that simple?

Was that why he asked her in that awful last encounter if she was "supremely happy"? She remembered telling him she was. And then he'd made sure to severe their relationship with his cruel behavior. *But what about Riley's happiness?*

"And Dan Freeman says hello," Charlotte concluded, then she cocked her head. "You seem distracted."

"I think I need to play piano. I've been slacking lately."

"Yes," Charlotte agreed, straight-faced, "Rose said you'd played for *only* four hours yesterday."

"I should have played for five," Sophie said, then offered her a wry smile.

"I am so very glad you put this off until now," Sophie said, as Egbert tucked a blanket around her and Carling. "I would have hated to miss this monumental trip." Which would be all the better if Riley were beside her.

Stop, stop, stop, she admonished herself for the hundredth time in a week. Put Riley in the past where he belonged.

"Go on with you," Carling said, squeezing her arm. "It wouldn't be the same without you."

They started out in a brougham for wine country with Sophie trying to take pleasure in the ordinary things in life. This *was* her life, after all. Riley had made his decision, and if, as she surmised, he'd made it without giving her a choice in the matter, then she could do nothing about it.

"So, what's the plan, soon-to-be-Mrs. Egbert Hull?" Sophie asked, inwardly begging to be distracted from her wayward thoughts. Even discussing her friend's impending marriage, with its double edge of happiness and loss, was better than brooding.

The ring Carling had waggled in front of Sophie when she'd returned from her trip to Boston contained one sweetly sparkling diamond, and held a promise of a summer wedding. The Hulls planned to move north immediately after.

Carling squealed with excitement, and Egbert leaned back from the driver's seat to kiss her full on the mouth. Sophie smiled, never expecting to see such an open display, but Carling was good for him and vice versa. Apparently, they were the opposite to her and Riley, whose paths had never been going in the same direction from the moment they'd met.

"We're going to visit Charles Krug," Egbert answered for her, "a super fellow. He apprenticed for Haraszthy at Buena Vista winery and then for Patchett, so he's full of information and tips. Says drinking wine keeps him young, but he's very long in the tooth, and I want to pick his brain a little before he . . . ," he trailed off and then coughed delicately.

Egbert patted the pad of paper beside him. "Anyway, I'm going to take all sorts of notes. We'll stay with the Burris family. They've got grapevines, too, and then we'll visit the land for sale in the morning before heading home."

Sophie felt a pang of melancholy. Riley had been the one to suggest they all stay with a friend of his father's, David Burris and his wife, Julia, on their three hundred acres when the trip was first discussed. Riley was so very far away, and it was likely she would never lay eyes on him again.

"What is it, love?" Carling asked.

Sophie shook her head. "Nothing."

"Why don't you tell us all about your new gentleman friend?" Carling suggested, going exactly in the direction Sophie wished to avoid—for despite letting one of the violinists take her to dinner now and again, it was a pale, watery version of spending time with Riley.

"There's nothing to tell."

"I could tell you about Haraszthy's *Report on Grapes and Wine of California*. It's a bit outdated, from 1858, but still very good information."

They settled back and let Egbert talk.

As Valentine's Day came and went, Sophie found herself with more suitors than she could ever imagine. A talented, educated, single female from the East Coast was rather an oddity in the sometimes rough-and-ready city of San Francisco. She was asked out by nearly every unattached man in the orchestra, as well as by some who were attached. She was asked out by audience members who lingered after the curtain went up. She was even asked out by men she met on the cable car.

To one and all, she said, "No, thank you."

She'd felt the kind of affection that grew steadily over time with Philip, and she'd experienced the type of love that hit her at first sight with Riley. She didn't want to feel either one for a while.

Instead, she had music and more music to occupy her. Henry talked of their young orchestra going on tour, not internationally, merely a few states will halls large enough. It would raise money and let them stretch their talents.

Sophie tried to gain enthusiasm for the idea of a late-summer trip. In truth, however, she'd had enough moving about on trains for a while. She loved the hilly city and her new apartment, and had no desire to leave either.

"You're getting all sedentary," Carling teased over drinks.

"Oh my goodness," Sophie exclaimed. "What will I do without you? Only a few more months and you'll be gone." She might cry as the realization hit her she would be alone in San Francisco. It was almost like having to start over. Again.

"We'll be so close, nothing compared to how far away your family is."

Sophie felt more tears prick. Could her music be everything for her? Was it worth missing out on her family? And the unbearable question that always cropped up in her mind—had her musical gift cost her Riley?

"Oh, dear," Carling got up and came around the table to hug her. "Sorry, that was stupid."

Sophie dabbed at her eyes. "No, it's fine. I'm all weepy today. Let's discuss the music for your wedding. That'll cheer me up."

"Did someone say 'wedding'?" Egbert asked, sitting down. "I have the license right here." He patted his pocket. "And I have great news. We have the title to the land in Sonoma, and it has a farmhouse on it, maybe nice enough to be a little inn someday."

Carling squealed and threw her arms around Egbert.

"And to think, a year ago, I thought you were Mr. Hoity-Toity Stuffy."

"What?" Egbert looked shocked.

"I thought that, too, when I first met you," Sophie confessed. "Starch in your unmentionables, and all that."

Egbert turned red at the mere mention of his unmentionables. "I'll have to work on the impression I give to people when I'm a winemaker and an innkeeper."

"Go on with you," Carling said. "Just be you, and I'll handle the social niceties."

They dovetailed into the perfect pair. Like Charlotte and Reed, and Sarah and Doc. That was how it should be. She and Riley would never have had that. He was a country doctor and she needed a city orchestra. It was clearly for the best he hadn't fallen in love with her after all.

She stood. "I'm heading home. I've a long day of rehearsing tomorrow."

Carling shook her head. "I don't understand this rehearsing business. You spend hours practicing something you already know how to do. You already play piano better than anyone in the world, don't you?"

Sophie laughed. "Not quite the *whole* world."

"Yes, but nearly," her friend persisted. "Why do you have to spend hours rehearsing?"

"Because I can always get better and we learn new pieces for each concert. Also, because the orchestra has to be knit together."

"Knit?" Carling repeated.

"The way you and Egbert are." Sophie gestured to their two hands, firmly intertwined. "That's how the symphony orchestra has to play. Unless we rehearse, we run the risk of being discordant."

"Discordant?" Carling wrinkled up her nose.

"Yes. Imagine if Egbert wanted to grow grapes and you wanted to grow beets."

"Why would I grow beets?" Carling scoffed. "You can't drink beets!"

They all laughed. Sophie hugged her. "Beet wine, indeed!".

Carling smirked. "Get on with you, then."

Sophie walked slowly home. Discordant, indeed. Similar to how her brain and heart wrestled over the puzzle that was Riley. She could recall each of their encounters from the first day onward. Certainly, she'd believed it was a mutual attraction, a desire that grew and blossomed into something more.

Yet exactly when they could have had a real relationship, he ended it. He said he didn't love her, and she ought to believe him. If he had, then he wouldn't have left her behind in the city, would he?

It still alarmed her, how greatly she'd mistaken the depth of his feelings. Lately, if a man showed an interest in her, she was immediately doubtful.

"Miss Malloy," an unfamiliar voice broke into her thoughts, making her heart race, as she was putting her key in the lock.

Turning, wary due to her assault the previous year, Sophie recognized her neighbor's son.

"My mother sent me with this. We got it by mistake." He thrust a letter into her hand and ran off home before she could even thank him.

Thinking it most likely from one of her sisters, Sophie tucked it under her arm and headed inside. Five minutes later, with her hat, coat, and shoes off, a cup of coffee in hand, she sat on her sofa and looked at the envelope. Sarah!

For the second time, her heart sped up. Simply knowing Sarah was in the same town as Riley, working closely with him, made Sophie all kinds of curious. She sniffed the paper, imagining he might have stood somewhere nearby when she wrote it.

Good lord, she was a fool!

Snapping the cream paper open, she scanned the letter. Riley's name jumped off the page almost immediately, and she began to read. In fact, Sophie read and then reread the letter, her coffee forgotten and cold when she finally put the paper down. Certain sentences were irrevocably stuck in her head:

"Riley has turned out not to be a blessing after all. He is surly and makes mistakes he would never have made before he went away to school."

"The townsfolk avoid coming in on days when Doc is off. He doesn't see how we can possibly leave. Doc is at his wits' end."

"Everyone is sure it's because of Eliza breaking off their engagement, but I think you and I know better."

Sophie did know better. Eliza setting him free had made Riley happy. So, what had gone so terribly wrong? Sarah seemed to be hinting whatever it was had something to do with her. Could Sarah be right?

There was really only one way to find out.

CHAPTER TWENTY-FOUR

Sophie saw Riley long before he saw her. With the early spring sunshine warming her on the outside, the sight of him made her go all-over hot on the inside. He was sitting with a boy on a bench outside Doc's practice, and to her shock, he was yelling at him.

"Just give me your hand," Riley shouted.

The boy, whom Sophie recognized as Ely's son, Jack, apparently refused.

"This won't hurt, I'm telling you." Riley grabbed for the hand in question, which the boy snatched away. "It's only a goddamned splinter," Riley roared. And this time he succeeded in securing Jack's hand.

"Maaamaaaaa," Jack wailed.

"Jesus!" Riley swore.

Sophie found herself running toward them. At that rate, the town would lynch Riley sooner than they'd go to him for healing.

"Jack," she soothed when she got close enough. "Why is a big boy like you crying for his mother?" she asked, even though he was all of five years.

They both fell silent. Riley's and Jack's eyes were equally large and round and shocked.

"Why don't we go inside where Dr. Dalcourt can better look at your hand." Goodness but that sounded strange to her ears. *Dr. Dalcourt.* But utterly right, too. "And I'll find you a hard-boiled sweet to suck on if you're very good," Sophie added, knowing Sarah kept them in the drawer of her desk for the youngest patients.

"Sophie," Riley finally managed, as he and the boy stood up. "What in the hell are you doing here?"

"You'd better mind your language, doctor," she said and led the little boy inside. The office was vacant. "Where are Sarah and Doc?"

"A lady's having a baby," Riley muttered, "and wanted them both with her."

"But not you."

"No," he admitted, his jaw tight, "not me."

She hefted Jack onto a table, and he obediently held out his hand. She turned it over and saw the wooden shard, tiny and sharp. "Good thing, or this little man would have to spend the whole day with a splinter in his palm."

She turned to Riley, who seemed mesmerized by her presence, standing stock-still and staring at her. In truth, she felt lightheaded. It was truly *that* good to see him, despite how they'd parted and despite his current display of uncharacteristic ill-temper. If he would let her, she would gladly smooth his brow with her fingers.

"Well, doctor?" She gestured toward Jack.

"I want Doc," Jack protested.

What on God's green earth had Riley done to turn the citizens of Spring City against him? He had seemed to be a favored son when she was there before.

"Doc is out," Riley said. "You got me."

Sophie sighed. "Jack, Dr. Dalcourt specializes in splinters. Let him take it out."

The boy still looked unconvinced. Sophie added, "How about you let him do it for my sake, so I can give you that sweet?"

Jack thought about it for a moment and then nodded, stuck out his hand in Riley's direction and scrunched up his face, eyelids firmly closed.

Riley rolled his eyes, but then, with the tweezers he already held in his hand, he removed the splinter in a heartbeat.

Jack remained frozen.

"You're all done," Riley said gruffly, lifting Jack off the table before he'd even opened his eyes. "Now get."

"Wait," Sophie said, finding the sweets in Sarah's desk. She held out the white wax-paper bag. "Why don't you take two for being such a brave boy?"

At last, Jack smiled and reached in the bag for his reward.

"Thank you, ma'am," he said, and he fled.

"Jesus," Riley said again. "How about 'thanks, Dr. Dalcourt'?"

"Indeed." She'd seen it for herself—a bad-tempered Riley—or she'd never have believed it. "What is going on?"

He stared at her. "Why don't *you* tell me what's going on? What are you doing here?"

He didn't sound pleased to see her at all. With her mouth suddenly dry, she swallowed and decided to be truthful.

"I got a letter from Sarah, basically saying you're a disaster."

"Shit!" Riley heaved himself onto the table and sat, head slightly bowed. "If that doesn't beat all."

"They're not going to go traveling and turn over Doc's practice to you, not as things stand. Can you blame them?"

"Nope." Then he lifted his head and looked at her directly, "but they'll go all right. I just need to slap on a smile and hand out the sweets."

He sounded so unlike himself. So jaded—yet he'd only been a doctor for a matter of months! Despite what he'd said to her in the coat closet at The Grand, she ached for him. Now, with his gaze locked on hers, she was transfixed.

"Isn't this what you've always wanted to do?" she asked, her voice softened by the longing that was starting to slide through her. Looking to where his hands gripped the table on either side of his muscled thighs, she wanted to close her own hands over his.

"Don't look at me that way?" he ordered.

She jumped at his harsh tone, but clung to the memory of a sweeter, gentler Riley. His feet hit the floor, and he closed the space between them.

"You shouldn't have come here. You can't help me." His voice was thick with unspoken emotion.

Her heart was breaking all over again, but this time, for his sake.

"Please, Riley, tell me what's going on. You remind me of a story I read as a little girl, about a lion with a thorn in its paw. The pain made him very angry, and he lashed out at everyone, until a slave came along and removed the thorn."

"Is that what you're here to do?" He lowered his voice as he took another step bring him nearly up against her. She had to look up at his handsome face, with its unfamiliar, stubble-covered jaw.

She didn't answer. Reaching up, she grazed his unshaven cheek with her palm before she realized what she was doing. And he captured her hand in his own. They stared at one another.

Her emotions were evident on her face and in her eyes. Riley would know she had no pride, could plainly see she loved him despite everything. However, it was an answering look on his own face that made her heart twist, even as it gave her a spark of hope.

"No," he ground out, denying what he was about to do before his mouth claimed hers. He released her hand, and she wrapped her arms around his warm, strong body, leaned against his hard, muscled frame, and felt she was home.

"No," he said again, against her lips before he forced hers open so he could deepen the kiss, far beyond what was appropriate in Doc Cuthins' surgical practice. His arms held her close, enveloping her in everything Riley, including his vanilla soap.

Embarrassingly, Sophie whimpered.

How could she live without this man? The question itself embarrassed her, too, even as his tongue touched hers.

What kind of nineteenth-century, independent-minded woman was she, to think such a thought? Yet, when his hands roamed down her back and he parted his thighs slightly so he could bring her in even closer, she had no answer.

The door swung open beside them.

"Oh, my!" said Jessie, still wearing her apron from Fuller's. "What in the world! Is that you, Sophie? Why, what . . . ? I mean, is Doc here?"

By this time, Sophie and Riley were standing a respectable three feet apart, both red-faced and breathing heavily.

"What do you need, Jessie?" Riley asked gruffly.

"I burned my forearm a little, but I can see you're busy." She started to back out.

"I was about to leave," Sophie assured her, despite how obvious it was she'd been doing no such thing.

"No," Jessie protested. "It's okay. I'll wait until—"

"Until Doc gets back," Riley finished, his voice thin, sounding tired.

"Well, that is . . . yes."

Sophie had to speak up. "Riley is a good doctor, Jessie. He attended one of the finest schools in the country. I think you can trust him to handle a kitchen burn."

"I couldn't last time," she said flatly.

Sophie looked from Jessie to Riley.

"I'm sorry," he said with a shrug. "I used the wrong ointment."

"It stung like the devil," Jessie protested.

"Burns will sting," he said cavalierly.

"Riley!" Sophie scolded. "Jessie, I'm sure he's got the right medicine now. Some lanolin balm, perhaps."

"Aloe," he corrected, looking at her. "With some acetylsalicylic acid and a little laudanum to deaden the pain," Riley added, sounding more like himself.

Still looking doubtful, Jessie let Sophie lead her to the inner surgery, with Riley following. Then she pulled up her sleeve to show a sore-looking red mark on her arm.

"A steam burn, would you believe? But I panicked and rubbed at it with my kitchen towel. Plum took the skin off."

"We're going to clean that first, so you don't get infected," Riley said. He talked to Jessie all the while he treated and dressed the burn.

Sophie watched him. He was calm, competent, and caring, the way he'd been during the train accident, and she couldn't imagine how the people of Spring City weren't thrilled to have him.

Jessie was nearly out the door, when she turned and said, "You can go back to what you were doing when I came in." She smiled at their mortified faces before adding, "It seems to have helped him no end."

After Jessie left, they both remained silent a moment.

At last, Riley asked, "Are you staying at the Sanborn place again?"

"Yes." Although she hadn't let Sarah know she was coming, so there would be no prepared bed and stocked pantry like the time before.

"I'll take you over," Riley offered.

"No," Sophie said, putting up her hand. "I'll make my own way. You need to be here in case you get any more patients, right?"

She was backing away, needing distance from him. "I'll speak to you later. If you see Sarah—"

She stopped and stared at him.

He half-smiled. "I'll tell her you're here, so she can start cooking."

She nearly had the door closed when he asked, "Sophie, how long are you staying?"

She hesitated. "A couple days, at the most." By her reaction to him, she knew it couldn't be longer or she'd never be able to leave. Even now, she could feel how painful it was going to be.

After Sophie shut the door, Riley counted to five and then whooped with joy. God, it was good to see her again. Better than good, it was incredible. He felt instantly alive and happy, carefree, and nearly singing like a wren in nesting season. The very same room and the exact same town that had been confining and drab and colorless, at that moment was exciting, simply because he knew she was near.

He had to shake his head, almost fearing she was a vision conjured up by his lonely, desperate brain. He still could barely believe Sophie had been standing there a moment earlier.

Over the past weeks, he'd resigned himself to never setting eyes on her beloved face again, and that reality had darkened every waking moment since he'd returned to Spring. Now, he was counting down the minutes until he could close the door for the night and see her again. He steadfastly refused to think past one plain and simple fact—Sophie was in town.

For the time being, he wouldn't acknowledge how nothing had changed regarding their impossible situation. She was there, and that was all that mattered.

His facial muscles actually hurt a few hours later because he'd been smiling so much for the first time in ages. Making sure the lamps were down and the medicine all locked away, he secured the door behind him.

Riley paused. He wanted to run straight to the Sanborn house, but he knew what would happen. He would take her in his arms, and then they'd be goners. It would be easier to catch a weasel asleep than to keep his hands off her, and it would be entirely his fault. She would only be there a couple of days, and he'd have to live with being a cold-hearted, selfish cad all over again.

How many times could he break her heart? Not to mention his own.

He went to Drake's barn where his horse was stabled and saddled him quickly. With supreme effort, he rode past where Sophie was staying and out toward his own homestead, unable to keep from turning his head, though, and looking for a sign of her.

Sure enough, lights were on and smoke was coming from her chimney. As he rode, he pictured her inside, playing on the upright piano. Maybe waiting for him to stop by.

Hell! It couldn't hurt to go say hello and hear the news from . . . He nearly thought of San Francisco as home. He *had* to stop doing that. Anyway, he'd promised to tell Sarah that Sophie was in Spring, and he hadn't yet done so. She probably had nothing to eat. He could at least take her to Fuller's for supper.

No harm in that, was there? He turned his horse around.

CHAPTER TWENTY-FIVE

Sophie had been waiting in the utter quietness of Charlotte's old house, tense as a cat on a floating log. She hadn't changed from her traveling clothes or hardly moved from the piano stool in hours. She missed the sounds of the city and wondered how she would ever sleep that night with so much vast emptiness around her.

Then he knocked.

Takin a breath to steady herself, she let it out slowly. He didn't love her. Plainly, he lusted for her, but he didn't love her. Knowing that, she could be strong enough to resist him. Then why was she really in Spring City?

She opened the door, and the sight of him sent a sizzling jolt right through her. Nothing fancy, just his narrow-lapelled sack coat and slim-fitted trousers, but it was the way his shoulders filled out the jacket and the way—she gulped—the way his pants fit over his rock-hard thighs.

Lord, have mercy!

He clutched his black hat in his hands and stared back at her.

"Come on in," she stepped aside, ignoring the clamoring of her body. It seemed the whole brass section was sounding at once.

"I thought you might be hungry," he said, not moving an inch forward but putting his hat firmly back on his head.

Surprised, she nodded. "I am. This place is completely cleaned out."

"Keeps away the rodents," he said, rocking back on his booted heels, hands in his pockets.

Hm. Silence. They stared at one another.

"Did you bring me something to eat?" she asked into the charged atmosphere.

"Nope."

She blinked. "Thanks."

"I thought we could go to Fuller's. Or even Ada's saloon. She makes some good chicken."

She took a couple steps backward.

"What about . . . I mean, everyone knows you were only recently engaged. What will they say if they see us together?"

"Hell, Jessie's already told everyone by now what she saw today. They'll figure we were having a flirtation when you were here before, or that we waited until I was free and are having one now."

She blushed. "A flirtation?"

"Whatever they'll call it. And I guess we were, at that."

"And now?" She bit her tongue. Why did she ask him that so blatantly? Was she inviting another "flirtation"?

His eyes darkened. "And now we're not. Look, Sophie, I'm sorry I grabbed you earlier. I wasn't thinking straight, if you know what I mean. I was so shocked you were here."

She watched him swallow hard and his jaw tighten, before he continued, "I'm offering you dinner between friends. All right?"

No, not all right. But she'd come all this way, and she'd helped him with Jack and with Jessie. Perhaps he did need a friend and would open up to her about whatever was eating away at him and making him the scourge of Spring City.

"All right. Let's go have some dinner, seeing as you're all scrubbed up."

She poked her hand into his stomach teasingly as she passed him, pausing long enough to get her cloak from the hall stand. That was the sole contact she permitted herself, except when he gave her his hand to climb into his wagon. She felt him squeeze her fingers ever so lightly before he released her, and they went in companionable silence to Ada's Saloon.

Sophie had not been inside before. A few men sat at the bar, leaning over, nursing their glasses of beer or whiskey, but no one else dined at the tables, which were small with mismatched chairs. A bartender wiped glasses on a rag, and a woman stood by the bar, young, scantily dressed with her face heavily made up. She stared at them as they entered.

Compared to the places Sophie had seen in San Francisco's red-light district on that fateful night, this looked like a church gathering.

"Riley," called a female voice belonging to another woman who rose from a stool at the far end of the bar.

Sophie assumed this was Ada, who sauntered over, dressed provocatively, although with kitchen stains on her satin gown. It was a strange combination of homey and harlotry, if she ever saw one.

"You got your pick, tonight," she said, eyes only for him, jerking her thumb at the tables behind her, as if on other nights the tables would be full. Not taking her gaze off Riley, she led them over to one, her rear end performing an exaggerated sashay, no doubt for his benefit.

Sophie didn't miss the way Ada eyed him appreciatively. How could she blame her? It wouldn't take long before another woman stepped into his fiancée's shoes, one whom he could share passion with in the way he hadn't with Eliza.

"I know what you're having, Riley," Ada said, familiarly, leaning down and exposing her ample cleavage above her low neckline.

Well, it was a saloon after all, Sophie mused.

Ada finally glanced at Sophie, "What'll you have, honey? Chicken or chicken?" She laughed at her own joke.

"We'll both have the roast chicken and potatoes," Riley said. "And a bottle of red."

Ada gave him a long look, then she sniffed. "Coming up." She strolled away with the same swaying saunter.

"I don't get a choice in the matter, I suppose," Sophie said.

"Not here. There's one good thing on the menu. Take it or leave it. Come to think of it, there isn't even a menu."

Sophie smiled at his joke, but couldn't help remarking, "She likes you."

Ada was older than them, but not by much. Perhaps she wouldn't make a good doctor's wife, at least, not one who greeted the patients and ran the office. But at least Ada wouldn't want to leave Spring City, not while she had her own business establishment.

He looked at her curiously. "Ada likes *every* man," he assured her. "And if you weren't with me, she'd be offering me dessert in her room upstairs. Hell, she might do that anyway," he added, shooting her a lopsided grin.

Sophie bit her bottom lip. "Would you go? Upstairs, I mean, if I weren't here?"

Thunderstruck, he grimaced. "Jesus, woman, that would be begging for trouble. The answer is absolutely no. Not if I know what's good for me and for my health."

Sophie got the message. But some men in this town had to partake of Ada's "dessert." Otherwise, with so few customers, how could she afford to keep the place open?

"Are you sure the food is safe to eat?"

He chuckled. "I've been eating here since I was in my teen years. Hasn't killed me yet. Ada takes pride in her one dish."

"Chicken," they both said at the same time.

Then they laughed. Sophie loved hearing his laughter. This was the Riley Spring City knew and loved.

She let him pour her a glass of wine, and then folding her hands around the stem, she decided to take the bull by the horns. "Why have you been such a bear?"

"A bear?" he asked, casually, but he put his head down to sip his wine, not looking her in the eye.

"Yes, you know all growly and mean, so half of Spring City hates you and the other half fears you."

Shaking his head slightly, he said, "I don't think I'm that bad."

"Bad enough for Sarah to mention it in a letter to me. Bad enough Doc is cancelling their trip."

He shrugged. "I'll talk to them tomorrow. No sense them doing that. People are simply used to Doc." Riley drummed his fingers on the table. "They'll get used to me."

"To you yelling at scared little boys?"

"That was a mistake."

"Speaking of which, it sounds as though you've been making some of them recently. Medical ones, according to Jessie, and in Sarah's letter."

"I'm a good doctor," he flared, raising his voice.

"I didn't say you weren't."

"Apparently, people here don't think so." He gave the table a thump with his open palm. "And I'm giving up everything for them."

Now, that was an interesting statement. "What do you mean?"

Riley took a long swig from his wine glass and shut the conversation down.

"Nothing."

The food came, and they lapsed into silence for a bit.

"You were right, the chicken is good here," she said.

"Not quite The Palace dining room," he quipped.

"Definitely not." Back on neutral ground, she said, "I didn't tell you, Carling and Egbert are getting married."

He nodded thoughtfully. "They seem made for each other."

"That's what I think, too. And we stayed with David and Julie Burris, as you recommended, when we went to Sonoma. They were lovely people. Very helpful to Egbert."

"They're really going to start a winery?"

"That's their dream, or at least, it's Egbert's. And Carling is more than happy to share it. Wherever her man goes, she goes," Sophie said teasingly, but the shadow that crossed Riley's face drove the smile from her own.

"What's wrong?" Unthinkingly, she reached across the table and touched his hand.

He jumped but didn't pull away. Instead, he stared down at her soft, pale hand over his own larger one, and then he stroked her knuckles with his thumb, sending shivers racing through her.

It was too easy to imagine him stroking other parts of her. Too easy to remember being in his arms, nearly helpless with the pleasure he gave her. Slowly, Sophie pulled her hand away, resting it in her lap. He hadn't answered her question, and it appeared he didn't intend to.

"I better get you home," he said, standing up abruptly.

"Sophie, are you in there?" A voice carried up the stairs waking her. Carling, she thought, confused for a moment. No, it was Sarah!

Glancing outside, Sophie saw the sun was high in the sky. Grabbing her dressing gown, she raced downstairs and found Sarah standing in the middle of the hall.

"Sorry to barge in, but you didn't answer the door. Riley said you were here. No food, no bed made up." She looked distraught.

"I'm fine," Sophie assured her. "I found clean sheets and blankets last night. And I ate at Ada's with Riley." She wondered if Sarah would have an opinion on that.

Sarah wrinkled her nose. "I haven't been inside for years. How was it?"

"The chicken was good. The atmosphere was not."

"How about the company?"

So, Sarah was interested in her dining companion.

Sophie hesitated. Did Sarah hold any animosity toward her for her "flirtation" with Riley while he was still engaged? She didn't think so. But plainly, Sarah cared about Riley and about her town.

"He is miserable, from what I can tell."

Sarah nodded. "I'll put the kettle on. Why don't you go get dressed? I've brought some food. We can have a late breakfast or an early lunch, and a good chat."

Sophie hoped it wasn't going to turn into a lecture or a scolding. Nevertheless, she went upstairs obediently and was back down in minutes to find the coffee made and sandwiches on the table.

"I guess I slept through breakfast this morning. That's not like me," Sophie began, feeling a bit shy suddenly.

"You probably had a lot on your mind last night."

That was an understatement. Sophie was grateful for what Riley had done after he'd brought her home. He'd practically shoved her through Charlotte's front door and pulled it firmly closed behind her. She'd heard his boots go crashing down the steps, and then he was gone.

She'd made up the bed and then taken the time to heat up water for a soothing bath, knowing sleep would evade her if she lay down immediately. Even so, it had been the wee hours before she'd finally drifted off.

"Thanks for writing me the letter. I don't like to think of him being unhappy. He's a good man and a good doctor."

"You wouldn't know that by the people of Spring."

"But remember how he was during the train accident?" Sophie pushed.

"Of course, I do, and many years before that. I know his skill, as well as Doc does. But he's been a changed man since he got back from San Francisco. It's as if he doesn't care about anything or anyone, not even himself. He doesn't even ride that blasted horse of his anymore."

That did shock Sophie. Riding long and hard was Riley's primary enjoyment.

"That's the answer, then. He probably has all sorts of pent-up energy and needs time galloping out in the open spaces or riding up in the foothills."

"Doc told him that, but he doesn't listen. When Riley's not on duty, he stays in his house. That's why I wrote you the letter. You have to put him out of his misery."

Sophie stopped with her cup halfway to her lips. "Excuse me?"

"I don't know what happened in San Francisco, dear, but you have to take him back. He loves you."

Too many things were wrong with what Sarah was saying. Sophie started to shake her head, but the older woman set her cup down with a thump.

"Please, Sophie. When Eliza broke it off with him, I never saw a happier man. He went charging out of here, ready to claim you. It was clear as day to me and Doc. And then, instead, the only happy news I heard was that he'd passed his exams and was coming back a licensed doctor."

Sarah released a long sigh. "Until he got off the train alone, I was certain he was surprising us by bringing you back as his bride."

Sophie's eyes had grown increasingly wider until she put her head in her hands and groaned.

Sarah stroke her head. "He's a good man," she said.

Sophie's breath felt ragged. She wanted to cry, this was so downright confusing. Instead, she raised her head.

"I cannot take him back because he was never mine."

"I don't understand." Sarah had a frown on her face perfectly mirroring Sophie's confusion.

"I don't either," Sophie agreed. Riley, alone, had those answers. "He never asked for my hand or declared his love. Well, he did once, but then, he changed his mind."

"Does he seem like a man who changed his mind?"

"Are you saying he's behaving this way because he loves me?"

"Pining for you, more like," Sarah guessed. "Missing you with an ache as big as his heart. Why, I saw more sparks between you and him in the short time you were here than I ever did between him and Eliza."

Sophie knew a thing or two about those sparks. She blushed.

"See, I was right." Sarah had a knowing glint in her eye.

"But I'm leaving soon," Sophie protested. "I have to go back. I have rehearsals and another concert in a week."

"Then I don't know what will happen after you've gone, but I know ol' Webster sent telegrams to two hospitals requesting a doctor come apply for town physician. He was that upset about how Riley treated Anna last week."

"I hadn't heard about that. What happened?"

"Anna came to the surgery, all in a tizzy, 'cause she thought she'd been bit by a rattlesnake. Nasty looking red mark on her leg. Riley started treating her, but when Doc came in, he took over so Riley could go find the snake, right where she said she'd cut its head off with a shovel."

Sophie cringed. Charlotte had told her about that particular method of protection, but she'd not seen a rattler and hoped to God she never would.

"When Riley got back, he was all yelling about the foolishness of women, and Anna started crying. He said it would serve her right if she died from fright. Then he dumped out the dead, headless snake right on the table next to the poor girl and said, 'It's a damn harmless bull snake.' And he walked right out of there. I saw it all myself."

Sarah refilled her coffee cup. "I tell you it took me a good while to get Anna to stop crying, and Doc was flabbergasted at his behavior. Webster was hopping mad, and still is."

Sophie had seen him with young Jack and had no doubt it was all true. However, she remembered his kindness with her when her hand was injured. It hadn't been a life-threatening injury at all, but he'd been patient and caring.

"He was never this way this before, though, was he?"

"Like I said, he's a different man, ever since he returned from San Fran. And unfortunately, no one likes him. No one blames Eliza, at this rate, either."

"I guess I better talk to him," Sophie offered. "I tried last night, but he got defensive."

"Webster's got a doctor coming to see if she—yes, *she*— likes the town enough to live here, so if Riley wants to keep his job, you'd better turn him around, right quick."

CHAPTER TWENTY-SIX

Sophie used Sarah's wagon to reach the Dalcourt homestead about twenty minutes out of town. In the mild weather, she could have walked, but it would have been a long journey, and she might be coming home after sundown. In any case, the rattlesnake story had given her pause about walking past the outskirts of town, such as it was.

Mr. Dalcourt, the elder, certainly must prefer his isolation, she thought, as she left any semblance of a road. All around her were the wide-open spaces Riley loved to ride. The grass was a yellowish-green after the long winter, and the sky was a cloudless blue. There were red scrubby plants, although she had no idea what they were, and plenty of white flowers. Foothills stretched away to bigger mountains in the distance.

It was beautiful and enormous, and it made Sophie want to run for the nearest cable car. Except there weren't any. She felt about an inch tall and a bit panicky. Yes, she decided, she preferred the paved streets of Boston or the masses of people in San Francisco.

Following Sarah's directions of landmarks—a large pine and a juniper, an old fence, and a strangely shaped boulder—at last, she saw a small, white house seeming to be growing out of the landscape, along with a barn. More pine trees shaded a fenced paddock, and a windmill was turning lazily. Riley's horse grazed behind the fence, keeping company with two others. There was also a goat grazing nearby. It looked at her idly as she halted the wagon and got down from the seat.

Suddenly, her hands were sweaty and her heart was pounding. This new Riley who yelled and thumped the table was daunting. But she didn't fear him. Not really. *Just a lion with a thorn.*

Swallowing, Sophie wiped her hands on her dress, arranged her bonnet that had fallen sideways, and walked up to the front door.

She knocked and waited. Silence. She knocked again. Should she be feeling as relieved as she did? She could turn around, go back to town, and tell Sarah she'd tried. But then Riley would lose his job, not to mention the respect of everyone in town.

She bit her lip. Where could he be? He wasn't in town. She knew that because she'd ridden right through it to get to Riley's. Besides, his horse was there. Three of them, in fact. He could have another one, she supposed, and be out riding. Or perhaps he was sleeping.

The thought of him in bed made her prickly and nervous. Riley's bed! What did it look like?

She tried the knob. It turned easily in her hand, and she pushed the door open.

"Riley," she called out. "It's Sophie." Still nothing. A thief could walk right in, but she guessed he didn't worry too much about anyone happening upon his place, way out there.

Venturing inside, she realized she was tiptoeing at first and started to walk with heavy feet, making as much noise as possible. If he was upstairs, she didn't want to startle him. He might come down shooting.

The house was very similar in style to Charlotte's home. She bypassed the empty front parlor and went down the hallway to the kitchen, which was also empty. Out the window was a beautiful view of the mountains. Then Sophie's gaze drifted over to a small wooden structure, and it dawned on her it was an outhouse.

Good God! If Charlotte's house hadn't had a real water-closet upstairs, why, Sophie feared she wouldn't have stayed even for a day. She was not the pioneering type!

Turning away, she considered venturing upstairs, merely to take a peek. Right then, she felt the hair on the back of her neck stand up, and at the same time, she heard boots on the back step.

"Sarah," Riley said coming in. He stopped short when he saw Sophie in his kitchen.

They stared at one another a moment.

"I borrowed her wagon and her horse, too, of course," Sophie said, clutching at her skirts nervously with both hands, needing something to hold onto. Indeed, the room seemed to shrink with his presence and tilt with the sudden rush of blood to her head. "Sorry to barge in. I knocked. More than once."

"I was in the barn," he said. That was obvious. His clothes were grimy and pieces of straw stuck in his hair. He had dirty streaks on his face and a cloth tied around his neck to catch the sweat. He looked more appealing than ever.

"I didn't think to look there," she admitted. "Not yet. I mean, I only just arrived."

He wasn't smiling. In fact, he hadn't moved an inch farther inside his own house. But he did close the door and lean against it, legs crossed at his ankles, arms crossed over his chest.

He looked utterly forbidding, Sophie thought.

"Why did you come? Does Doc need me?" he asked.

"No. I came to talk to you."

"About?" he prompted without warmth.

"About whatever is going on with you. Sarah said—"

"Sarah sent you?" He made a sound of disgust and pushed away from the door. He wrenched off first one boot, then the other, and dropped them onto the varnished wooden floor.

She shrank aside as he approached her, but he went to the sink, pumped the handle, and started washing his hands. She heard him sigh, and when he was done, he just stared out the window while he dried them, leaving a bunch of dirty streaks on the kitchen towel.

Finally, he turned to face her again, his lustrous eyes so deep she could fall right into them.

"What did Sarah say?" he asked.

She couldn't tell him all Sarah had said, in case Doc's wife was plain wrong about Riley's feelings.

"She said you're acting differently than you did before you went away the last time."

He shrugged. "We went over this at Ada's last night. I'll talk to Doc later."

She hugged herself. "It may be too late for that."

"What do you mean?"

"Mr. Webster has an open invitation to any doctor who'll come fill the position. And already someone's coming to answer his request."

"Well, damn." Riley ran his hand up the back of his head. "I don't think Doc's really going to replace me, but I owe it to him to do better. I'll do whatever the good people of Spring want."

"What the people of Spring City want," Sophie tried again, "is for you to be happy."

He shook his head. "That's not going to be easy."

"Why?" she asked.

He stared hard at her a moment, then seemed to dismiss her question. "Are you staying long? 'Cause I need to take a bath."

"Are you refusing to talk to me?"

"Suit yourself and stay." He put on a large kettle and two pots of water to boil. Then he opened a cupboard and dragged out a tin washtub. Sophie's mouth opened.

"No bathroom upstairs," he drawled. "My parents weren't quite as modern as the Sanborns or just about anyone else in town, for that matter." He removed his dirty neckerchief with a tug.

Poor, unfortunate Mrs. Dalcourt, was all Sophie could think. Riley's mother hadn't any luxuries to speak of. Come to think of it, whomever Riley took for a wife probably would be expected to live there. Except Eliza. Sophie couldn't picture the tidy blond woman bathing in the kitchen. If he'd married her, they would most likely have lived in the Prentice home in town. Besides, his parents still lived there sometimes, didn't they?

She had no more time to ask questions because he was stripping off his dirty shirt faster than she could blink. Suddenly, she was staring at his rippling flat stomach and the barest amount of dusky hair tapering right down to his—

"Riley!" she warned, but he undid his belt and put his hands to the button fly of his denim pants. Since she remained standing there, watching him, he shrugged and opened a button, then another, and she started to see more dark hair. In fact, she could tell he wore nothing under his blue-jean trousers.

Sophie fled before any more skin or anything else was exposed. She was sure she heard him laugh at her.

Well, he wouldn't get rid of her that easily. From the front hall, she listened for the sounds of water hitting the tin tub and then heard him splashing as he bathed. She paced the hall, sat a moment in the parlor on a worn chair, and then paced some more. At last, she heard his footsteps and turned when he opened the kitchen door.

"Sweet mother!" she muttered, as he stood there in nothing but a small, bleached-white towel, with his damp, brown hair curling everywhere on his head at once. Everything else was flesh and muscle. She hadn't seen that much of him in any of their previous encounters, and she couldn't stop gawking.

His body was the exact likeness of the statue of David she'd seen in Florence, not to mention any number of paintings of Adonis. Not that she'd ever say such a thing to fill his head.

Even the light hair on his strong arms and muscled legs fascinated her. She wanted to run her hand over it and over his sculpted chest, where it ridged down to his waist. She recalled the feel of his firm chest from their encounter in her hotel room. That was all she'd had the chance to caress before he'd deflowered her.

He didn't look like he wanted her to caress him right then, though. If she had to name his expression, it would be annoyance.

"It's not polite to stare," he rasped.

But she only stared harder when she thought she saw his towel move, all of its own accord. Then she swallowed.

"If you're going to prance around—"

"—in my *own* house. And, Sophie, I don't prance."

"Still," she said, blushing red and unable to keep her eyes from roaming over his body, and then her mind went blank.

"I was in such a hurry to get clean, I didn't get any clothes from upstairs, or even a bath towel. Besides, I wasn't sure you were still here."

"I think you knew I was here," she countered.

He tilted his head. "Maybe I hoped you weren't."

That stung, and without warning, she felt tears in her eyes. Crying was the last thing she wanted to do in front of him. He didn't want her in his home. He didn't want to talk to her. She couldn't help him anyway, and she had no idea what would make a man happy.

Turning away, already blinded by her unshed tears, she made it to the front door, hand on the knob, when she realized he was close behind her. For a second, his fingers rested very lightly on her shoulder, before he pulled away quickly.

"I'm sorry," he said, his voice so low and rough, it sounded raw. "You shouldn't have come here, not alone."

She nodded, but she had no idea what he was talking about. She didn't fear him. How could she? But she couldn't face him either, not while on the verge of breaking down. She pressed her free hand to the door frame and rested her forehead against it.

"I'm sorry," he said again, but he hadn't moved an inch away from her.

She knew she had to leave before she broke down completely and embarrassed herself. But in the next instant, she was enveloped in Riley's arms, pulled back against him, his torso plastered against her back. She felt him press his face into her hair. Then he was motionless, except for the throbbing of his warm body, answered by the strumming in her ears of her own coursing blood.

Despite his bath, he held the scent of leather and sunshine, mixed with his vanilla soap. Utterly intoxicated, she nearly relaxed into his embrace. Then his words replayed in her brain: *Maybe I hoped you weren't.*

With the back of her hand, she dashed at the tears that began to fall. *Damnit.* No more tears over men, she told herself sternly, trying desperately to get control. He turned her gently in his arms, then raised her pale face to his, groaning at what he saw.

"Sophie, don't cry," he whispered. And he kissed the path of a tear down her face until he was at the corner of her mouth. "Not over me. I'm not worth it."

Shocked he would say such a thing, she pulled back. "Of course you are."

"I've treated you badly," he said, "from beginning to end. You were an unattainable shooting star, and I had no business roping you in." His eyes stared into hers, warm, intelligent, and haunted. "But I couldn't leave you alone. I had to know you and talk to you." He paused and then he ran his hand over her cheek. "And touch you."

She could barely breathe.

Slipping his other hand behind her head, he cradled it in his large palm before pulling her mouth against his. His kiss was sweet and desperate, filled with all the yearning they both felt.

His words filled her ears but made no sense. The only thing that made sense was how she felt in his arms. She returned his kiss, returned his touch, slipping her hands into his damp hair. Then his towel moved again, low against her stomach. She pressed against his erection and moaned, hearing his answering growl.

In a swift movement, he lifted her into his arms. Silently, he carried her up the stairs to his room. She didn't notice the surroundings, until she felt the bed under her back and his fingers at the buttons of her blouse. She did notice he'd lost his towel along the way and was, for the first time, buck naked in front of her.

She sucked in her breath. *Was a more magnificent sight ever beheld?*

In a few minutes, she was as bare as he was. He'd even removed all the pins from her hair, so it fell around her shoulders and pillowed her head. They had nothing between them but what they'd come into the world with. And then they started to explore.

He was bolder than her, at first, kissing a tingling trail down her arched neck and between her breasts. He didn't linger at her nipples, but went down to her bellybutton, dropping a kiss on it before inserting his tongue. She giggled.

She sobered up with lightning speed when he went lower. His mouth explored her, as if she were a delicacy, dropping kisses all along one thigh and calf and ankle, then all the way up the other side. All the while, he rested one hand almost lazily over one of her breasts and with his other hand, he began to play her body with earnest, until she breathed out his name.

Feeling as though she were sizzling with her desire for this man, she tugged at him, demanding to feel his whole hard body over her. It was the only thing that stopped her from floating away, she thought, parting her legs so Riley could settle between them.

He covered her mouth with his own, kissing her deeply, and she grabbed his hair with both hands, holding him, afraid he would disappear—or change his mind—the moment she let him go. Until she looked into his eyes and knew he wasn't going to change his mind this time.

No words passed between them as he rose and put on protection. She couldn't help watching, her gaze roaming up and down his body and settling on his shaft.

Rejoining her on the bed, he ran his hand over her taut stomach and then bent to kiss her nipple, stopping to suck first one, then the other, as his fingers played over the curls between her legs.

"*Mm*," she said, pressing up against his hand.

"*Mm*," he answered against her breast. His finger slipped between her silken petals and she gasped. Clearly, she was ready for him, and he didn't make either of them wait any longer. Pressing his arousal to her core, he slid gently inside her.

"*Mm*," she sighed again. And then, "*ohh*" as he went deeper, filling her, stretching her.

He rested on his forearms, his hips moving back and forth, and she easily matched his pace, delighting in the sensation as he drew back almost all the way out of her and then surged forward. He kissed her again and again, moving his tongue in sweet mimicry of his lower body.

The feelings swept over her like chords of music, vibrating through her entire frame. And then the tempo increased, and she had to hang on to him, her fingers sliding from his shoulders to his waist. His lips found the pulse at her neck, rasping her skin with his teeth.

"Sophie," he said, his voice hoarse and strained.

"Yes?" she asked, equally breathless.

"God knows I love you."

She heard an eagle cry overhead as their crescendo built. Her entire body was coiling like a spring. Gliding his hand between their bodies, he lightly slid a finger between the sensitive folds, touching her where she throbbed.

Climaxing fully, intensely, her body clenched and unclenched, squeezing around his hard shaft, milking him. A moment later, he pumped faster, surging into her before he peaked.

Afterward, his whole body seemed to grow even hotter and become spineless, as he melted onto her, seemingly spent. When Sophie thought she might have to poke him to let her breathe, he rolled to the side. She watched him remove the protection and place it on his bedside table.

Her heart was quivering along with the rest of her, on the brink between joy and sadness. All the pain he'd given her, she now knew could have been avoided.

"You lied," she declared. He did love her. "Why did you do it?"

Riley lay back down and pulled a blanket over them both.

"You know why," he said. He rolled on his back and put his arm over his eyes. "Can you imagine living here?"

"With you?" she asked, surprised.

"Yup, right here in Spring City. In this very house."

She hesitated, and he laughed abruptly and without humor.

"That's what I thought," he said.

"Wait. You didn't give me a chance," she protested, trying to think through the idea. No San Francisco Symphony, no exquisite grand piano, no orchestra to play with. The thoughts stole her breath away.

On the other hand, she'd have Riley, every day. His smile, his eyes, his sense of humor, his intelligence, his company. Could she live for him alone?

"Are you asking me to marry you?"

"No," he fairly grunted his reply. Then silence, but he wasn't trying to hurt her. Her whole body still tingled with how much he loved her.

"You won't ask me to marry you?"

"That's right. You might talk yourself into it, and then you'd hate me."

"I wouldn't," she protested.

"Well, *I* would hate me. I've seen you perform, heard your music in that concert hall. That's where you belong, on the stage. That's what you're supposed to do with your life."

She'd always felt that was the case. However, she didn't like him making the decision for her.

"I could perhaps teach piano here."

He snorted. "Where? On Charlotte Sanborn's old piano? Or, maybe you didn't notice the little upright at Ada's. The only time I've heard it is when some guy drinks too much and backs Ada up against it. Her butt plays two octaves."

She puffed out her disapproval. He wasn't making it easy. "I could have my own piano shipped from Boston. I could set up a music school."

He rolled over onto his side and rested his head on his arm, looking directly at her.

"Sophie, I know you would try to make it work. But, in case you haven't noticed, Spring City has a couple hundred people. Plenty to keep me busy, but very few who'll be interested in piano lessons, or who could afford it."

"You lied to get rid of me?"

He traced a finger over her cheek and down her throat, stopping in the hollow between her breasts before he looked up at her again.

"Yup. I figured if you knew how I felt, you would sacrifice your dreams for mine, like a sweet, selfless martyr. It killed me to hurt you like that. You know that now, right?"

She couldn't speak. She could hardly think with his finger still resting between her breasts.

Then he added, "You're a huckleberry above most people's persimmon."

She chuckled. "You sound like Charlotte."

"Do I?" he asked.

"So, you *do* love me?"

Slowly, idly, he circled each of her nipples, making them pucker and pearl. "Yup."

"And you know I love you?" she asked.

He broke into a slow, broad smile and leaned down to kiss her, sending warmth sparking through her body clear down to her toes.

"Yup," he answered.

"And you'd like me to be your wife?"

His face darkened, and he sighed. "Nope."

"Damn it, Riley!" Sophie sat up in bed, then realized her own nakedness and grabbed the blanket as she stood, not caring that she left him entirely exposed. She wished there was a bathroom she could storm into. She ought to be over the moon—the man she loved and had yearned for all these months loved her, too.

Instead, she was angry.

"Turn around so I can dress," she ordered and, with a bemused expression, he complied.

"Seems a bit late for that," he muttered, facing the wall.

"It's never too late for courtesy," she said, putting on her stockings and her shift before hauling on her skirt and then her blouse, starting to work on her buttons with shaking hands.

"Can I turn around now?" Riley asked.

"Yes," she said, sitting on the bed to lace up her ankle high shoes. She couldn't do much about her hair without a brush and a mirror.

She felt him move and then heard him pull out a dresser drawer. When he came around to her side of the bed, he was wearing a clean pair of blue-jeans and was pulling on a shirt. It was easier to address him after he was covered.

"I'm going now," she said.

He nodded.

"Well? Don't you have anything to say?"

"I told you, Sophie, you shouldn't have come." He ran a hand through his still-damp hair that was already standing up in a million different directions. "I guess I should tell you again that I'm sorry. But, hell, if the woman I love is going to show up in my kitchen like a fanciful spirit, looking so damned beautiful, then I'm going to make love to her in the middle of the afternoon." He dropped to his knees in front of her.

"And I've missed you so much, Sophie. It's hard to be sorry about what we just did."

The anger emptied right out of her.

"I missed you, too."

He closed his eyes a moment before his soft, tawny gaze fixed on hers. "Now for that, I *am* sorry. I tried to be such a bastard you'd hate me and not miss me at all."

"You're not very good at being hateful." Actually, he had been pretty darn convincing, but that was neither here nor there.

"Tell that to the good folks of Spring City."

She could think of nothing more to say, except, "I'm willing to stay here and be your wife, Riley. I want you to know that."

He stood and pulled her up with him, holding her close and kissing her tenderly, a gentle caress across her lips. It was all too brief, and then he stepped back.

"I won't let you throw your gift away, Sophie Malloy. How could any man who loved you do that?"

He grabbed her by the hand and led her downstairs. She found herself out on the front step before she could say "boo." She was being shown the door by the most grim-faced Riley she'd ever seen.

He didn't even let her say goodbye.

CHAPTER TWENTY-SEVEN

Sophie's heart felt about as light as lead. She cried herself to sleep and woke up feeling beyond desolate. Desperately, she wanted to be at the perfectly tuned piano in San Francisco, healing herself with its magic. Charlotte's untuned upright was simply not doing the trick. She needed the rich, soul-soothing sounds of her grand on stage at the concert hall, or even her own beloved piano in Boston.

On the other hand, she couldn't face the train trip that would take her away from Riley. Again! Perhaps forever. Truthfully, she didn't want to live in Spring City. She felt out-of-place, and the one person who could make it seem like home wouldn't ask her to stay anyway.

Regardless, he *was* hers. Clearly, he belonged to her, both body and soul, as she did to him, and to be alone without him in California was far worse than being there in Colorado without her orchestra.

If only, he would let her make the decision. Instead, he seemed hell-bent on forcing her onto the first train out of Spring. He'd sent Dan over with a ticket for the next morning's train, as if he couldn't risk coming over himself. She knew why. Sparks would fly as soon as they were alone, and they'd end up in bed again.

Not that that was such a bad thing, Sophie mused, wearing a sad smile as she sipped her coffee, sitting on the piano stool, thinking of the ardent afternoon they'd shared the day before. She picked up the ticket she'd placed on top of the piano. Tomorrow, she would use it. She had no other choice.

It was after supper when apparently Riley couldn't stay away any longer. She was on the porch swing when he rode up.

"I wondered if I would see you before I left." Her calm words belied the quickening of her pulse.

"Honestly, I didn't intend to come by." Nevertheless, he dropped onto the swing beside her. "I just finished with my last patient, a ferocious sore throat that I treated with the utmost kindness, even though I know it was brought on by Mrs. Fisher yelling all day at Mr. Fisher."

She nodded, unable to speak for a moment.

"You would have been proud of my courtesy," he finished.

It occurred to her right that instant after tonight, she might never see him again, hear his voice, or touch him, and she put her hand on his leg. His muscles tightened beneath her hand. Life without him would be absolutely bleak. Why wasn't he moving heaven and earth to keep her?

"Why aren't you . . . ?" she trailed off, her voice barely above a whisper.

He put his hand over hers and leaned closer, until she could smell the familiar scent that was Riley. "What?" he asked.

"Why aren't you going to fight for me?" she managed, her voice thick with emotion.

His eyes widened momentarily, then he shook his head.

"Sophie, sweetheart, I am. I'm fighting myself every damn day to make sure you stay where you belong."

She paused, feeling the tears prick at her eyes again. She waited till the feeling passed so she could speak once more.

"Why aren't you fighting to keep me?" She realized that's what hurt most of all.

He didn't say anything at first. Then he stood, letting her hand drop away from him. Leaning his hips against the porch rail, he faced her.

"I'm doing the best I can do for you while keeping my promise to Doc. Don't you think I want this to go another way?"

"You'll give me up for duty!" she spat out, allowing her anger to overtake the pain. It was easier to be angry than hurt. "First, for a promise to Eliza, you would throw our love away. Now, for a debt you owe Doc!"

"What kind of man would I be if I chucked aside everyone and everything else?"

"I guess you'd be a man in love," she stated, defeated, devastated, and utterly exhausted.

"Not fair, Sophie."

"I don't feel like being fair. I'll get on that train tomorrow, and I'll return to my blessed life in San Francisco, but it will be diminished—everything will be—knowing what we could have had."

He swore. "That's why I didn't want you to know how I felt. If you hadn't come here, you never would have known."

His words felt like a knife in her ribs. "Don't I deserve to know how much a man loves me? Especially one whom I love back?"

"You'll find another—"

"Please," she got to her feet. "Don't you dare say it. You're not so easily replaced and my passions aren't so fickle." She crossed her arms. "Why? Are you planning on marrying the next single girl who comes your way?"

"No."

"You will eventually," she said, her voice lowering, talking more to herself than to him.

"Sophie, please." He took a step toward her and reached for her hands.

"Don't," she warded him off. "You go back to being surly and sad. I'm going home."

Turning on her heel, she went to the screen door.

"You know, Riley, I don't believe you do love me the way I love you. I'm willing to stay here, perhaps teach piano or . . ." *Blast!* She couldn't think of anything else she could do in this ridiculous town. "Or something, just to be with you because I simply cannot imagine my life without you. But tomorrow, on that train, I'm sure as hell going to try."

She slammed the screen behind her, but as she turned to close the door, she was unable to stop herself from looking once more at his face, so somber in the shadows, so dear to her.

Riley rode home ever so slowly. He couldn't bring himself to spur his horse to a flying gallop. He didn't feel like enjoying the ride. He didn't feel anything but numb. When Sophie left tomorrow, the rest of his life would be colorless without her. Despite what she might think, he couldn't imagine hitching himself to any other woman, marrying merely for company.

Even if he wanted to care for another, in his heart, Sophie would still be there, taking up all the room, being an impossible comparison for any other female. He sure hoped he was easier to replace, for her sake. If not, it seemed as if he'd damned them both to hell on earth.

Her face, so sweet, so wretched, right before she closed the door. It broke his heart. *Fight for her? Hell!* He was doing exactly that, fighting his weaker self that wanted to keep her with him. Fighting to make sure she didn't look at him one day with resentment, if not downright hatred, for ruining the life she could have had.

"Hi-ya!" he yelled at last, and his horse took off at a cantor.

He shouldn't have made love to her. He should have been stronger. As soon as he'd seen her in his kitchen, he'd known how it would end if she didn't leave right then. After all, she belonged to him, unquestionably and absolutely, just as he belonged to her. It would have been ungrateful not to take the gift he'd been given—one perfect union with her.

And it had been exactly that, perfection. Beyond his dreams. Beyond anything he deserved.

He pulled his horse up short.

It seemed ungrateful not to take the gift.

He sat in his saddle in the middle of nowhere, the only sounds being the heavy breathing of his horse and the occasional owl's call. Riley let all his thoughts rush through him—hopes, dreams, love, Sophie. Everything good in his life led back to her, a gift that had ridden into Spring City on a train, not once, but twice. Twice!

Slowly, he took a deep breath and, looked around him, up at the stars. *What the hell was he doing throwing away such a miracle?*

Shit! It was late, but Doc was used to late nights and emergencies. Riley turned his horse around.

It was unseasonably warm as Sophie walked to the station, very happy not to be dragging a trunk. With her, she had her carpet bag in one hand and her coat draped over her arm. She was clenching a handkerchief, just in case. After all, she had a lot of quiet hours to fill on two trains and hoped she wouldn't spend most of them crying.

Passing Ely's and Dan's, she had her foot on the first step of the station platform, such as it was, merely a few planks of wood on the edge of a dusty town.

"You need help with that?"

She whirled around, nearly losing her balance. Her heart sank. She couldn't take another brutal round with Riley, exposing her heart and having it handed back to her. She'd hardly slept and felt almost like an invalid.

"No answer?" He was smiling at her, looking as he had the first time they'd met.

How could he come to say goodbye and actually smile at her? But if he could do it, then she could, too. Girding her heart—after all, it should be made of steel by now—she played along.

"Are you going to knock me into the street?"

"Is that the only way I'll see your purple drawers again?"

She gasped. After all, there were other people around. Besides, he was still wrong.

"Lavender," she corrected him, but with a ghost of humor in her voice.

He crossed his arms. "As a doctor, I better check them out for myself. I'm licensed, you know."

Despite herself, she smiled. "To look at ladies' undergarments?" What was up with him? He seemed giddy, precisely the opposite to how she felt.

"You'll have to stay another night," he said, coming closer.

"So you can check my unmentionables?"

He barked out a laugh. Then shook his head. "No. . . . Well, maybe! But I need a day to pack my things."

She swallowed. "What are you saying?"

Everything happened at once. She saw Doc and Sarah coming along the sidewalk with Jessie not far behind. Mr. Webber was sitting on a chair outside his store as if he had a seat at a show. Just then, Riley dropped to his knees, giving her a view of Dan leaning against the wall outside the feedstore, smiling at her.

"Sophie Malloy," Riley said, looking up at her, and it seemed as if all the other sounds hushed. No more footsteps or horse's hooves or birds singing or people talking. Only Riley.

"Will you do me the extreme honor of becoming my wife?"

"Riley?" she asked uncertainly. But she could barely hear her own voice for the buzzing in her ears.

She was lightheaded. Surely, it was due to lack of sleep and not eating anything the previous night or that morning. And the sun was already hot on her head. Stupidly, she'd put her bonnet in her bag.

That was the last thought she had before she started to crumple, feeling Riley's arms catch her as she collapsed.

How long she was unconscious, Sophie didn't know, but she awakened on the bed in Doc's surgery, her head feeling achy.

"Drink a little of this as soon as you're able," Riley said, lifting her head slightly. He sat beside her on a stool. She saw he had a glass in his hand of what looked like water. Taking a sip, she swallowed and let him wipe her chin.

"Yuck." It was salty and bitter.

He chuckled. "Tastes nasty, but it'll make you feel better."

She coughed before taking another sip.

"You ready to sit up?" he asked.

She nodded.

"Slowly, all right?" He helped her reach a seated position, and quickly stuffed pillows behind her to keep her that way. Doc and Sarah were at the end of the bed.

"You didn't eat, did you?" Sarah said. "And folks are always making fun of my fussing about feeding everyone. Nothing good comes from starving yourself. You fainted, right in the middle of Main Street."

She had a familiar box on her lap, which she tapped with her hand. "I went straight over to Fuller's after you dropped like a stone and got the tastiest item on the menu."

She handed the box to Sophie, who looked down at it, then up at Riley.

"Lemon cake," they said together.

"What's the matter?" Sarah asked. "Don't you like it?"

"I don't know. I've never had it."

Riley opened the box and held it in front of her. Sophie breathed in the heavenly fragrance of lemons and vanilla wafting up at her. Her mouth watered and, without waiting, she picked up the slice in her hand and took a bite.

"*Mm*, it's so light and delicious." She took another bite, unable to stop herself. Soon, she'd eaten the whole thing and was licking her fingers.

Doc laughed. "That's what I do, too. Why, you're going to be fine. Rest here till you feel like we can take you back to Charlotte's."

"Oh," Sophie exclaimed, dismayed. "I missed my train."

Sarah and Doc looked at each other, and Sarah gaped. "Don't you remember—?"

Doc cleared his throat loudly, cutting her off. "My lovely wife and I are going to leave you two alone to have a chat," and he hustled Sarah out the door.

Sophie looked at Riley again, who was grinning in a way that made her want to kiss him. All at once, she remembered him on his knees.

She gasped. "Dear God! Did you ask me to marry you?"

"I did, but you didn't react the way I expected."

He leaned down and kissed her, then he licked his lips. "Lemony. I'd give you another piece just to watch you lick your fingers again."

"Riley," she scolded. Had he been thinking that while Sarah and Doc were in the room?

"The only person I've ever known who didn't like that cake was Eliza."

Sophie snorted. "What are you talking about? I was there when you bought her a piece."

"No," he corrected, stopping to kiss her again, "it's the other way around. I stopped to buy her a piece of cake because *you* were there."

"Oh." That meant a lot to her. And suddenly, his expression became more serious.

"You know and I know the reason I've been such an ass is because when I'm not with you, Sophie Malloy, I have no heart. I came back here and realized I'd left my heart in San Francisco."

She gazed at him thoughtfully. "Something about that would make an excellent song."

"Sophie, please focus. Are you going to give me an answer?"

She wanted to be serious, but she simply couldn't stop herself from smiling, even as she did, finally, answer him.

"Yes, I'll marry you."

"And you'll live with me in San Francisco?"

"Yes, I'll live with you in—wait, what do you mean?" Excitement fluttered in the pit of her stomach.

"I can't give you up, but I can't let you give up your dream, either. We're going back to San Francisco and you're going to marry me."

"What about Doc?" she asked, tossing the box off her lap as she reached up to hug him.

"He's already married, and I don't fancy him."

She laughed hard. Everything was funny or happy or . . . perhaps she was dreaming.

"Pinch me," she said.

Without hesitating, he responded, "Roll over so I have access to your rosy round cheeks."

"Stop teasing, Riley. No, don't ever stop," she ordered. "But what will happen? What about Doc's practice. And Sarah's long-awaited trip?"

"Doc will interview those doctors Webster invited, and he'll pick one. End of story. I had it in my head it was me or no one, and that I'd be letting down the whole town of Spring, as well as Doc. But that's ridiculous." He paused while he stroked her cheek, then he held her chin still and looked into her eyes.

"I realized the only person I shouldn't let down is you. If I did, I would deserve the hell I've been living in."

He brushed his thumb over her lower lip, and she trembled slightly.

"I went to Doc last night and told him I felt terrible leaving him in the lurch, but I had to leave. He said if it were him, he'd choose you and San Francisco, too. Actually, what he said was, if Sarah wasn't in Spring, he wouldn't be, either."

She smiled at Riley, feeling absolutely blessed. "Smart man, that Doc Cuthins."

His arms encircled her. "Lucky man, this Riley Dalcourt."

And then Sophie's new fiancé kissed her."

EPILOGUE

Riley didn't sit in the front row anymore. Seats at the concert hall were in too high a demand. He had a chair offstage for the evenings when he could attend one of his wife's performances. That night was special, indeed, for when she finished, he was going to whisk her away to Egbert and Carling's lovely inn in Sonoma, so they could meet Carling's new baby. He hoped to spur a little baby envy in Sophie, or at least have fun trying.

It was nice to be alone, just the two of them, after the hullabaloo of the past year. Their courtship had been a whirlwind at best, for neither could wait to share a bed every night. And they hadn't waited. *Damn propriety!* They had been through too much separation to let a little thing like a marriage license keep them apart.

For their wedding vows, however, they'd dutifully allowed Sophie's extended family to take over the Trinity Church on Post and Powell streets. Not only were Sophie's mother and sisters in attendance with Elise's husband and her children, naturally Reed and Charlotte came with baby Emory and their two older adopted children, Charlotte's brother, Thaddeus, who was Riley's childhood friend, along with Doc and Sarah, but also most of Sophie's orchestra, and, thanks to Henry Hadley's connections, many of the notables of San Francisco, as well.

And in the midst were Riley's parents, who'd learned of their son's wedding in time to stop surveying the territory on the northern border with Canada and make it to the church for the ceremony.

It was an uncommonly clear day with no fog. With Dan as best man and Carling as maid of honor, Sophie's sole disappointment was not being able to play her own wedding march, which Henry performed admirably on her behalf.

Evelyn Malloy insisted on remaining in San Francisco with the happy couple for an extra week to help her middle daughter set up a home.

"I'm sorry to say you're utterly unprepared for such a thing" her mother declared. "What with no maid or cook." She'd given Riley a stern glare. "I'm sure you'll hire help soon."

In fact, they were going to get both, since their salaries permitted it. Nevertheless, Sophie learned to cook a few dishes and even to beat a rug, but she drew the line at darning stockings.

"I'll buy new stockings," Riley whispered in Sophie's ear, before nibbling her ticklish lobe, as his mother-in-law huffed over "young people with their strange ways."

His parents had stayed for an extra week at The Palace, where many of the wedding guests from the East Coast and from Colorado were enjoying its comforts. Egbert used his former connections to get them all a good rate, while inviting guests to come to the wine country and stay at Hull Inn.

"If you have time, we'd love to have you," he kept repeating, handing out the inn's brochures at the crowded reception.

On the Dalcourts' last day, they presented the newlyweds with a framed map of the United States with a marked trail from Boston to Spring City to San Francisco. Riley hung it immediately in the parlor.

"My sweet boy," Mrs. Dalcourt proclaimed, pinching her son's cheek. Sophie reached behind and pinched Riley's nether cheek, making him jump.

"That's *Doctor* Sweet Boy," quipped his father, who'd seen Sophie do it.

Sophie decided her in-laws were odd and delightful, but she wished them gone, along with her mother.

"Don't forget," Mrs. Dalcourt said, as she adjusted her hat, "I love babies."

"So much," Mr. Dalcourt added, "that she had only the one."

"I love *other* people's babies," Riley's mother amended, and his parents were still discussing it as they went out the front door of Sophie and Riley's new home on Alamo Square.

That night, Riley thought Sophie played better than ever, but then, he thought that every time he heard her play. When the final notes died away in the depths of the packed concert hall and the applause had reached a crescendo and faded, after the musicians had bowed, smiled, and clapped for their conductor, Sophie came directly into his arms.

He kissed her, fully, passionately, in front of all the musicians who, so used to seeing the adoring couple, continued around and past them without a second glance.

"*Mm,* that's my favorite part of the evening," Sophie said, when he let her breathe.

"I think I can do even better," Riley promised.

She bit her lip. The anticipation his words provoked coursed through her, as her passion for her husband always did, always would, leaving her tingly and excited. Like hearing an irresistible melody.

"God knows I love you, Dr. Dalcourt."

"God, I wish I could take you on top of your grand piano, Mrs. Dalcourt."

She laughed. She laughed so hard she almost choked, and he had to thump her on the back.

"You two are making a spectacle of yourselves, as usual," Henry said, tossing his cape about his shoulders. He looked at Sophie, "As your conductor, all I can say is 'Carry on.'" He walked away.

"Oh," Sophie remembered. "We're going to Carling's tonight, aren't we?"

"You know," Riley said, tilting his head, "we might want to put that off until the morning. I'm prescribing a few hours in bed for you."

His grin turned wicked, her knees went weak, and she decided her husband was positively genius.

"Well," she said, taking hold of his outstretched hand, "you're the doctor."

Finis

AN INESCAPABLE ATTRACTION
BOOK 3

and the rest of the Defiant Hearts series
including

AN INTRIGUING PROPOSITION
PREQUEL

AN IMPROPER SITUATION
BOOK 1

AN IRRESISTIBLE TEMPTATION
BOOK 2

AN INCONCEIVABLE DECEPTION
BOOK 4

AN IMPASSIONED REDEMPTION
NOVELLA

are available in print and ebook.

ABOUT THE AUTHOR

USA Today bestselling author Sydney Jane Baily writes historical romance set in Victorian England, late 19th-century America, the Middle Ages, the Georgian era, and the Regency period. She believes in happily-ever-after stories with engaging characters and attention to period detail.

Born and raised in California, she has traveled the world, spending a lot of exceedingly happy time in the U.K. where her extended family resides, eating fish and chips, drinking shandies, and snacking on Maltesers and Cadbury bars. Sydney currently lives in New England with her family—human, canine, and feline.

You can learn more about her books, read her blog, sign up for her newsletter (and get a free book), and contact her via her website at SydneyJaneBaily.com. She loves to hear from her readers.